BABY CHRISTMAS
Pamela Browning

D1007584

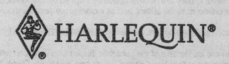

HARLEQUIN®

TORONTO • NEW YORK • LONDON
AMSTERDAM • PARIS • SYDNEY • HAMBURG
STOCKHOLM • ATHENS • TOKYO • MILAN • MADRID
PRAGUE • WARSAW • BUDAPEST • AUCKLAND

ISBN 0-373-16854-3

BABY CHRISTMAS

This edition published by arrangement with Harlequin Books S.A.

® and TM are trademarks of the publisher. Trademarks indicated with
® are registered in the United States Patent and Trademark Office, the
Canadian Trade Marks Office and in other countries.

Visit us at www.eHarlequin.com

Printed in U.S.A.

ABOUT THE AUTHOR

Pamela Browning is the award-winning author of thirty romance novels—many of which appeared on numerous bestseller lists. Her books consistently win high ratings from reviewers and readers alike. She makes her home in North Carolina.

Books by Pamela Browning

Dear Reader,

A baby was the last thing Rachel needed. She'd lost her own family at Christmas five years before, and she never wanted to celebrate the holidays again.

But finding Baby Christmas in the nativity scene gave Rachel a reason to open her heart to a wonderful, kind, caring man. From him, she learned to love and to hope again.

Which is really the message of this book. No matter how dark the days, no matter how lonely we feel, we need to know that our hearts are still open to those most precious treasures, love and hope. And sometimes we find them in the most unlikely places!

May peace be with you this holiday season—and ever after.

Love,

Pamela Browning

Prologue

"And what do you want for Christmas, little girl?"

Rachel nudged the package of printer paper toward the jovial Santa who was manning the cash register at the discount store and said blankly, "Excuse me?"

He raised bushy white eyebrows and looked faintly apologetic. "I guess I want to know why a nice girl like you is out buying office supplies tonight instead of at home with the special people in your life." His eyes were a warm, twinkly blue, and he had a birthmark in the shape of a crescent moon high on his cheekbone.

Rachel's heart sank, but she was instantly comforted by the certain knowledge that he couldn't know her secret. No one in the small island resort town of Coquina Beach, Florida, knew. Nevertheless her mouth went dry.

"I—" She didn't know what to say.

The Santa studied her face intently for a moment. "You don't have to talk about it if you don't want to," he said. He dragged the package of paper across the electronic scanner and popped the drawer of the cash register.

Rachel fumbled in her purse and handed him a twenty-dollar bill. It was all she could do not to burst into tears.

He dropped the change into her outstretched hand, and she picked up the package.

"Make a wish," he said suddenly.

Rachel, whose mind was a million miles away, pulled herself back to reality. She wasn't sure she had heard him correctly. "What?"

"Make a wish. Any wish." He was staring at her in a way that made her think he could see to the bottom of her soul.

She mustered a comeback. "You're joking, right?"

He didn't crack a smile. He only gazed at her with an intensity that might have frightened her if his overall demeanor hadn't been one of kindness and compassion.

"Who *are* you?" Rachel said, the words catching in her throat.

"It doesn't matter. But make a wish and it will be granted."

Rachel couldn't breathe. She felt caught up in something that she didn't understand, and the beating of wings brushed against her heart, and the singing of angels filled her ears. Or was it only her blood pounding and Christmas carols playing over the store loudspeaker?

Before the Santa could say another word, Rachel fled. But because she believed that wishes sometimes came true, she made the wish anyway.

I wish I had a reason to celebrate Christmas again.

Of course she knew she was only being foolish. Christmas was over for her. It had ended with a fire on Christmas Eve four years ago, and it would never come again.

Chapter One

Yes, Rachel was alone. And yes, she minded it. But, she reflected as she pulled herself together after the strange encounter with the Santa at the cash register, soon she would be back at work.

Work. It was her solace and her lifeline. It was the only thing, she sometimes thought, that kept her going.

As she slid out of her car in the parking lot of the Elysian Towers condominium, Rachel couldn't help hearing the strains of a Christmas carol wafting on the balmy tropical breeze. She ignored it. By holing up in Mimi's apartment, she'd somehow thought that she would be able to escape reminders of the season. That's why she'd agreed to house-sit for her globetrotting grandmother when Mimi decided to go gadding about the Orient.

Thinking about this, Rachel rounded the corner of the Nativity scene near the front portico. The manger was brilliantly spotlighted to showcase the details of the plaster representations of Mary and Joseph and the baby Jesus, incredibly lifelike statues.

"'The cattle are lowing, the poor baby wakes.
The little Lord Jesus no crying he makes—'"
"Wah!"

Rachel stopped dead in her tracks. That noise sounded like a baby's cry, and it—

"Wah! Wah! *Waaah…*"

It *was* a baby's cry. And it was coming from the manger.

"'I love thee, Lord Jesus, look down from the sky,
And stay by my cradle till morning is nigh.'"

Incredibly, above the side of the wooden cradle a tiny fist flailed in the air.

Rachel looked to the right; she looked to the left. Not a creature was stirring, not even a—well, anything. No one was in the parking lot. No one was driving past.

She tiptoed closer to the scene. She peeked into the manger. And there, amazingly, lay a tiny pink-and-white baby wrapped in a nondescript cotton flannel blanket.

A real baby. Not a plaster baby like the one Rachel had seen there this afternoon. But a real, live, honest-to-goodness baby!

Insects batted against the spotlight. A breeze, fresh with salt spray from the nearby ocean, ruffled palm fronds overhead. The baby stopped crying and snuffled. Then it sneezed.

The sneeze galvanized Rachel into action. She bounded over the low hedge of flowering ixoras separating grass from sidewalk and knelt beside the manger in utter disbelief. The baby, wide-eyed and silent now in its bed of straw, stared into her face. It had fat rosy cheeks and a captivating fluff of golden hair combed into a peak on the top of its head. She could have sworn that the baby smiled.

Rachel still didn't know why a real baby would be part of the Nativity scene. And she didn't care. She dropped the package she was carrying. Slowly, reverently, she slipped her hands under the baby's soft warm body and lifted it out of the manger. The baby smelled sweetly of talcum powder. And it sighed and settled against her breast as if it belonged there.

The weight of the child in her arms felt right somehow. Rachel had always considered herself born to be a mother, and it had been so long since she had held a baby. So heartbreakingly, miserably long.

"Look! I...I...I just found a baby in the manger!" Rachel blurted as she burst into the lobby of the building.

An angel seemed to be hovering over the bank of elevators. It looked as lifelike as the plaster figures on the lawn.

Stunned, Rachel blinked her eyes and saw belatedly that this wasn't an angel at all. It was a man, a handsome man who was balancing ever so precariously atop a ladder. He was tall and muscular with an appealingly open face, and he wore a blue chambray shirt and jeans so soft that they clung in all the right places. A leather tool belt was slung low on his narrow hips, and his dark, rugged good looks would have totally captured her attention if the baby hadn't started to whimper.

"You found a baby, did you? Well, so did the three wise guys," the man said. It was only after he spoke that it registered with Rachel that water was gushing out of the ceiling above the ladder and that much of the lobby was awash in four inches of water. As her mind grappled with this additional oddity, the flow from overhead slowed to a trickle and then a steady drip.

The man on the ladder observed the *plink, plink, plink* for a moment and then began to descend slowly, confidently, with an air of self-command. Interested eyes looked Rachel over; she realized that she must look a fright with her hair teased by the coastal humidity into a frivolous mass of curls around her face, and she was wearing her oldest shorts and sandals. But she couldn't worry now about the way she looked, not with the baby in her arms. The baby stopped whimpering and hiccuped.

Rachel thought she'd better explain. "I came in from the parking lot—I had to run to the store to buy printer paper because I suddenly remembered that tomorrow is Christmas Day and nothing will be open—and I was walking past the Nativity scene and I heard a baby crying. And then I saw it move. And I thought, 'A plaster baby isn't supposed to move' or something like that, and when I went and looked, it…it smiled at me!"

The man remained calmer than Rachel thought he had a right to be under the circumstances. His eyes focused on her face. They were an arresting silvery color, the irises as pale as water and rimmed in gray, and they crinkled appealingly at the edges. They were regarding her with a slightly incredulous expression. She supposed she couldn't blame him for being perplexed, astonished and amazed. *She* certainly was.

"Who could have left a real baby in the Nativity scene?" Rachel wondered, on the verge of becoming even more distraught. Before the man could reply, a head wearing a baseball cap backward appeared around the door from the utility area.

"Hey, boss," said the man whose head it was, "I've turned off the water upstairs, so now all we have to do is—um, is anything wrong?"

Silver Eyes leaned against the ladder and thrust his thumbs through his belt loops as he surveyed the scene. "Well, Andy, it's Christmas Eve, water is raining from the ceiling, and this lady insists that she found a live baby in a manger. Why would you think there's anything wrong?"

"Yeah, I see your point." The man disappeared around the corner.

Indignation supplanted the shock and numbness that Rachel had been feeling ever since she first saw the baby. She didn't know who Silver Eyes was, but he must be uncaring and unfeeling not to sympathize with the baby's plight. Certainly he was unhelpful.

Rachel drew a deep breath and willed herself to be calm. "Would you mind telling me what's going on here? When I left, there was no water in the lobby. When I left, carolers were going from floor to floor singing Christmas songs. It was normal around here when I left. And," she said, focusing on Silver Eyes, "where's Sherman?" Sherman was the doorman. He should have been manning the lobby desk.

"Sherman hightailed it into the manager's office with a committee of residents to telephone the condo manager. Excuse me, but I'd better introduce myself. I'm Joe Marzinski, president of Condo Crisis Control. Sherman called my company when a bathroom upstairs starting pouring water down four floors into the lobby."

Just seeing the lobby's lovely turquoise-and-coral-print chairs rising above the flood like islands in a stream was enough to make Rachel feel depressed. "I'm Rachel Hirsch. I live here, and I was hoping Sherman could suggest what to do about this baby," she said. She felt perilously near tears for the second time that night.

"He'll be back. Why don't you—"

She couldn't take this man's lackadaisical attitude for one more moment. "Why don't you be more helpful?" she snapped. She couldn't help it; she was losing patience.

Joe Marzinski, who, she noticed, was wearing heavy and presumably waterproof boots, sloshed toward her.

He studied the baby coolly and judiciously, pursing his well-sculpted lips, but even though he was looking at the baby, he sent out vibrations to clue her in that he was aware of her in a particularly avid way. *She* was certainly aware of *him*. Vitality radiated from him, and energy, and something far more potent. Although he was looking at the baby, she was sure that he had noticed the shortness of her khaki shorts, the unbuttoned top button of her simple red jersey, and the fact that she wore almost no makeup. She wished suddenly and irrelevantly that she'd dabbed on a bit of lipstick for her late-night foray to the store.

"It's a pretty baby," he said.

"*What's* a pretty baby?" demanded a strident voice.

"Behold, the condo committee," Joe Marzinski said under his breath.

They were friends of her grandmother's from the community theater group, and they all lived in this building. Rachel privately called them the Theatrical Threesome. Gladys Rink, seventy years old but lithe and suntanned from spending hours on the tennis court, waded out of the manager's office. She was barefoot. Right behind her was Ivan O'Toole, a white-haired elderly man who was steadfastly clutching a copy of the condominium bylaws. Accompanying them was Ynez Garcia, her salt-and-pepper hair held fast in pink foam-rubber curlers, the corners of her mouth turned down in her typical woebegone expression. Sherman, the doorman, who followed, gave a worldly wise roll of his eyeballs and did one of his notably stealthy disappearing acts out the door to the utility area.

Mrs. Rink immediately spotted the baby in Rachel's arms and indulged in a quick double take. "Where did *that* come from?" she snapped.

"I found it in the Nativity scene. In the manger," Rachel said.

"Oh, great. As if we didn't have enough trouble around here tonight."

Mr. O'Toole waved the condominium bylaws a mere two inches from Rachel's nose and quoted verbatim from the text. "'No children shall be allowed to abide within the Elysian Towers condominium unaccompanied by their parents. Children must be accompanied by adults at all times when using the swimming pool, and children—'"

"Oh, Ivan, I don't think this baby is old enough to use the swimming pool, do you?" said Mrs. Rink impatiently.

Mrs. Garcia, who had remained quiet while gazing reverently into the baby's small face, broke into a beatific and rare smile. "A baby arrives on Christmas Eve. It is a miracle! A miracle from God!"

Mr. O'Toole bent to roll up his pants legs, presumably so he wouldn't ruin his new suit. "The baby may be a miracle, all right, but I'm certainly not capable of walking on water, and who's supposed to be cleaning up this mess, anyway?" he said.

Joe stepped forward. "We've turned off the water at the source, and my clean-up team is on the job. If you'll all go to your apartments, I'm sure we'll be able to set things straight in no time." With an air of forbearance, which was not lost on Rachel, he shepherded the disgruntled committee members toward the elevator and guided them inside. The last thing Rachel heard as the elevator doors closed was Ynez Garcia saying, "It's a miracle, I tell you! A Christmas miracle!"

Joe Marzinski indulged in an audible sigh of relief. Into the subsequent hollow silence punctuated only by the *drip, drip* of water from the ceiling, Rachel said plaintively, "But what am I going to do about the baby?"

Joe's eyes met hers. "Condo Crisis Control takes pride in handling any crisis. Come with me," he said, cupping a firm hand under her elbow and urging her toward the office. Rachel, mesmerized by the way the baby felt in her arms, was agreeable to someone else's taking charge, because she truly believed that she was incapable of rational thought at the moment. All the maternal feelings that had been buried so long had unexpectedly surfaced, and she felt overwhelmed by memories. Oddly enough, they weren't sad memories this time but the happy ones that she sometimes tended to forget.

The manager's office at Elysian Towers was a spare white cubicle adorned by a dusty potted palm and amateurish seascapes. Joe, businesslike and efficient, sat down behind the vacant desk and poked around wordlessly for a moment or two before he found a phone book in the bookcase.

Rachel sank down on a chair opposite him. The baby was rooting with its mouth and making little sucking motions. She felt a wave of helplessness that she couldn't feed it. She had always prided herself on nursing her babies, had nursed them longer than her friends thought necessary, and she had reveled in the warm moist sensation of the tiny mouth against her nipples and the gentle tugging in her abdomen as they suckled. It had been a sexual feeling almost, and Nick had pretended to be jealous of the baby, and she had teased him about it, and—

"Here it is," said Joe, breaking into her reverie. He underlined a number in the book. "Department of Health and Social Services. They're the government agency responsible for abandoned children. Do you want to call or shall I?"

Rachel swallowed. She wanted to go on holding the baby. "You'd better," she said.

Joe punched out the numbers on the phone and waited while it rang on the other end. "It's a recording," he said in exasperation as he slammed down the phone. "It's a sure bet nobody's there because it's the Christmas holiday. And this is Wednesday, which is Christmas Eve, and Thursday is Christmas Day, and a lot of state government offices are closed on Friday. Do you realize that there may be no one in their office until Monday?"

"Oh, dear," said Rachel.

Joe stared at her for a moment. "You're enjoying this, aren't you?"

She was uncomfortable with his being able to read her so well. "Enjoying! That's not exactly the word. It's a beautiful baby, that's all, and I can't imagine who could have left it in the manger, and—well, I'm worried. But I'm somehow glad that I found it."

"Why?" Those incisive eyes were direct and honest, and they demanded the same from her.

But she couldn't tell him why. She never talked about it. She never mentioned Nick and Lolly and Melissa and Derek. She shrugged and looked down at the baby so that Joe Marzinski wouldn't see the desolation in her eyes.

The baby began to squirm.

"I think we'd better change its diaper," Rachel said. She was glad for the diversion.

"Couldn't we stop referring to the baby as 'it'?" Joe's voice held a hint of teasing.

Rachel lay the baby flat in her lap and unwrapped the blanket, exposing a chubby little body. She peeked inside the diaper. "It's a girl," she said.

The baby, perhaps feeling the cool rush of air from the

air-conditioner vent overhead, began to cry even louder, transforming herself into a tiny package of pure misery.

"Mrs. Rink's niece visited last month and brought her baby along. Maybe she has some diapers left over," Rachel said over the din.

"What?" It was hard to hear anything over the baby's cries.

"I'm taking her upstairs." And Rachel got up and walked out into the lobby, where two men in coveralls bearing logos saying Condo Crisis Control were sucking water up into large vacuum cleaners. Joe gave them a pleased thumbs-up sign, but the roar of the vacuum cleaners in addition to the baby's wailing made it impossible to talk, and Rachel was surprised when Joe stepped into the elevator with her. As it began its upward journey, she shushed the baby, who refused to be calmed.

Rachel stared at Joe in the bright light from the fluorescent fixture overhead. "You don't have to come with me," she shouted.

"I want to," he shouted back.

When they reached the eleventh floor, Joe followed her out of the elevator to the door marked 11E. Rachel fumbled in her shorts pocket for the key to Mimi's apartment.

"You better let me hold the baby," Joe said, and Rachel, seeing the sense of this, deposited the squalling infant in his arms. Joe began to rock back and forth, an instinctive movement, but it surprised Rachel nevertheless. She hadn't thought of Joe Marzinski with his brisk no-nonsense air as knowing what to do with a baby.

She dug the key out of her pocket and inserted it into the lock. The door swung open on Mimi's startling yellow-and-white decor.

Joe blinked his eyes at the brightness within.

"Mimi—my grandmother—wanted something to cheer

her up after my grandfather died,'' Rachel explained loudly as Joe took in the overwhelming decor.

"Looks like she got it," Joe muttered. He looked slightly stunned.

"I'd better run over to Gladys's about the diapers," Rachel said.

"What?"

No surprise; he couldn't hear her. "I'D BETTER GO OVER TO GLADYS RINK'S ABOUT THE DIA-PERS," she repeated more loudly. Joe grinned and shook his head. But she thought he got the message.

As she ran down the long hallway, Rachel dreaded knocking on the formidable Gladys's door. But the baby needed a clean diaper right away, and this was the fastest way Rachel knew to get one.

JOE MARZINSKI, surrounded by yellow walls, yellow furniture, yellow everything, gazed down at the angry red-faced baby screaming in his arms and thought with some annoyance, *How did I get involved in this?*

But then again, how could he not? His firm specialized in controlling condominium crises. If this wasn't a crisis, what was? The baby was clearly abandoned. Joe, as he tried his best to calm the baby, couldn't imagine how anyone could leave a kid right out in the open like that, manger or no manger, and on Christmas Eve to boot. A baby was to be cherished and loved, nurtured and adored. Like a woman, but more so.

Oh, he was accustomed to babies. Joe came from a large Polish Catholic family, and his five fertile sisters and their husbands kept the family well supplied. Mary Cecilia had five children, and Gracie had three, all boys. Then there was Lois with her brood of four and one on the way, which would catch her up with Mary Cecilia, much to her delight. And then there was Tonia and her twin girls, and Jenn with her four-year-old son. Jenn lagged behind the others, but she was the youngest.

His sisters and brothers-in-law, immersed as they were in the joys of child rearing, pestered him a lot for not upholding the family tradition in producing offspring. "When are you going to get married?" they kept asking. Up until recently, Joe had only smiled or deflected their inquiries with a lighthearted comment of some sort. It wasn't that he didn't want to get married. The trouble was that he hadn't found the right woman.

At Thanksgiving only a few weeks ago, Jenn had bugged him again about remaining a bachelor for so long. He'd recently been out with a local schoolteacher a few times, so he'd dropped that information right into the middle of the family razzfest. What the rest of the Marzinskis still didn't know was that Joe had already crossed the schoolteacher off his list of possibilities because she'd made it clear that she didn't want kids.

The truth was that Joe was thirty-five and tired of looking. All the good ones, he suspected, had been picked off long ago by guys who didn't have to spend all their time building a business. Now that Condo Crisis Control was thriving, Joe could afford to take time off. He couldn't find anyone worth spending it with, that's all. It was sad in a way, but what was a guy to do?

He wished this baby would stop crying. Maybe a view of the scenery would help. He wandered over to take in the wide-window view of Coquina Beach and the Intracoastal Waterway to the west. At this time of year with all the colored lights adorning the houses on the other side, the view was spectacular.

"Look," he said to the baby. "See the lights? Pretty neat, huh?"

Not that she seemed to pay any attention. If anything, the crying intensified. And she was kicking so hard that the blanket fell away. His admiration of the Christmas scene across the water paled when he touched one little foot. Now here was something to admire: five little toes. He uncovered her other foot. Five more little toes. Her toenails reminded him of tiny pink seashells.

The baby was a newborn. Joe was pretty sure of that. She was a chubby baby, maybe weighing seven and a half pounds or so, and she seemed alert. Hell, she was more than alert. She was energetic. She was robust. And there was certainly nothing wrong with the kid's lungs. Her screaming was probably audible all the way up to the penthouses on the sixteenth floor.

"Hey," he said softly. "Do you think you could stop making such a racket?" The baby cried even louder.

"Rachel and me, we're doing our best," he said in a reasoning tone, forgetting for the moment that babies didn't take to reasoning. Not knowing what else to do, he hummed the lullabye his mother had always sung to him when he was a kid. Before he knew whether this measure was likely to have any effect, the front door swung open and he swiveled around to see a harried Rachel followed by Gladys Rink carrying a box of disposable diapers.

Rachel headed straight for him, her hair bouncing around her shoulders. She was beautiful. And she was all eyes for the baby. Suddenly he wished she would look at him with that same interest.

"I'm going to change her diaper, and then..." Rachel was saying as she took the baby in her arms.

Changing diapers was something Joe knew about. "Wait," he said, and marshaling his thoughts, making himself concentrate on the matter at hand, he went into the kitchen where he rummaged in the pantry and found what looked like an old but waterproof-vinyl patio tablecloth, which he took into the living room and spread over the couch.

What he'd done was no big deal, but Rachel smiled her thanks with eyes so big and brown that he felt as if he could sink into their velvety depths. For the first time he noticed her short tip-tilted nose and her full rosy mouth that looked for all the world as if it needed kissing.

Kissing. Now why was he thinking about that? *Get a grip, Marzinski,* he told himself sternly.

The door to the hallway hung ajar, and in crept Ynez Garcia, her hair still snaked around those awful pink curlers. "I happened to have some cans of infant formula sitting around. I fed it to Rubio when he was sick." She sounded slightly apologetic.

Rachel, sitting on the couch and applying the clean diaper to the baby, whose cries had diminished somewhat, said blankly, "Mrs. Garcia—Ynez—you fed infant formula to your cat?"

"*Sí,* poor *gato,* it was the only thing he'd eat before he died."

"Well, you're sure it's infant formula, right?"

"Oh, certainly, I wouldn't offer it if it could harm our little Christmas miracle. See, it mixes right out of the can half and half with water. I'll make it up for you if you want."

"Okay," Rachel said. "The can opener is in the middle kitchen drawer." She jiggled the baby while Ynez rummaged in the drawer and washed off the top of the can.

"Rachel, there is a problem," she called over her shoulder. "The can opener broke."

"I'll see if I can fix it," Joe said, but after one look

at it he tossed it in the garbage can. "It's too bent to work. Is there another one?"

"No," Rachel said distractedly. "At least not the punch type."

"I'll get one from my place," said Gladys. As she was preparing to leave, Ivan O'Toole walked in, grumpiness written all over his wispy, lined face. "I couldn't concentrate on TV with all the noise in the hall. I heard everyone milling about."

Gladys drew herself up to her full height, which was somewhere short of a self-important five feet. "We weren't milling, Ivan. We are helping, which is more than you can say, I might add."

Ivan took in the box of diapers on the couch and Ynez in the kitchen measuring formula into a pitcher. "I could do something, I guess," he said reluctantly.

"You could sit down and be quiet," said Gladys.

"Aw, Gladys, you underestimate me." With that, he withdrew a cellophane-packaged pacifier from his shirt pocket and dangled it in front of the baby.

"Now where did you ever get that?" demanded Gladys.

Ivan looked proud of himself. "From the drugstore. I picked up a bunch of baby items that they donated to the condo's hurricane-relief supply a few weeks ago, and this didn't get included because it fell behind the couch. Maybe I better wash it off before you give it to the baby." He hurried into the kitchen.

"I thought you were going to get us a can opener," Rachel reminded Gladys gently.

"Humph, yes," Gladys said before bustling out. She soon returned brandishing the required utensil. "We're bearing gifts," she sniffed. "Like the three wise men."

"It's a Christmas miracle, I tell you," Ynez reiterated from the kitchen.

Ivan O'Toole objected strenuously to this viewpoint, and Gladys tossed in her few cents' worth. While the others continued to take issue with each other over every possible aspect of the situation, Joe said quietly to Rachel, "What can I do?"

Rachel turned to him with a tentative but grateful smile. "If you don't mind, you could get on the phone and call the Health and Social Services people again. Maybe you can leave a message for someone to call here. I mean, I found a baby. An abandoned baby. We really need to report it to someone, don't you think?"

He smiled back. It was easy to smile at Rachel. "We should." He reached for his cell phone, realized he'd left it in the company van. "Is there a phone in the kitchen?"

Rachel glanced over her shoulder at the group, which Gladys was attempting to organize into some semblance of order. "Better use the one in the master bedroom." She gestured with her head toward a door at the far end of the room.

Happy to absent himself from the contentious crowd, which Rachel was now trying to mollify, Joe ambled into the bedroom, which was decorated in a delicate lemon shade of yellow with sheer white draperies pulled halfway across sliding glass doors leading to a balcony overlooking the ocean. The moon was rising now, unfurling ripples of light on the water.

He had to look the number up again before dialing. He tried not to wince as the tinny answering machine message at HSS grated in his ear for the second time that night. "Sorry, but we're out of the office for the Christmas weekend. Our regular office hours are…" and the message droned on as Joe listened. At the end the voice said, "In an emergency, please leave a message," before a beep threatened to separate his ear from his head.

"This is Joe Marzinski," he said impatiently, wondering if anyone in the annals of human history had ever gone deaf from listening to answering machine beeps. He thought he himself might be a likely candidate.

"It's Wednesday night, Christmas Eve, and we've found an abandoned baby at the Elysian Towers condominium. Please have someone call—" and at this point he had to look at the phone to find out the number "—as soon as possible. It's *very important*," he said, emphasizing his words, but the machine cut him off before he could get in the last two syllables of the last word. He slammed the phone down in anger at the unwieldiness of bureaucracies.

Reluctant to rejoin the group until he had calmed down, he glanced around the bedroom. Rachel had said that the apartment belonged to her grandmother, and on the dresser he spotted a picture of a smiling Rachel with her arms wrapped around a beaming older woman who was wearing a wide-brimmed flowery hat. That must be Mimi, he thought. But he doubted that the lacy rose-and-violet-print satin bra looped over the doorknob was Mimi's; ditto the black ribbon-trimmed nightie folded neatly on the nightstand.

He grinned at the thought of Rachel wearing that nightie and was titillated by the unbidden vision of her sliding out of bed in the morning with one strap slipping down her shoulder. He caught himself up short. He had only just met Rachel Hirsch. He had no business thinking intimate thoughts about her. He noted with a not-so-dispassionate interest that there were no signs of a man around.

"Joe! Are you off the phone?"

Feeling undeniably hopeful about where all this might lead, he sauntered out of the bedroom to see Rachel holding the baby over her shoulder and gently rubbing her back. The baby was sucking vigorously on the pacifier, and Mrs. Rink and Mrs. Garcia and Mr. O'Toole were hovering with hushed reverence in the background.

"I left a message with HSS. How's the baby doing?"

Rachel looked worried. "She's hungry. No telling how long it's been since she ate. And, Joe, we don't have any baby bottles. Ynez has mixed the formula, though. The problem is that we can't get it into the baby."

"I'll run to the drug store."

"No point in it. Every place is closed at this hour. It's Christmas Eve."

Joe raked an impatient hand through his hair. "Can't you use an eyedropper or something?"

Rachel patted the baby's round little bottom. "Babies have a sucking instinct, and she wouldn't be able to suck on an eyedropper."

Gladys Rink cleared her throat. "Nellie Winstrom on the seventh floor collects dolls for a hobby, and she showed me a baby doll that came with a nursing bottle. It looked exactly the same as a real bottle only smaller. Want me to go see if she's home?"

"Please," said Rachel.

Gladys returned in a few minutes, triumphantly waving a doll's bottle. "She said we could use it," she said. "Until we can get the baby a real bottle, that is." She rushed to the kitchen to fill it with formula.

Ivan stepped forward. "We can't go on calling this child 'the baby.' She needs a name."

"A name?" said Ynez. "Why, we should call her Christmas. Because she's a Christmas miracle."

"I was thinking of Noel," Gladys called from the kitchen in a tone that brooked no protest.

"Christmas, Noel, what's the difference?" huffed Ivan impatiently. "It all means the same thing."

"She can be Christmas Noel," Joe said in an effort to keep peace, and Rachel smiled at him gratefully and said firmly, "Christmas Noel is a lovely name. We'll call her Chrissy for short."

"Little Baby Christmas," breathed Ynez, clearly captivated.

"Well, Chrissy's a nice enough name," agreed Ivan in a tone of resignation.

"I say we call her that." This from Gladys, which clinched it.

Joe cleared his throat. "I'd better check on the clean-up downstairs. Be right back." He left everyone but Rachel debating the proper temperature of baby formula and how much the baby might drink at one feeding.

As soon as he stepped off the elevator, Joe saw that Sherman, the doorman, had reappeared and was conversing in his usual nasal tones on the phone behind the lobby security desk. Andy, Joe's second in command, was energetically heaving folds of soggy carpet out the open front door where a truck waited to haul it away.

"Hey, Andy, you're doing a great job."

Andy stopped what he was doing and tossed Joe a bag. "I found this near the Nativity scene. Maybe it belongs to your lady."

Joe peeked inside. The bag contained a package of printer paper. "If you're talking about Rachel Hirsch, I might as well inform you that she isn't my lady."

Andy removed his hat and wiped his brow before jamming it on again. "Whatever. Say, Joe, you can go now. Me and the guys, we've got everything under control."

"Who's the boss around here, anyway?"

"Oh, you're the boss, which is why you should take Christmas Eve off." Andy grinned at him.

"I *am* the boss, which is why I'm dealing with this. That way more of my employees can spend the evening with their families. You and the crew can make like a tree and leave now, Andy. I'll take over," Joe said. He was accustomed to filling in for people on holidays since he didn't have a wife and kids of his own. He always felt guilty if his employees had to miss out on their home life due to a holiday mishap.

"We're almost at a stopping point," Andy said. "Besides, I saw how you looked at the woman. She's a knockout, that one. Can't blame you if you got a thing for her." Two of Joe's employees glanced at him and smiled.

Joe drew himself up to his considerable height. "I do not have a 'thing' for Ms. Hirsch or anyone else," he said indignantly. Of course, he wasn't about to admit it to Andy and the crew, but it was true that the thought of spending the evening with Rachel had crossed his mind.

"Well, boss, want to come along with us? We're gonna be leaving in a few minutes." As if to emphasize the truth of this, Andy went outside and slammed the tailgate on the truck. The workers gathered there were already shucking their damp coveralls and exchanging lighthearted banter.

But Joe didn't want to leave.

Before Andy could embarrass him further in front of his employees, Joe adopted what he hoped was a noncommittal expression, hastily stepped back into the elevator and pushed the up button. "I'll see about getting someone out to repair the ceiling tomorrow," he said to a bunch of upraised eyebrows as the door closed in front of his face.

His lady.

A thing for her.

Right now Andy and his cohorts were probably gleefully elbowing each other in the ribs and speculating on the boss's chances of getting lucky.

Joe inhaled a deep breath. Well, okay. He was fascinated by Rachel Hirsch. Who was she, and why was she alone on Christmas Eve? And what exactly was it about her that made him want to stick around on a night when he could be going home to his family?

Well, for once thing, he'd begun to feel alone even when he was in the midst of family activities. No one at those regular gatherings of the Marzinski clan was exclusively his, no one had his welfare primarily at heart. Even a Marzinski could be lonely sometimes.

If he allowed himself to be completely candid, he had to admit that a Rachel Hirsch under his Christmas tree would be a welcome present indeed.

Chapter Two

When Joe arrived back in the apartment on the eleventh floor, Rachel was sitting on the couch in the midst of a fascinated group. She was feeding the baby and retelling with much animation the story of how she found Chrissy.

"What I want to know," Ivan said loudly when Rachel had finished, "is where did the baby come from?"

"We should not question Christmas miracles, Mr. O'Toole," Ynez reminded him gently.

"Christmas or no Christmas, babies don't just happen."

"Well, Ivan, it appears that this one did. Goodness," said Gladys, glancing at her watch, "I still have to call my son in Seattle. I'd better get going. Rachel, are you sure that's going to be enough diapers?"

"They should get us through the night."

"You're planning to keep the baby here all night?" Joe asked, somewhat disconcerted.

"If the HSS is shut down for the holiday, I may have no choice," Rachel said. Something in her tone, something raw and revealing, made him shoot her a keen look. In that moment he thought he saw desperation flare behind her eyes and a pain that surprised him. He would have thought that Rachel Hirsch, in her snug T-shirt and wild blond hair and short flippy shorts, didn't have a care in the world except whether, say, the latest shades of fingernail polish complemented her suntan.

Gladys gathered herself together and patted Rachel's shoulder. "Well, I'm sure the baby will be safe with you. Good night, Rachel, dear. See you tomorrow."

"Now, Rachel, you call me, I'm just a few doors away, and you have my number if you need anything at all." Ynez Garcia spared Rachel a nervous smile and headed for the door.

"Good night, and merry Christmas," said Ivan. He chucked the baby lightly under the chin before following the others out.

"Whew," said Rachel dispiritedly after Joe had closed the door behind them. "I'm sure my neighbors mean well, but I'm glad they've gone." With her left hand she brushed her hair back behind her ear. Joe had noticed before that she wore no rings, and there wasn't even a telltale white band of skin where one had been recently removed.

He took off his tool belt and slung it over a chair back, then sat down opposite Rachel and leaned forward, his elbows on his knees. "How's the baby doing?"

"She seems healthy. And she's eating well. The doll's bottle works fine." She grinned over at him, her face lit with pleasure. Her skin had the texture of a sun-burnished apricot, and her lips were luscious and full.

"I don't know when the HSS people will call back. We've got to keep in mind that it's Christmas Eve, you know."

"I know," she said softly. For a moment she looked inexpressibly sad. The expression was a fleeting one. Was she sad because she was alone? He saw no signs of the season in the apartment at all. Most people he knew went overboard with decorations—wreaths made of seashells were big this year, and so were electric candles in windows and Christmas trees trimmed all in one color.

While he was pondering the lack of ornamentation in the apartment and its possible relation to the sadness he sensed in Rachel, she arranged the newly named Chrissy over a clean dish towel spread across her shoulder and began patting her back. Rachel handled the baby with gentle competence as if she were well experienced at motherhood. That was odd, too. Joe didn't peg Rachel for a mother, since her personality was anything but matronly. He detected a mystery about her. A mystique. He considered himself a down-to-earth kind of guy, but he liked mystique.

Chrissy began to wriggle. "I can't get her to burp," Rachel said.

"Give her to me," Joe said with assurance born of long experience with all his nieces and nephews. He took the baby from Rachel and propped her on one of his knees in a sitting position, one big hand gently cupping the baby's chin. With the forefinger of the other hand, he rubbed Chrissy's delicate little spine up and down, producing a burp after only a few seconds.

Rachel shot him a frankly admiring look. "You know your stuff, Marzinski. You must have a couple of kids of your own."

He felt slightly abashed. "No. I'm not married," he said, and the conversation paused a beat until he jumped into the awkward silence and told her about his big family and how all Marzinskis pitched in to help whenever one of them had a new baby.

"You know, it must be nice to have so many sisters," Rachel said, looking wistful. "I was an only child, and my father died a long time ago. My mother's in a nursing home and doesn't even recognize me anymore.''

This, then, could account for the sadness. But before he could reply, Rachel glanced down bemusedly at a damp spot on the front of her shirt. "While you're holding Chrissy, do you think you could feed her what's left in the bottle? Before I changed her diaper, I got a little wet. I'd like to put on dry clothes.''

The mention of clothes caused a vision to flit across Joe's mind of Rachel wearing that pretty satin bra he'd seen in the bedroom. *Ho-ho-ho,* he thought.

"I don't mind feeding the baby," he said. "The guys have finished with the mess in the lobby, and it's not as if I have to go anywhere.''

Rachel's eyes held a teasing light. "Don't you have to put together a swing set or something? For one of those nieces or nephews of yours?''

"I wiggled out of helping my brother-in-law assemble bikes for his twins after Sherman called about the leak from the fourth floor. So, no, I don't mind bottle duty.''

She smiled at him. "Thanks, Joe. I'll be right back," she said, and her bare knee brushed the leg of his jeans as she headed toward the bedroom. He caught a whiff of the fresh fragrance of her skin as she passed. She smelled like rain-drenched flower buds—the heady scent of night-blooming jasmine, maybe.

While she was gone, he allowed himself to imagine Rachel walking toward him carrying great bunches of jasmine, her hair loose and free, and she was wearing—well, she wasn't wearing much. She wasn't even wearing the satin bra. As she was bending over to kiss him, the phone rang.

Almost immediately Rachel, the real Rachel, strode out of the bedroom wearing jeans and a loose, yellow short-sleeved sweatshirt so short that it left a band of skin exposed at her midriff. A cordless phone was pressed to her ear, and she looked distressed.

"Oh. Okay. Right," she said. She hung up with a beep.

She stared at Joe blankly. "It was a social worker from HSS. She says she's the only one on call tonight, but she'll be over soon to take the baby." She seemed agitated, on edge. She hadn't been that way when she'd left to change clothes.

"The HSS people are trained to deal with situations like this one," he said, thinking that she needed reassurance. "The baby will be fine. They'll find a foster home with people who will love and care for her, and—"

To his dismay Rachel's face crumpled, and her brown eyes, her beautiful eyes, filled with tears.

"Rachel?" He couldn't believe this.

Tears ran down her cheeks, and she buried her face in her hands.

Joe let her cry, not knowing what else to do. His instinct was to go to her and wrap his arms around her, but he intuited that she wouldn't welcome such familiarity. Besides, he was sure he couldn't put the baby down without her starting to cry, too. That would mean he'd be trying to calm two weeping females, and after growing up with five sisters, it was a task to which Joe knew himself to be unequal.

Finally he shifted the baby over to one arm, hanging on to both baby and bottle with one hand as he dug a handkerchief out of his pocket. He silently offered the handkerchief to Rachel, and she accepted it and mopped her eyes.

"Sorry,", she mumbled. "I think I've bonded with this

baby, believe it or not. You wouldn't think I'd be so emotional about her, would you?''

"Don't apologize," he said sharply. He softened his tone. "What I mean is, you don't have to hide the way you feel. You seem very real to me because you're being yourself."

"Yep, this is the real me, all right." She didn't sound happy about it.

"In our big Polish family," he said, "emotion is standard. For instance, you should hear my mother every time one of us gets on a plane. You'd think we were going to the North Pole instead of Atlanta or Denver. She cries and brings fried chicken to the airport so we won't have to eat airline food. It's not good for us, she says. And she's totally oblivious to the fact that fried chicken isn't the most healthful of foods itself. What makes this all so funny is that Mom has no firsthand knowledge of airline food because she's never been on a plane in her life."

Rachel managed a tentative smile before she sank down on the couch beside him. She looked drained.

"Rachel," he said carefully. "I don't mean to minimize what you're feeling. I only want you to know that you're entitled to feel it and to express it. Okay?" He was touched that she could feel so much for this baby after so short a time.

She looked rueful and studied his expression for a long moment before she spoke. "All right." She made a visible effort to pull herself together. "How about letting me hold her again?" she asked in a small voice.

If that was all it would take to make Rachel feel better, then she could hold the baby. She could hold a million babies as far as he was concerned.

"Sure," he said easily. "I think this kid's eaten all she wants for the time being." He carefully massaged

Chrissy's back until she brought up another air bubble, then he checked her diaper and settled the baby in Rachel's outstretched arms. Chrissy made little smacking motions with her mouth, and he was prepared to pop the pacifier into her if necessary, but the motions subsided and the baby looked around wide-eyed until her eyes fixed on Rachel's face.

"She'll probably fall asleep now," Rachel said. She gazed at the baby with an expression of such devotion that Joe might not have been there at all. Rachel's long eyelashes curved shadows on her cheek; Joe had never seen such abundant lashes.

Suddenly restless, Joe stood up and walked over to the sliding-glass door leading to the balcony.

"Nice view," he said.

Rachel glanced up. "I know. I feel really lucky to be here for the season. Mimi won't be back for another month or so."

He kept his back to Rachel, but he could see her reflection in the glass.

"Where are you from?" In the mirror of dark glass, he watched her.

"North Florida originally. New Jersey lately," she said. She left it at that.

He waited for her to elaborate, but she didn't. Suddenly he remembered something. "I brought a package upstairs. Andy found it near the Nativity scene."

"Oh, it's my printer paper. I was going to work tonight. That's before I found you," she said to the baby. Her voice changed when she talked to Chrissy: it became gentle and solicitous. She sounded the way his sisters sounded when they talked to their babies.

"You work at home?" Through a door to the left of

the kitchen he'd spotted a computer monitor and stacks of papers strewn across a desk.

"I have my own secretarial service. In the past couple of months I've developed a steady client list of businessmen who live in Coquina Beach during the winter season and need a personalized typing and faxing service. One of the men I work for has a major report due on the last day of the year, so I've been working steadily for the past couple of days." She looked worried for a moment. "I should be working now," she said.

"I'll be glad to look after the baby until the social worker gets here if you need to be doing something else," Joe offered.

"Thanks, but I really want to hold her until she leaves." Rachel nuzzled the baby's cheek. "She's so adorable. So sweet."

"Who could leave a child like this, that's what I'd like to know. If you hadn't come along, there's no telling what could have happened."

"It was a good thing I had to go buy paper," she said. She paused, and then her eyes widened. "Oh, Joe, I'm not much of a hostess am I? Would you care for a drink? There are drinks at the bar."

Joe had noticed the well-stocked wet bar in the corner earlier. He shook his head. "Nothing for me."

He wanted to add, *I could be happy looking at you all night.* He wanted to say, *When the baby's gone, don't kick me out, too.* But he said nothing. He only watched Rachel, admiring the curve of her high cheekbones and the swanlike elegance of her long neck. He had pegged his initial reaction to Rachel Hirsch as primal, a born instinct. But what had kept his attention after the first few minutes was his sense that she needed someone, that she was lonely. And vulnerable. And she was immensely appealing to him because of that.

She saw that he was staring at her, and he thought she flushed slightly. "Tell you what," she said. "You deserve a reward for not leaving me in the lurch with the baby. After Chrissy is gone, we'll see if we can do justice to those brownies I made earlier today. I used Mimi's recipe, double-chocolate-chunky everything. How does that sound?"

"Like dessert. I didn't eat tonight. How about if I order out for dinner first?"

She looked taken aback. "I didn't think to offer you a meal."

"No matter. I like Chinese food. How about you?" He reached across for the phone and sat down facing her. He didn't want to position himself where he couldn't see her.

"I ate earlier."

"You might want a midnight snack. Do you like moo goo gai pan?" he asked as he dialed Fat Choy's Chinese Take-Out.

"Oh, I don't think—" she began, and he thought that maybe she didn't want him around that late. But then, "I am a little hungry," she admitted.

"Egg roll?" he asked. She nodded.

"You knew the phone number by heart," she remarked after he'd hung up.

"I eat a lot of take-out."

"Don't you cook?"

"I often get home late from a job and don't feel like making a mess in the kitchen. Especially since it's only me."

She treated him to a measuring glance. He wasn't sure what it meant. "Don't you have girlfriends?"

He shook his head. "Not lately. The women I meet aren't usually willing to wait around while I rescue some condo's swimming-pool pump or track down the only repairman in town who knows how to fix a certain kind of card-system entry gate."

"You must have a terrific business," she said.

He warmed to this topic. "It's growing," he said. "I have three offices now along the coast."

"So many! How'd you get into this line of work?"

"I started from scratch when I realized that these big buildings on the beach had a real need for someone they could call when things break, as they inevitably do. We handle plumbing failures like the one tonight as well as electrical problems and air-conditioning malfunctions and, well, almost anything that can go wrong. Usually it happens on holidays. Like Christmas Eve." He didn't tell her that he planned to be a millionaire before he was forty. And would be, barring unforeseen circumstances.

"Wouldn't you rather be with your family tonight?" she asked. He couldn't help noticing that she had a way of cocking her head to one side when she listened, her eyes fixed on his with an intensity that signified total interest. It made him want to talk to her for a long time, to bask in her approval.

"I'm not leaving until after the baby's gone." *And hopefully much later,* he added to himself.

"But—"

"There'll be time for my family later."

Rachel caught her lower lip between her teeth, clearly unsure what to make of this. Of him. At that moment the baby stirred in her arms, restlessly tossing her head from side to side. "Is anything wrong, little Chrissy?" Looking grateful for the distraction, Rachel pressed her lips to the fuzz on top of the baby's head.

"You and the baby," Joe said suddenly. "You're a lovely picture. You look like a composite of every Madonna and child painting I've ever seen."

Rachel's eyes, startled now, focused on him. They held his for an endless moment before she glanced away in confusion. She didn't seem to know what to say.

Joe was afraid he'd made her uncomfortable. He cleared his throat. "What I mean is, you're beautiful when you look at the baby the way you do."

Rachel started to shake her head in denial.

"No, I mean it," he said. "If I've offended you in some way—" Perhaps he was pushing too hard.

She flushed, whether with pleasure or not he wasn't sure. "I don't hear many compliments," she said. Her features seemed softly etched in the dim light from the lamp on the other side of the room.

"I can't imagine why not."

"Are you always this nice?"

He hadn't expected a blunt question. He smiled at her. "Am I nice?" he said.

"Very."

"Let's just say I'm glad to help." Their eyes held for a long moment of understanding, and Joe thought, *Where did that come from?* And he knew that it didn't matter why they could reach out to each other in these unusual circumstances. It only mattered that they had.

The delivery girl from Fat Choy's brought the food, and Rachel refused to put the baby down even to eat. She held Chrissy carefully in her lap and brandished a plate off to one side so that moo goo gai pan wouldn't fall on the sleeping child, and when she couldn't open the little packet of hot mustard for her egg roll because her hands were full, Joe opened it for her.

"This is good," she said. "Really good."

"I'm glad to see you chowing down."

"I haven't had Chinese food in a long time. I didn't know the best place to get it here."

"Fat Choy's has the best take-out, but if you want a restaurant, then we should go to the Oriental Garden," he said without thinking. He realized too late that this implied a continuing relationship with her, but she had given him no signal that she would want to see him again.

She glanced at her watch. "I wonder what happened to that social worker," she said.

Chrissy opened her eyes.

"There, there," Rachel said in that solicitous tone of hers. "We're not trying to get rid of you. No, we're not. We're not, I promise."

Chrissy sighed, brought her knees up, screwed up her face and began to wail.

"Shh," Rachel said. "Hush now." She offered the pacifier, but the baby spit it out.

Joe bent over them. "Could she be hungry again?"

"She only ate an hour ago."

"Maybe she needs water," Joe said.

"Would you mind getting it?"

Joe went into the kitchen and after a while came back with a bottleful of water, which they tried to give to the still-screaming infant, who only thrashed her head back and forth and screamed with even more gusto.

"Maybe she needs to lie on her stomach," said Rachel, looking worried. She eased the baby onto her lap, stomach down, but the baby cried harder than ever.

"She must have colic," Joe said bleakly. Not that he thought Rachel could hear; the baby had a marvelous set of vocal chords that seemed to be stuck on high volume.

"I'd better try calling the HSS people again," Joe muttered. He picked up the phone and stalked into the bedroom. If he hadn't closed the door, he wouldn't have been able to hear the number on the other end ringing.

He was forced to listen to HSS's full recorded announcement in order to leave a message of his own.

"This is Joe Marzinski again," he bellowed into the recorder without much patience. "I called earlier. We've still got the baby we found in the manger, and we're waiting for the social worker who said she'd come and get her. The baby is crying." He opened the door to the living room and held the phone out so that the cries would be recorded. "Hear that? The baby is crying *hard*." A thought occurred to him. "You can hear the baby crying, right? So you know this isn't a sick joke. Uh, goodbye." He hung up, wishing that social worker would show up now. Or a minute ago. Or a half hour ago.

"Any luck with the HSS?" Rachel asked when he returned.

"The recorded message again."

They exchanged a look of pure futility.

"Well, Rachel, do you happen to know what we need to do for colic?" He balanced his hands on his hips and stood looking down at the two of them, Rachel and the baby. The neckline of Rachel's shirt had slipped sideways, revealing a seductive bit of cleavage. He realized with a start that she wasn't wearing a bra.

"I always—" Rachel began, then clamped her lips together. It was a long moment before she spoke again. "In Mimi's linen closet is a hot water bottle. We could try that."

Joe was barely paying attention to what she was saying. No bra. Why wasn't she wearing one? Maybe she hadn't had time to put one on when the phone rang earlier. He imagined her shrugging into the sweatshirt, yanking it down over her bare breasts as she grabbed the phone. He was tantalized by the thought of her loose breasts shifting under the fabric, rubbing against the soft nap of the sweatshirt.

"The linen closet is the door next to the bathroom," Rachel said.

Linen closet. Bathroom. Hot water bottle. Right. Joe hurried to get the hot water bottle as he willed his anatomy to calm down.

Joe had just filled the hot water bottle with water from the bathroom sink when Rachel called, over the sound of the baby's wails, "I love holding her, but maybe Chrissy would be more comfortable in a crib. I wish we had one."

Joe looked around the apartment, eager for something, anything to do. There was nothing that could be pressed into service as a baby crib. "How about a dresser drawer?" he asked with sudden inspiration.

Rachel waved him toward the bedroom, with which he was becoming very familiar. Although not in the way he would like, he thought to himself.

"Will any drawer do?" he called toward the living room, but Rachel was cooing to the baby and the baby was still screaming, so in the end he pulled out the top drawer of the dresser and dumped everything in it on the floor. Out rolled skimpy bikini panties in rainbow colors and bras to match and panty hose in unopened packages and a fragrant sachet packet. Jasmine. Just as he'd thought.

A folded blanket from the closet made a cushion for the bottom of the drawer, and he grabbed a pillowcase out of the linen closet for a sheet. He would have liked to add something waterproof between sheet and blanket, but he couldn't find anything that would do, so he carried the drawer out into the living room where Rachel was now pacing back and forth with the squalling child draped over her shoulder. He set the hot water bottle on top of the makeshift mattress.

Together they eased the baby onto the hot water bottle, and she settled down to an occasional whimper. Joe brought an afghan from the foot of the bed to cover her, but it turned out to be too big. Rachel produced a crocheted shawl of Mimi's and tucked it around the now-sleeping infant. They were sharing a smile of triumph when the phone rang.

"Get that, will you, Joe?" Rachel said.

He clicked the phone on and crooked it between his neck and shoulder as he smoothed the shawl down over the baby's feet. He listened while the person on the other end talked.

"Oh. I see," he said, his hopes for a romantic evening fading.

Rachel glanced up at him as he hung up. One hand rested on the baby's back, and the other was gathering her hair back from her face, exposing the smooth and delectable line of her jaw.

"Who was it, Joe?"

"A police officer. She says that the only social worker on duty has been in an automobile accident and has been taken to the hospital emergency room. They don't think it's a serious injury, but she won't be here tonight. Police headquarters is going to send a policeman over to talk to you about how you found the baby as soon as they get a chance. They'll probably take the child into custody." He glanced at his watch. It was a few minutes before midnight.

"Well," he said, a little too heavy on the irony. "Merry Christmas, Rachel."

"Merry Christmas," she replied faintly. But her voice held a sense of wonder, and there was nothing ironic in the way she said the words at all.

Chapter Three

Joe's hands, Rachel thought dispassionately, were huge.

The two of them sat at Mimi's tiny kitchen table, their knees bumping occasionally because they were in such close quarters. Rachel had cut the brownies into nine squares, and they had eaten six of them. Well, Joe had eaten five. She'd only had one.

Her own hands were folded demurely in her lap, whereas his were wrapped around one of Mimi's coffee mugs. This one said, The Hurrier I Go, The Behinder I Get. Rachel tried not to think about getting behind in her work; this was an emergency.

No. The baby was an emergency. Joe was not. But all the same it was fun sitting across from him, looking into his eyes and developing an intimate knowledge of his kneecaps. She could tell that Joe was deliberately keeping his gaze above her neckline, which amused her slightly. She already knew that he thought she was pretty. Did he also think she was sexy?

"So," he was saying, "after my old man raised six kids on a machinist's salary, I figure he has a right to do whatever he wants. He's got the greenest yard on the east coast of Florida, works in it all the time, loves gardening.

And my mom, well, she's busy with her grandchildren and her charity work. You'd like my mom."

"I'm sure I would," Rachel said. She paused, wondering about him. "Did you grow up here in Coquina Beach?"

Joe flashed a grin. "Around here, you don't grow up on the wrong side of the tracks. You grow up on the wrong side of the Intracoastal, like me. We had a big stucco house near the church on the mainland. Come on, I'll show you." He stood up and rinsed his coffee mug in the sink; he seemed at home in a kitchen.

He took Rachel's hand—it surprised her, this contact, but she didn't pull away—and led her to the sliding-glass doors. "See the church steeple? No, we'll have to go out on the balcony."

Rachel cast a glance toward Chrissy. She was sleeping peacefully. Joe slid the door open quietly and they stepped out into the cool night air.

Joe gestured toward the mainland. "The steeple of St. Marina's is to the left of the docks over there, see how it's lit up red and green for Christmas? Okay, count over four rooftops, and that's our house. The one with a banyan tree to the side."

Rachel could just make out the lights in the windows of a house that appeared to be white stucco with a red Spanish-tile roof. "Do you think your parents are up this late? It's after midnight."

"Oh, sure, they're probably wrapping presents, and Mom's doing something in the kitchen, baking maybe."

"You'll be having Christmas dinner there tomorrow then." For a moment she felt a pang of nostalgia for all the Christmas dinners she'd eaten in the past—roast goose, with her mother's special wild rice stuffing, fresh cranberry-and-orange relish, mince and pumpkin and apple pie with a slice of cheddar cheese melted on top.

"I may not have time for dinner tomorrow," he said. "I've got to make sure this job downstairs gets done."

Rachel wrapped her arms around herself and leaned on the concrete railing. The lights across the water were a spectacle of red, green, yellow and blue. Maybe because there wasn't snow on the ground to lend a Christmasy atmosphere, Floridians went wild with colored and lighted decorations. On one of the boats alongside the municipal dock, a cheery Santa Claus figure bobbed on top of the tuna tower, his hand raised in greeting. Eight blinking reindeer danced across the roof of an insurance office nearby. Reflections of the colored lights mingled with the reflections of the stars and rippled merrily across the dark water.

"The lights are prettier than snow for Christmas," Rachel said almost to herself. "Snow only stays perfectly white long enough for someone to take its picture for next year's Christmas card."

"To me, a warm climate is right for celebrating Christ's birth," Joe said. "After all, the first Christmas took place in a place a lot like this. And it's not as if we don't have most of the trappings. Every mall has a Santa to take orders from the kids, and we even have more than our share of Salvation Army bell ringers."

They smiled at each other in easy agreement. Suddenly self-conscious, Rachel looked away first. "It's certainly lucky for Chrissy that it's warm," she said. True, this was a convenient change of subject, but all the same, she didn't like to think about the baby's lying abandoned in the Nativity scene. In fact, she shivered at the thought.

Joe noticed. "Let me get a wrap for you," he said.

Rachel wasn't cold at all, but she said nothing to correct

his misunderstanding. Instead she said, "Why don't we go back in."

Joe hurried inside, anyway, and came back with the afghan that they hadn't needed for the baby.

"Is Chrissy—"

"Sleeping soundly." He draped the afghan around Rachel's shoulders. "Better?" he asked.

Joe seemed to want to make her more comfortable, which touched her, so Rachel only nodded and tilted her face slightly until she was looking at him. The moon above was flat and shining with a silvery light; it cast his features into sharp relief. Rachel thought how strong Joe's profile was and yet how tender he could be. She warmed toward him as he moved closer and slid his arm around her shoulders.

"I like looking at the Christmas lights from this side of the water," Joe said quietly. "It's pretty, isn't it? Kind of gets me in a holiday mood." Up here the traffic sounds were muted, but they could still hear the crash of breakers upon the beach.

"We really should go back in. What if the baby cries?"

Joe laughed. "If that baby cries, we'll hear her. *Everybody* will hear her. Still cold?"

Rachel shook her head. She didn't know where this was going. On the one hand, she thought she should put a stop to it—right now, before any expectations developed. On the other hand, the expectations that were developing might be only hers. She sneaked a look at Joe. He looked quiet, contemplative, and if he noticed that she was looking at him, he gave no sign.

"Someday," he said suddenly, "I'll have a house on Coquina Island. A big one on the ocean."

"Seriously?" she said.

"Sure. Why not? I can't go on living in a two-bedroom apartment the rest of my life. Besides, I find the ocean soothing and restful, not only to look at but to listen to. To get up in the morning and take my coffee out on a deck overlooking the beach instead of grabbing it on the run would be heaven."

"Hmm," Rachel said, picturing it. He would be wearing shorts, she thought, in the morning as he walked out to survey the beach, and his big hands would be wrapped around a mug much as they had been earlier in the kitchen, and for a moment she had a vision of those hands doing something much more exciting than raising a mug to his lips. His lips. For a moment she imagined how soft they would feel. Oh, God, she must be losing it.

"And then," he was saying, "every morning after I call my office and check on the jobs we've got going, I'll go for a swim. Maybe about twenty minutes of swimming and then I'll call my office again and then," and here he stopped.

"And then?" she said.

He slid a glance in her direction. "Well, I was just thinking how lonely it would be without kids. A big house like the one I want should have kids hanging out every window and falling off every deck." He looked sheepish.

"These, um, children," she said, trying to picture them. "Are you planning to start an orphanage or something? Because we may have found your first candidate tonight."

"No, I'll only start an orphanage as a last resort. Hopefully they'll be *my* kids. My sisters are all having conniption fits because I'm the only Marzinski who hasn't reproduced."

"Failing to conform to the family standards, huh?"

"Afraid so. My business has taken a lot of time up until now. I've recently hired an administrative assistant and a new receptionist, which should free me up to have more of a life, but now that I've got time to think about it, I haven't decided which should come first—the kids or the big house."

He seemed to be poking fun at himself, and she smiled. She could imagine Joe as the patriarch of a large family, a galloping gaggle of small Marzinskis with gray eyes flashing and black hair curling and—big hands?

One of those hands was now massaging her shoulder through the afghan. "Don't you dream of a home and family, Rachel? You're so good with the baby."

Rachel was stunned. She hadn't expected this. She drew in her breath sharply, but even as she did, Joe tucked his free hand under her chin and tipped her face toward his. The Christmas lights across the water seemed not mere red but crimson, not only blue and green and yellow but azure and emerald and topaz. And then, as her heart started beating crazily in her chest, Joe's face angled toward hers and his eyes started to whirl as her vision got all mixed up, and she saw the stars and moon and eternity momentarily reflected in their pinwheel depths as his lips found hers.

She couldn't resist. Didn't have the strength for it, and then didn't want to. The kiss deepened, lengthened, his lips caressing hers, her soul rising up to reacquaint her with needs long dormant. She hadn't been kissed in so long that she had forgotten what it was like, had forgotten how it could make her lose all track of time or place or self. She had forgotten how a good kiss could touch places that she didn't know existed and how it could make her forget things she'd rather not remember. She had forgotten.

It was he who pulled away first, and when his face came back within her field of vision and looked like his face again, a very handsome face, all she could do was stare.

"Ah, Rachel," he said, sounding pleased, "wasn't that nice?"

"Y-yes," she said.

"And wouldn't you like me to do it again?" He smiled into her eyes and slid his hands under the afghan until she felt his thumbs resting on the bare skin above her waistband, treating her to a shimmering delight of goose-flesh.

"Yes," she whispered, lifting her lips, and he slid her closer to him this time, wrapped her tightly in his arms and kissed her until she was dizzy and could no longer breathe. His lips tasted faintly of coffee and Mimi's double-chocolate-chunky-everything brownies, and probably hers did, too, and she'd never been kissed in that flavor before. She'd never been kissed with such intensity, either, she thought. At least that's what she thought when she could think.

His hands pressed her so close that she could feel the rippling of his chest muscles through their clothing, and she felt her nipples hardening and tightening against the pressure. And as her mouth sank into his she wound her hands around his neck, tangling them in the hair at the nape and glorying in the coarseness of it and then the smoothness. She expelled a sigh from deep in her heart and felt filled with the peace and richness of the night. Joe moaned low in his throat as her hands moved around his head so that when he pulled away his face was framed between her palms. She felt the firm cartilage of his ears warm beneath her fingertips.

"This," he said unsteadily, "is a Christmas present."

Christmas.

Christmas, the holiday she'd never wanted to celebrate again.

Suddenly four dear faces danced before her like tree ornaments: Nick, smiling at her in that quirky fun-loving way of his; Lolly, missing her two front teeth; Melissa, her wispy hair held back by twin barrettes; Derek, flashing the dimple in his chin.

All of them.

"Joe," Rachel said. "Joe, I can't do this."

He stared at her, puzzled.

"I'm not asking—"

She trembled so violently that he dropped his arms and took a step backward. She wrapped the afghan tightly around her.

"I know you're not asking," she said, drawing herself up with what she hoped was dignity. "I think we should go inside."

"Rachel—"

"Please," she said dully, and then she whirled around and slid the door open, went through it into the living room. The bright-yellow decor hit her right between the eyes; it was exactly what she needed to bring her to her senses.

She was bending over the baby when Joe came in and closed the door behind him. He yanked the vertical blinds closed, shutting out the view of the lights and the stars and the moon. She couldn't look at him; she knew she'd led him on and felt guilty that she couldn't follow through.

"Maybe I'd better go," Joe said with obvious reluctance. He didn't sound angry or upset; he only sounded confused.

She straightened, trying to think of what she could say

to him that would explain without really explaining, and
wondering if she was stupid to think she had to explain
at all.

And then Chrissy woke up and let out a wail, and the
phone and the doorbell rang at the same time.

Joe grabbed the phone in one swift motion as Rachel
lifted the baby.

"There, there," Rachel soothed as Joe made a beeline
for the door. Expecting the promised policeman, he flung
it open without asking who was there and barked,
"Hello?" into the phone.

Rachel looked up to see a costumed Santa Claus standing in the hall.

"Merry Christmas," said the Santa over the din issu-
ing from the baby.

"Merry Christmas," Joe said blankly. He was still
holding the phone to his ear and trying to listen.

Rachel rocked the baby. "Time for a bottle, I'd say,"
she said to no one in particular.

"It's your grandmother," Joe said. He waved the
phone at Rachel. "Won't you come in?" he said to the
Santa.

"Ho-ho-ho," said Santa. "Yes, I think so."

Rachel took the phone. "Here," she said to Joe, dump-
ing the baby in his arms. "Mimi's calling from Singapore."

"Is there anything around here to eat?" Santa asked
with mild interest.

"Right this way," Joe said, raising his eyebrows. He
led Santa into the kitchen. "Brownies," he said, pointing
toward the plate. He shuffled the baby over to one arm.
Rachel had prepared a bottle earlier, and he took it out
of the pan of warm water and tested it on his forearm.

"Mmm, are these ever good," Santa said with his

mouth full. Joe noticed that he was taking care not to let crumbs sully his fluffy white beard. It didn't look like one of those fake beards, either. It looked real.

"Mimi, it's after midnight," Rachel was saying into the phone. "Don't you pay attention to time zones?"

Joe popped the nipple into Chrissy's mouth. She sucked hungrily, greedily, keeping her eyes on his face. They were a deep blue-gray, and their unusual shape reminded him of someone. He couldn't decide who.

"Yes, well, I'm okay, but we've had an unexpected turn of events," Rachel said into the phone.

"You'd be surprised what some people put into their brownies," Santa said in a conversational tone. "Last year I had a fruitcake brownie. A fruitcake brownie! With candied orange peel and cherries. Can you imagine?"

"No," Joe said, hardly paying attention because he was more interested in what Rachel was saying.

"The baby was just lying there in the manger," Rachel said, "and I met this man—no, not one of the men who live at the Elysian Towers. Joe was here fixing the ceiling in the lobby." A pause. "Water was pouring out. Of course Mrs. Rink found out about it. Is there anything Mrs. Rink doesn't find out?" Another pause. "His name is Joe Marzinski. He knows all about babies. He's helping."

Joe removed the nipple from the baby's mouth and flopped her over his shoulder with a practiced flip of the wrist. "Time to burp," he said to Chrissy. He patted gently until she brought up a big moist bubble of air, and before she could cry, he stuck the nipple back in her mouth.

"Looks like you really know what you're doing," said Santa, helping himself to another brownie.

"Yeah, well, just call me Mr. Mom," Joe said. For

the first time he noticed that the Santa had a birthmark in the shape of a crescent moon high on his cheekbone just above his beard.

"No, Mimi," Rachel was saying in the living room, "he's not trying to steal your jewelry. He's a kind man. Right now he's feeding Chrissy. No, not *Misty,* Mimi, her name is *Chrissy.* Well, actually it's Christmas Noel because we found her on Christmas Eve. It'll do till the HSS people find her parents or place her in a foster home."

"Well," said Santa. "I'd better be on my way. Just thought I'd stop by and check on things. Looks like everything is okay around here. You never know about Christmas wishes."

"I'm sure Rachel will be off the phone in a minute if you'd like to stay awhile longer," Joe said politely.

"I'm kind of busy tonight." Santa dabbed at his mouth with a napkin and started toward the door. "On Dasher, on Dancer, and all that," he said.

Chrissy chose that moment to grunt meaningfully, and Joe thought, *Oh no.* By the time he looked up again, Santa had gone.

"Okay, Mimi. Merry Christmas to you, too. I'm fine. No, I mean it. Yes, I love you too. Right. 'Bye."

"I think she's really messed up her diaper," Joe said apologetically to Rachel as she tossed the phone onto a handy chair.

"Give her to me," Rachel said. She made little clucking noises, and Joe thankfully transferred Chrissy to Rachel's arms. Rachel conveyed Chrissy to a small wheeled cart that she'd converted to a diaper-changing table and, moving with crisp efficiency, began to clean the baby.

"Mimi says the weather in Singapore is lovely and that

she's going to a noodle show today. I wonder what's a noodle show.''

"I can't imagine. Hey, who was that guy playing Santa? He said he couldn't stay."

Rachel zapped the tab closed on the diaper and blinked at him. "I thought he was a friend of yours," she said.

"I thought he was a friend of *yours.*"

"Are you sure he wasn't one of the guys on your work crew?"

"Believe me, they're all home with their families by now."

Rachel gathered the baby into her arms and went to the couch. She sat down. She looked baffled. "Well, if you didn't know him and I didn't know him, who could he be?"

"Maybe he's one of the guys who live here, who decided to dress up in a Santa suit and go around to wish everyone a merry Christmas."

"I don't think so. He didn't resemble anyone I know."

"His beard was real. And he had a birthmark, a moon-shaped discoloration on his cheek."

Rachel sighed in exasperation. "Okay, so we have a guy with a real beard and a birthmark. There are definitely no guys with real beards like that and moon-shaped birthmarks who live at the Elysian Towers. I don't even know anyone with a beard." She paused as a thought occurred to her. "I'll bet it was one of Mimi's actor friends. She does a lot of community theater. She also knows a couple of practical jokers. Old boyfriends. I don't recall ever meeting one with a birthmark on his face, though."

"He didn't mention your grandmother," Joe said.

"Well, hand me the phone. I'll call the doorman and

ask if he let a Santa in." She thought again. "No, Sherman will be off duty if it's after midnight."

"Whoever he was, Santa liked the brownies."

"That's no clue. Everyone likes brownies, especially Mimi's recipe. What did you two talk about?"

Joe had been so busy with the baby that he hadn't paid much attention. He thought for a moment. "Santa said— he said that he'd stopped by to check on things."

"Check on things? Maybe he was from HSS."

"Rachel, if he'd been from HSS, would he have been wearing a Santa suit? On the other hand, maybe he was the policeman that the HSS was going to send over."

"I'm sure he would have mentioned it if he was a policeman. Anyway, the police are much too busy to go around wearing Santa suits and eating people's brownies."

"Another thing he said was that you could never tell about wishes, or something like that. Christmas wishes. You could never tell about Christmas wishes."

"Oh," Rachel said. She seemed taken aback, as if she were running a thought through her mind and then discarding it. She looked slightly shaken.

"Is something wrong?"

"At the moment I feel like you did when we were standing in the lobby with water gushing out of the ceiling. We've had a minor flood, somebody left a live baby in the Nativity scene, the social worker on the case has been in a car wreck and we've had a visit from a Santa Claus that neither of us seems to know. Wrong? There must be something wrong because nothing is going right. And where is that policeman, anyway? Am I supposed to wait up all night until he shows up? And don't you want to go home?"

Joe had no intention of leaving at this point. "No,"

he said flatly. "And I'll call to find out when the policeman will be here."

"Fine. Whatever." Rachel went and got the one remaining brownie while he called police headquarters, silently offered him half and ate all of it when he refused. When he hung up, a faint dusting of crumbs remained on Rachel's lower lip, and it was all he could do not to kiss them away.

"The dispatcher who answered the phone said they've been trying to get a policeman over here ever since the HSS called them and that he should be here before long," he told her.

"Sherman is gone for the night. I'll have to go downstairs and open the door for the policeman," Rachel said gloomily. Her shoulders sagged, and for the first time Joe noticed that Rachel looked flat-out exhausted.

"Tell you what, Rachel. I'll go down and let the policeman in when he comes."

"That would be great," she said. She didn't seem overly enthusiastic.

"Why don't you go lie down for a while?" he said. "I'm an experienced baby-sitter."

"I couldn't."

"You could go in the bedroom and close the door. So I'll know you won't take advantage of me."

"I'd be a fool to try it, don't you think?"

"Few ever have."

She smiled at him, and he smiled back. He touched her arm. "You don't have to worry," he said.

She didn't seem to know where to look, and when her glance fell on the baby she said, "At least one of us is getting some rest." She avoided his eyes.

"One out of three isn't good enough." He slid his hand under her arm and pulled her into a standing position. "Come on, Rachel. Nap time, even for grown-ups. You look beat." He spoke cajolingly, as he would to one of his sisters.

"Do I?" she said. She tried to pull her arm away, but he held fast, and then he was propelling her across the room and into the bedroom. She went willingly, stifling a yawn. He twitched the bedspread of the queen-size bed down to reveal pristine white sheets and lace-edged pillow cases.

"Sit," he commanded, and when she did, he bent and slid her sandals off her feet. Her feet were tanned and tiny, no more than a size five, he'd guess. She swiveled so that her legs were on the bed, and he handed her a pillow.

"I'm only going to close my eyes for a few minutes," she said. "When the policeman shows up, will you come and get me?"

"Of course. He'll want to talk to you, not me, since you found the baby."

Rachel yawned. "If Chrissy wakes up, come and get me. If that strange Santa comes back, come and get me. If you have to leave—"

"If I have to leave, I'll come and get you. But I'm not leaving, Rachel." He stared down at her, at the way she took up less than half of the bed. Plenty of room for another person there.

She sighed deeply, and her eyes drifted closed before her head even touched the pillow. Lying there like that with her hands folded gently across her midriff, her chest rising and falling with each breath, she was more beautiful than ever. He replayed their kisses inside his head, then rewound the scene and started it again. He'd thought she was gorgeous from the first moment he'd laid eyes on her, and he'd pegged her right away as a sensuous woman, but he hadn't been sure until she'd responded to his kisses that she was a passionate woman. And having had a taste of it, of her, he wouldn't be satisfied until he kissed her again.

She must have sensed him standing there because her eyes flew open, startled. She pushed herself up on her elbows, and just as quickly he pressed her back into the pillows.

"Is it—?"

"It's only been a few minutes. Everything's okay. Chrissy is sleeping."

She lay back down again, her face gilded by the light he had left on in the closet. The golden glow, gentle as candlelight, glinted on her hair. It really was the most remarkable hair.

"You must be tired too," she murmured.

"I've been up since five this morning."

She smiled faintly. "Poor you. Why don't you sit down?"

"No chair." He hoped she wouldn't suggest that he go back into the living room.

"I meant on the bed." She patted the place next to her, and his heart, so help him, leaped in his chest. Still, he knew it wasn't an invitation. Or at least the kind of invitation he'd like.

He walked around the end of the bed and sat. The bed didn't give; the mattress was covered with something. It felt like armored plate.

"What...?" he said, mystified. Her mouth formed into an *O. Perfect for kissing*, he thought, but he knew better than to try it.

"That's Mimi's magnetic pad. I left it on the bed under the sheet when she left because I never sleep on that side." She drew the covers back and said, "Feel it. Weird, huh?"

He felt. The pad was made of a stiff fabric. It felt as if it was filled with little wires that yielded only slightly under his weight. "What in the world is it for?"

Rachel giggled. "Mimi has back trouble. She got the pad in Japan and is convinced that it takes away the pain. There's some theory behind it, something about the iron magnets realigning the magnetism in the body's cells."

"Poppycock. Lunacy," Joe muttered.

"Don't tell that to my grandmother. Lie down and see what you think."

She didn't have to issue the invitation twice. Joe lay down beside her, settling uncomfortably into the pad. "I don't feel anything except wired," he said, and Rachel laughed.

"You're not supposed to feel anything yet. But if you have back pain or arthritis or something, it's supposed to make it feel a lot better."

Joe lay there. He was wildly aware of Rachel only inches away. He hoped the magnetism in the pad didn't have any other effects, such as making every cell in his body more aware of every cell in her body or increasing the attraction so that suddenly they found themselves inexplicably stuck together. Now that would be a hoot.

He snickered. He couldn't help it.

"Something funny?" she said, sounding half-asleep.

"Yeah. Really," he said.

"Joe?"

"Yes."

"One other thing about the pad. Mimi says it makes you have the most vivid dreams you've ever had in your life."

"I think this whole thing is a dream. It couldn't be

real,'' he said, thinking of the baby found in the manger, the strange Santa and lying in bed next to the most beautiful woman he'd ever met. He hoped he would never wake up. He couldn't imagine having any dream more amazing than this.

But just in case Mimi was right about the dreams, he closed his eyes and waited to see what happened.

Chapter Four

Morning. Warm sunlight on her cheek. A baby crying.

Rachel stirred and rolled over on her side. Maybe if she didn't wake up, Nick would see to the baby. He was good that way, always eager to help with the children.

The baby kept crying. No, she was howling, poor thing. Rachel's eyes opened slowly, squinted at the numerals on the alarm clock on the bedside table. Why hadn't Nick—

The man beside her was staring full into her face, and he wasn't Nick.

Rachel's consciousness catapulted into the here and now. The *here* was Mimi's condo at Elysian Towers. The *now* was Christmas morning. The baby was no baby of hers. And the man was—

Who *was* he? Her mind grappled with his identity even as she pushed herself upright beside him.

Last night. The baby in the manger. The man on the ladder. Joe Marzinski. Condo Crisis Control.

Memories of last night flooded over her, a jumble of faces and names and phone calls and a kiss that she'd rather not think about. To make herself stop thinking about it, she swung her legs over the side of the bed.

"Better see what Chrissy wants," she mumbled before she jumped up and fled into the living room.

The baby was squirming in indignation at the lack of food. Rachel immediately went into the kitchen, scooped the prepared bottle from the refrigerator and settled it in a pan of hot water to warm.

By the time she returned to the makeshift crib, Joe was lifting the baby up. This morning he was tousled of hair and scruffy of beard, and he looked—well, he looked wonderful. His shoulders seemed very wide, and his height was imposing, but his strength and presence were offset by the gentle way in which he tucked the baby close to his chest.

"She's wet," he said.

Chrissy rooted for a nipple against the front of his T-shirt, but he only grinned and said, "Sorry, sweetkins, you'll have to wait." Then he proceeded to change her diaper, and skillfully, too, even though she was waving her fists and making every effort to wriggle off the table.

Rachel decided that there might be no better time to retreat and regroup. "I'd better go brush my teeth," she said. Joe only grunted.

In the bathroom she stared gritty-eyed at her reflection in the mirror. Her hair was matted on one side, and her cheek bore the mark of a wrinkled sheet. She looked awful. And she'd just slept with a man—well, in a manner of speaking—she didn't even know. Not very well, anyway. She must have been out of her mind for letting him sleep beside her all night. He could get ideas. He could have...

She felt a flush rising up the sides of her neck when she thought of what could have happened. He could have reached over and pulled her to him, and he could have kissed her. Again. And she could have kissed him back. Again. Worse yet, she might have liked it.

She washed her face more vigorously than usual and ran a brush through her hair. She was trying not to panic, but she had no idea what her next move should be. Should she ask him to leave? Or would he volunteer to go? Or did she want Joe Marzinski to stay?

She found a scrunchie and bundled her hair into it. *Think, Rachel. Think.* But she couldn't think.

When she went back into the living room, Joe was situated on the couch and Chrissy, curved into the crook of his arm, was going at the bottle for all she was worth.

"Here, let me take over," Rachel said as she sat beside him. Smiling over at her, he transferred the baby into her arms.

"Not that I wasn't enjoying her," he said thoughtfully, looking at Rachel with an expression that she couldn't read.

"Well," Rachel said. "I wonder what happened to that policeman who was supposed to pick Chrissy up last night."

"Want me to call the police department?"

"I wouldn't want them to come before she's eaten properly," Rachel said, thinking that she was worrying entirely too much about this baby.

"She's making a pig of herself all right," Joe replied. As if to prove his point, the baby slurped and gave a kind of snort. "You see?" Joe said, smiling indulgently.

"You'd better call and see what's keeping the police officer," Rachel said with reluctance.

"Okay." He went and looked up the number of the police station in the telephone directory, and Rachel heard him speaking tersely to someone on the other end of the phone.

When Joe came back, he looked resigned. "It seems that they think someone did come to pick up the baby last night."

"But no one—"

"I know, I know. I told them that. We were both here last night, and if anyone had rung the bell downstairs, one of us would have heard it. And it wasn't someone dressed up in a Santa suit that supposedly took custody of the baby. It was a police lieutenant that the dispatcher didn't know, but he had forms to prove that they'd been here. He read them to me on the phone."

Rachel was at a loss to deal with the surge of emotion that accompanied this news. She was inwardly overjoyed that the baby could stay with her, at least for the time being. But the baby couldn't stay forever. She knew that. Maybe today would be long enough. Maybe she could bear to let her go later. In the meantime she tried to concentrate on what Joe was saying.

"It's a bureaucratic snafu, that's all. I guess we'll just have to live with it until we can raise someone at HSS. I can't say that I mind. She's a cute little thing."

As Rachel was absorbing this, Joe bent over and waggled his eyebrows at Chrissy. "Merry Christmas, kiddo. Sorry about all this. Since it's Christmas, we'll have to see about getting you some presents."

"Presents?" Rachel echoed.

Joe straightened. "Well, sure. It *is* Christmas."

"I don't have any presents for her," Rachel said slowly. She never bought Christmas presents anymore. Well, except for Mimi, of course.

"We're not talking anything major, Rachel. What I have in mind is diapers, formula, and if Chrissy's a good girl, maybe a mobile to put over her crib."

"She doesn't have a crib," Rachel reminded him.

"I'll get her one."

The way Joe was talking, it didn't sound as if he were going to go away anytime soon. The baby's hand clutched at the front of Rachel's shirt, and she focused on the small face. Chrissy's eyes were closed, her expression dreamy. Babies were so delightful, so much fun. It was funny how you didn't really mind the work it took to maintain them, odd that you just kept wanting to do more for them even when they were ungracious about it. And this wasn't even her baby.

"Presents later, but what can I do to help now?" Joe prompted.

She'd almost forgotten he was sitting there, and she had to think for a moment.

"You could put the coffee on," she suggested, realizing too late that by asking him to start the coffee, she'd made a tactical blunder. A few minutes ago she'd wanted this guy out of there. Now he would stay until he'd drunk at least a cup. Would she have to offer breakfast, too? She didn't know.

"Coffee. Will do," Joe said. He disappeared into the kitchen.

"Coffee's in the freezer," she called after him. She heard him opening and closing the freezer door, running water in the coffeepot.

"Is it okay to nuke a couple of bagels or would you rather have them toasted?" Joe stuck his head around the corner of the kitchen.

"Nuked is fine." He certainly knew how to make himself at home, but at the moment she didn't mind a bit. She would rather tend to this baby. She removed the nipple from the baby's mouth and eased her over one shoulder.

"I could scramble eggs," Joe called from the kitchen.

"Well," she began. She frowned. "Don't you want to get home to your family?"

"Too late. I've already missed all the fun and games. It's eight o'clock already, and my nieces and nephews have all probably been up since five."

"Oh, that's too bad. Maybe you'd better—"

Joe appeared at the kitchen door. He was drying his hands on a dish towel. "After breakfast I'll call HSS again, see if anyone's there."

"I doubt it. It's Christmas morning. No one will be in the office today."

Joe grinned. "Not to worry. Chrissy is in good hands. Say, before I get down to the mechanics of breakfast, you wouldn't have an extra toothbrush, would you?"

The man had no qualms about moving in and taking charge. Rachel supposed that wasn't so surprising in view of the way he made his living. She sighed. "In Mimi's travel supplies she's got toothbrushes from all over the world. You know, all sealed up in plastic wrap from different hotels. Look in the basket on the top pantry shelf."

Joe went to look, and the aroma of the coffee began to waft into the living room. Rachel rocked the baby and gazed down into the solemn blue-gray eyes. "I bet you wish you had a family for Christmas, don't you?" The baby kept her eyes on Rachel's face, and then, much to Rachel's surprise, she winked.

But of course a baby this age couldn't possibly wink. Still, Rachel had the unsettling feeling that this baby had understood exactly what she had said. And that Chrissy knew all about Rachel's history and why she never wanted to celebrate Christmas again.

Which was ridiculous in the extreme. She'd better stop these fanciful flights of imagination and get serious. She had a baby who needed to be put in foster care, and she had a report to type for a businessman who was going to be hopping mad if it wasn't finished on time.

And she also had a house guest who seemed to have no intention of leaving. He emerged from the kitchen brandishing a razor in cellophane.

"I found this in the basket with the other travel supplies. You don't mind if I shave, do you? And how about a shower?" At least he waited until Rachel nodded faintly. Then he disappeared into the bathroom. She heard him turn on the shower behind the closed door.

Rachel smoothed the baby's soft hair and cuddled her close. If only she didn't have the distracting presence of Joe Marzinski to worry about, she could enjoy this. As it was, she half expected him to walk out of the bathroom with a towel around his waist, demanding to know if it would be all right to toss his clothes in the washer while they ate breakfast. She wouldn't put it past him.

"WELL, NO ONE'S ANSWERING at HSS. Same old recorded message," Joe said, clicking off the phone and tossing it on a chair. They had finished eating, and Joe had stacked the dishes in the dishwasher.

"It's because of the holiday. Everything shuts down," Rachel said, and she could hardly keep the bitterness out of her voice.

He spared her a sharp look but didn't comment.

Rachel smoothed the baby's fluff of hair. "So it looks like we keep you for a while," she cooed to Chrissy, whose sweet soft shape seemed perfectly molded to her own.

"Not without more diapers and formula," Joe reminded her.

"I'll call up Mimi's pharmacist friend and ask if his drugstore will deliver today," Rachel said.

"Don't pester him on Christmas morning. I'll get whatever we need." He whipped a small pad of paper and a pen out of his pocket. "I can get a crib from one of my sisters. We'll need diapers, newborn size. Formula. A real baby bottle, so we can stop using that doll's thing. Clothes." Joe scribbled on the pad. "Anything else?"

The "we" hadn't escaped Rachel. "Not for such a short-term visit," she said pointedly. Chrissy stared up at her and waved her arms. Rachel had second thoughts. "Maybe a rattle," she amended.

"A rattle. Check. Okay, I'm going to get this stuff and I'll be right back."

"Joe," Rachel began. She meant to tell him that he didn't have to do anything, that she could handle it. But the look of bright expectancy on his face made it impossible for her to force the words from her lips.

"You were going to say?" His eyes were on her face, too disconcerting.

"Um, nothing. Maybe if she goes to sleep I'll be able to get some work done."

"Hey, it's Christmas. Don't count on it. Speaking of which, you need to get into the Christmas spirit, Rachel."

"I don't think—"

Joe walked to the radio in the kitchen and flipped the on switch. The annoying cadences of "The Little Drummer Boy" filled the air.

"That's better," he said.

"No, it's not. That's the worst Christmas song ever written."

Joe twirled the tuning dial until he found some cool Christmas jazz. "Okay, so I agree with you about 'The Little Drummer Boy.' The point is that it's Christmas. You can't just sit around here like a lump. You need to get with the happiness of the season."

"You don't understand. I can't take time out."

"Circumstances have changed. You have a baby to take care of now. As for me, I'm out of here. See you later." Meeting her outraged expression with a grin and an expressive shoulder shrug, he was gone.

In spite of herself, Rachel smiled. Joe's mood was infectious. Never mind that she hadn't planned to celebrate anything, never mind that Christmas was a sad time for her. Joe Marzinski was like a walking, talking, breathing Christmas card, delivered right to her doorstep at a time when she was most vulnerable.

The trouble was, he was really pushing the envelope.

RACHEL WAS STEPPING out of the shower, dripping wet, when she heard Joe come barging in the front door. She'd forgotten to lock it, and she'd left the bathroom door open in case Chrissy cried.

"Rachel?" he called in a low voice.

She almost couldn't move. Then she had enough presence of mind to grab the nearest towel, a small one that she normally used for her hair. She was clutching it around her when Joe appeared in the doorway, his face barely visible behind a bedraggled Christmas tree that he had evidently found somewhere.

"Oh. Sorry," he said, taking in her wet hair, the towel and the fact that she was cringing behind the shower door. He did not look sorry, however. "I found this tree in an alley. It's slightly damaged on the bottom, but I brought a saw along so I can fix that. I might have to rearrange a few branches, too, but that's okay."

"Uh, Joe," she began.

"And ornaments. I brought ornaments. I had them at my place, never used them."

"Oh. Fine. I'll be right out," Rachel said despairingly

and with as much dignity as she could summon, which wasn't much.

As she was pushing the door shut, she heard him say, "Wear something pretty. We're going to dinner at my parents'."

She thought she hadn't heard him correctly. She opened the door slightly and took in the presents and ornaments and the small Christmas tree that he was now sawing with a hand saw both noisily and energetically.

"Excuse me?"

He stopped sawing. His expression was detached, but determinedly so. "Dinner. At my parents' house. With my family."

"I can't," she said, not so patiently. How many times did she have to tell him?

"Think about it, Rachel. This is the baby's first Christmas. We'll tie a red bow around her bottle, and look, I brought her a dress. A Christmas dress. What every well-dressed baby should wear." He held up a tiny hanger, and on it hung a tiny red velveteen dress. It was cunningly smocked and embellished with delicate white lace.

Rachel didn't know what to say, so she merely shut the door and stared through the steam at her reflection in the mirror. In the living room Joe was humming along with the radio. Dinner with his family? No way. He'd said they were a big family. She didn't know any of them. She'd be lost in a group like that, wouldn't know what to say, how to act. How to celebrate.

Joe's back was turned when she tiptoed out of the bathroom and toward the bedroom. By this time she'd wrapped her hair in a towel turban-style and was wearing a chenille bathrobe. She sniffed appreciatively at the pungent scent of blue spruce needles.

"You don't need to walk so softly. I don't think Chrissy will wake up. She's sacked out." He didn't turn around. He was hanging ornaments on the Christmas tree with meticulous care. A sunbeam touched on each one as he placed it, twinkling on the gilt.

"I'm not walking softly. I'm barefoot. And you might as well know, Joe, I'm not going to Christmas dinner with your family."

He pivoted and eyed her speculatively. "So where else are you going for Christmas dinner?"

"I'm going to stay home and work."

"Would you mind if I take Chrissy? I stopped by Gracie's house to get the car seat and the portable crib—" and he gestured toward it with his thumb "—and she knows all about how you found a baby in the manger. Not only that but her kids are fired up about it, and if I don't show up with at least a baby, they're going to be hopping mad. It won't be pretty. They got high-powered squirt guns for Christmas."

"Look, Joe," Rachel said, wrapping her robe more tightly around her. She thought he might be able to see right through it, the way he was looking at her.

He raised his eyebrows inquiringly. He had the expression down pat. It said, *How dare you challenge my authority. Why don't you just give in?* It even said, *I think you're cute when you put your foot down,* which was the worst of all.

She drew a deep breath. "I don't think it would be appropriate for you to cart this baby off somewhere. I'm the one who found her, I'm the one who will have to answer to the HSS, and I feel the responsibility very strongly."

"That," he said with equanimity, "is why you're invited to come along. Nice tree, isn't it?" He tore open a package of tinsel with his teeth and began to drape each strand meticulously over the branches of the tree, which was centered on the table next to the couch and, now that the damaged part had been cut away, was full and nicely tapered. The tree actually didn't look too bad. In fact, it looked pretty good.

"Yes, it's a lovely tree. You're not paying any attention to what I'm saying. What do you think gives you the right to come in here and start ordering me around? To kiss me, for heaven's sake? To just…just—"

Joe regarded her silently for a moment. "To tell the truth, I thought you might be lonely. You latched on to that baby as if you'd never let go. And as for kissing, you liked it. Didn't you?"

If she'd thought her annoyance would send Joe Marzinski slinking away with his tail tucked between his legs, she'd been wrong. Boy, had she.

"There's a question on the table," he reminded her. "I asked you if you liked the kissing?"

"I don't have to answer that. You've been most helpful, but right now the most helpful thing you could do would be to leave."

"You liked the kissing, then. I knew it." He favored her with an expression that might be classified as a smirk, only it was offered with too much good humor.

"You don't take hints very well," she said, her voice rising.

"Hints? I'd say that asking me to leave was more than a hint. It was a demand. But if I leave here, you and the baby will be going with me. By the way, I need to call my service and make sure there haven't been any major eruptions of plumbing or glitches in electrical systems in any of the condos on my watch. Do you mind?"

"Go ahead," Rachel said wearily. "I guess I should be surprised that you requested permission."

While Joe dialed on his cell phone, Rachel padded into the kitchen. The counters and sink were spotless. Joe had even rinsed out the dish towel and hung it on its little rack. She poured herself a glass of cold water from the refrigerator and forced herself to think.

She had a report to get out for Edgar Millhap of Green Star Tool & Die. He wasn't known for being patient, and his assistant at corporate headquarters in Ohio had already called twice and inquired when the report would be ready. Rachel had promised that she'd have it tomorrow. And she could hear her fax machine beeping even now as it received a new transmission.

Thinking she'd better check up on things, she went into her office and found a stack of faxes from Viento Communications in Mexico City. She was to forward them to Gilberto Perez, who was spending the holidays in his condo down the beach.

Rachel shoveled the faxes into a file folder. She couldn't go to the Marzinskis' for dinner today. She would have to be firm with Joe. She'd run the faxes down to Gilberto's condominium, drop them off with the doorman, hurry back. Chrissy could go with her.

Joe appeared in the doorway. "Nothing much happening today on the condo crisis front. So everything's cool."

"Lucky for you, but what about me? Joe, I can't go to your parents' with you. I have too much to do."

He stuffed his hands into his pockets and grinned at her. "When I bring you home afterward, I'll stay for a while and help you with this stuff. Or I'll take care of the baby while you work."

Rachel raised her eyes to his face. He was staring

down at her, and those remarkable silver eyes held a kind of glow.

"Well," she said, because she didn't want to say no to such a thoughtful offer. True, he wouldn't be much help with the report, but at least he could manage the baby.

"Say yes. It's the best offer you're going to get today." He favored her with a coaxing smile.

"I'll have to take Gilberto his faxes," she said dubiously. "They need to be delivered right away."

"We'll drop them off. And, Rachel, I hereby declare you an honorary member of the Marzinski family for the day. By the way, we'll need to leave at one o'clock. Marzinskis eat Christmas dinner in midafternoon so the little ones can nap afterward and the adults can visit."

Rachel glanced frantically at her desktop clock. "One o'clock? It's twelve-thirty now," she squeaked.

"That means you'd better get a move on. We're a casual group, but no one's ever shown up for Christmas dinner in a bathrobe."

Muffled snuffles came from Chrissy in her crib, and a glance told Rachel that the baby was indeed waking. "Now you've done it," she said. "She's waking up. She'll need to be diapered and fed and—oh, Joe, why don't you just go home! Alone!" This last was uttered on a wail to mirror Chrissy's.

"I'm not going anywhere without you, and that's that. I'll take care of Chrissy. I know what to do. And I'll get her all dressed in her new dress and she'll look like a picture of perfection, won't you, Chrissy girl?" He picked up the baby and dropped a kiss on her small head.

"Ohh," Rachel said, clenching her fists, and she went to get dressed.

She heard Joe talking to the baby in a conversational tone.

"Rachel may be hard to convince, but she's worth it, don't you think?"

Rachel brushed a hand across her eyes. She felt the hot prick of tears behind her nose, and she willed herself not to get all emotional.

It had been so long since she thought she was worth much at all. And now here was Joe Marzinski, who thought she was better than she was.

Maybe there were such things as Christmas miracles after all.

Chapter Five

Some things in life you had to learn to accept.

This was a lesson Rachel had learned. Or rather, she thought she had learned. But just when she began to believe she had accepted things as they were, something always happened. First she'd decided to accommodate Mimi when her grandmother decided to go jaunting around the Orient. On short notice, Rachel had subleased her New Jersey apartment, piled her computer and printer and office records into her little sedan and headed south. She'd endured the curiosity of the other residents at the Elysian Towers condominium and settled in.

And now here was something else to accept. A really great-looking guy who insisted that she was supposed to celebrate Christmas with his family. She was terrified.

"And then there's Greg, who is married to my older sister, Mary Cecilia. They have five kids, an assortment of boys and girls. Gracie is married to Tom, her college sweetheart. They have three boys, all terrors. Lois and Jackson have two boys and two girls and she's expecting another one in June. Tonia married Reggie right out of high school, and their girls are twins—Liza and Katie. Then there's Jenn and her husband Elliott, who have

Carson. He's three or four. Four, I think. And Mom, a real doll, and Dad, who adores her. That's about it.''

Thoroughly intimidated by the thought of meeting all these people, Rachel adjusted Chrissy's dress, flicking an imaginary piece of lint off the red velveteen. They'd delivered Gilberto Perez's faxes, and now they were sailing across the concrete bridge traversing the Intracoastal Waterway, the metal bridge spacers thumping rhythmically beneath the tires of the Condo Crisis Control van. Rachel saw that below the bridge some people were waiting in their boats for the bridge to open and let them through. At that precise moment Rachel wished that she were on a boat, floating along toward somewhere. Somewhere else.

They arrived at the end of the bridge and slid through a yellow caution light, then turned right. Past the post office, past the church, past a park where little children in helmets were riding spanking-new bikes on wobbly training wheels. There were teenagers, too, on Christmas-morning inline skates, shiny fresh-washed hair flying out behind them. Everything about Christmas was designed for families—toys, kids, warmth, emotion. It was almost more than Rachel could take.

''Well, here we are,'' Joe announced as he pulled up in front of the big two-story white stucco house.

Bright sunlight bounced off the shiny finishes and chrome of several cars and minivans parked out in front. Joe eased the van into a space and came around to open the door for Rachel, who was unbuckling the baby from the car seat.

Rachel, unaccustomed to wearing a skirt, tried to maneuver herself out of the high van. Her skirt inched higher on her leg and caught on the seat lever so that it revealed a quick glimpse of thigh.

Joe raised his eyebrows, and Rachel used her free hand to tug the skirt lower, but not before she caught the gleam in his eye. All right, so he was a leg man. Every man had his preferences. There was nothing surprising about that. What Rachel found surprising was that Joe was at all interested in *her* legs or anything else about her.

There wasn't time to ponder this because all at once the front door of the big stucco house flew open and a slew of children spilled out.

"Uncle Joe, Uncle Joe! Where's the baby?"

"Wait till you see my bike, it's awesome!"

"What did you bring me?"

"Did you bring a baby? Tommy said you were bringing a baby!"

"Guess what, Carson ate six candy canes and threw up all over Jamie's new fire truck!"

"What did you bring us! What did you bring us?"

Joe patted a red-haired boy on the head, slid a hand down his ear and produced a shiny dime.

"How about this, Tommy?" he said, and the boy grabbed it.

The resulting clamor from the other children woke Chrissy, who had been dozing, and she started to fuss.

"Oh, what a tiny baby!" This exclamation was delivered with a lisp because the speaker was missing her two front teeth.

"This is Chrissy, Katie," Joe said. "And this is Rachel." He slid an arm around Rachel's shoulders. She wanted to shrug it off; he was embarrassing her in front of these kids. But it felt good there, felt good to be included. It made her feel less like an interloper at this family event.

"Are you going to get married?"

"Not today, Jeffrey," Joe assured the boy, who appeared to be about eleven.

"A baby! Uncle Joe has a baby!" yelled Tommy. He raced back inside the house.

Joe smiled down at Rachel. "That was Tommy. This one with the tattoo is Megan, and that's Carson," he said. A red-haired prepubescent girl with a fake tattoo on her cheek stuck her tongue out at him, and he made a grab for her ponytail but missed.

Rachel tried to memorize the names, but she was sure she would never get them straight. Liza, Katie, Mary Grace, Jeffrey and Todd. All little whirlwinds, all dressed up in honor of the occasion. As they swirled around her, she was propelled up the steps and into the house where Marzinskis seemed to spill from every nook and cranny and where Joe's mother greeted her with a big smile.

"We're so glad you could be here, Rachel," she said, and Joe's father grinned his welcome, too. Mary Marzinski wasn't what Rachel had expected. She'd thought Joe's mother would be a little dumpling of a woman, very old-worldish, but she was slim and fashionably dressed in a white tunic-and-pants outfit, her hair swinging in a chic blond bob. Joe's father, Jim, was tall and balding and tanned from many hours in the sun.

One by one Joe's sisters emerged from the kitchen to meet Rachel. It didn't escape Rachel's attention that they were exchanging significant looks. At first she was barely aware of this byplay, but it became much more obvious when, even though Joe was explaining about the baby, everyone was paying more attention to Rachel.

Fortunately Chrissy was at her cutest, yawning widely once and letting out a little coo when Rachel leaned over to adjust her blanket. The cuteness seemed to refocus everyone's attention, for which Rachel was supremely grateful.

"An honest-to-goodness baby in a Nativity-scene manger? Well, that takes the cake," said Jenn, the youngest sister.

"I want some cake too," said Todd, an outspoken five-year-old, and that made everyone laugh. The ice was broken, and everyone began to resume whatever activity they had been pursuing when Joe, Rachel and the baby had arrived.

The Marzinski house was bright and airy, with worn furnishings but with many decorations of the season. An enormous Christmas tree rose almost to the high cypress-beamed ceiling, and lopsided crayoned stars hung from the chandelier over the dining room table. One of the children, Jenn told her, had painted the charming Santa-and-elves mural on the glass of the door between the living room and the wide sunporch. Mistletoe hung from the hallway light fixture.

"I'd better put Chrissy's formula in the refrigerator," Rachel said, and so Joe's sister Gracie showed her where it was.

Joe had brought the portable crib for Chrissy. Joe and Lois's husband set it up in an alcove off the kitchen, and Rachel, who waited in the kitchen where she was studied carefully by a silent toddler named Melinda, settled the baby in it. After she was tucked in, Chrissy stared up at Rachel for about ten seconds and then her little eyelids began to drift closed. Melinda deserted when it seemed that nothing exciting was going to happen, running in search of her own bottle.

Distracted by all the commotion around her, Rachel bent over the crib and focused on the now-sleeping baby. *Easy for you to handle this situation,* Rachel said in her mind to the baby. *You can just close your eyes and shut everyone out. But I've got to deal with all these people with names that I'll never remember, and they're going to wonder why I don't have any family of my own, and then I'll have to tell.*

But she wouldn't tell. Not in a million years. No matter how nice everyone was. If they knew, they'd think she was a bad person, they'd understand that she'd failed the people who depended on her.

Blinking away the sudden sting of tears, Rachel backed out of the alcove straight into the path of Mary Cecilia.

This elder sister of Joe's was the most formidable of the family members Rachel had met so far, with her stern, pulled-back hair and eyes that could pierce right through a person. At least that was the way they seemed to Rachel.

"Oh...excuse me!" Rachel said.

"It's okay, I saw you coming. Would you mind grabbing that head of romaine off the table? I'm trying to put together a salad, but every time I start to do it, someone yells something and I have to go fix it."

"I'll help," Rachel offered, and Mary Cecilia looked surprised and then relieved.

"You could wash the lettuce, if you don't mind," she said.

Rachel was happy to have something useful to do. She ran water in the sink and held the lettuce leaves under it, a few at a time. Mary Cecilia dragged a salad spinner down from a top shelf, and Rachel put the lettuce in it after she'd washed off the worst of the grit. She didn't know what to talk about with this woman except for the children.

She was about to inquire as to how many of the children were hers when Mary Cecilia said abruptly, "We didn't know our Joey had a girlfriend until he mentioned it at Thanksgiving.''

Rachel dropped a paring knife with a clatter and watched helplessly as it clunked into the yawning black hole of the garbage disposal.

''I'm not—'' she began, but her words were lost in a series of bumps from the back porch followed by a long piercing wail. Carson had ridden his new scooter down the back steps and hit his head.

Rachel, after initially ascertaining that Carson was all right except for a nasty bruise, fished the knife out of the disposal and went on making salad while Joe's youngest sister, Jenn, Carson's mother, tended to his injuries. Mary Cecilia hurried off to find bandages.

While she was blessedly alone in the kitchen, Joe came in the back door and let it slam behind him. ''Just another Marzinski Christmas,'' he observed as he helped himself to a slice of tomato. ''Never a dull moment.''

''They think I'm your girlfriend.'' Rachel hissed through her teeth as she snatched a piece of celery out of his hands so she could slice it.

''I don't have a girlfriend. And, anyway, so what?''

''So I just met you last night. Your sister said you told them about a girlfriend at Thanksgiving. I'm *not* your girlfriend.''

''We did sleep together,'' Joe said in a reasoning tone.

Rachel almost gasped, but it turned into a gulp. She looked around to see if anyone could have heard him, but the only person in the room was a blond moppet of indeterminate sex who was crawling around under the table pushing a truck. ''That didn't mean anything,'' Rachel said.

''It did to me.''

A quick glance told her that Joe was grinning at her.

"It didn't mean anything to either of us," Rachel retorted in righteous indignation. "I was sleepy, that's all, and you were supposed to wake me up but you didn't."

"Next time," Joe said seriously, "I will."

Rachel wagged the paring knife at him. "You are one pushy guy, Joe Marzinski."

"Hey, that's my brother you're talking about! And why didn't you tell us right off the bat that Rachel is your fiancée?" said Jenn playfully as she bustled in.

"Fiancée?" said Joe.

"Well, Jeffrey said you weren't going to get married today, so I figured you must have another day in mind."

Rachel shot Joe an outraged glance.

"Not exactly," Joe hedged.

Jenn, who had been peeking through the glass window in the door of the oven, turned to Joe. "Did you know we're having a surprise guest?"

"No," Joe said. "I thought I'd brought the surprise guest of the day." He winked at Rachel.

"Well, not entirely," Jenn began, but then the doorbell rang and someone shouted, "Oh, look, it's Gina! Gina's here!" Jenn exited hurriedly.

Gina? thought Rachel. *An old girlfriend of Joe's? The schoolteacher he mentioned at Thanksgiving?* Thoroughly confused by this time, she slanted a look at him out of the corners of her eyes. Joe, true to form, was poking around in the pots and pans on the stove and counter, acting completely unconcerned.

"Joe, you'll have to set things straight," she said.

"I'm having too much fun," he said with a roguish quirk of his eyebrows. "And everyone's much too hyper at the moment. What can be the harm of letting them think we're an item?"

From the living room came a lot of loud talking, all of it centered around the newcomer.

"Gina, guess what happened! Carson ate a bunch of candy canes and threw up all over Jamie's new fire engine!"

"Gina, Gina, look at my new Barbie!"

"Gina, are you going to stay for dinner?"

Gina this, Gina that, and Joe, who was sampling the orange sauce that was destined for the duckling, still didn't seem in a hurry to join the group in the living room.

"Who's Gina?" Rachel blurted, and then was sorry. She didn't want to know more about the Marzinski family than she already knew, and most especially, she didn't want to know about Joe's girlfriends, past or present. Nor did she want to be mistaken for one, come to think of it.

Joe dropped the lid back onto the pan and licked the spoon while leaning up again the counter. "Gina's an eighteen-year-old girl who used to live here. My parents took her in when she had no place to go. Her father died, and her mother took off, leaving her with her two older sisters, who could barely cope with their own lives, much less Gina's. Come on, I'll take you in to meet her." He ran the spoon under the faucet.

Rachel reluctantly dried her hands and followed Joe into the living room. The newcomer, a pretty dark-haired, almond-eyed teenager, fashionably dressed in a red-plaid shift and sandals, was surrounded by a bevy of little bodies but looked up quickly when Joe entered the room.

The kids made way for Joe, who kissed Gina on the cheek and pulled Rachel forward. "Gina, this is Rachel. I invited her to spend the day with us. Rachel, Gina's almost a member of the family."

"So is Rachel," chimed in one of the kids, and everyone laughed and smiled indulgently, which made Rachel feel even more uneasy.

Gina seemed distracted and ill at ease. Well, Rachel could identify. She felt the same. She eyed Joe, willing him to speak up about their status. He ignored her.

"Gina, honey, you look so pale," said Jim, Joe's father, as he took Gina's hand.

"Just getting over the flu," she said, punctuating the words with a negligible shrug of the shoulders. Gina pecked Jim on the cheek and tendered Mary a self-conscious hug. Her movements seemed more choreographed than spontaneous, which caught Rachel's attention.

"All right, Gina, we'll fix what ails you," Jim said. "How about a little glass of wine? My father in the old country used to swear by it as a blood-building tonic."

"Okay," Gina said, allowing herself to be led away.

Joe, for some reason, was frowning. Rachel was on the verge of pulling him into the nearby hallway and asking him if he was out of his mind and if he really expected her to go along with this farce about their supposed relationship, but before she could, Gracie pressed a glass of mulled cider into her hand and two of the children almost pulled the Christmas tree over onto the dining table after which the house erupted into a melee unequaled in Rachel's experience.

Through it all, she heard a slight whimper from the direction of the kitchen and hurried to see if Chrissy was hungry. But Joe had beaten her to the little alcove where the baby slept, and when she came around the corner, there he was, the baby in his arms.

Her heart warmed to him in that moment, though she wasn't sure why. Maybe it was the concern in his expression, or perhaps it was catching him in a tender moment when no one else was around.

"I'm warming her bottle," he said, and, looking over her shoulder, Rachel saw it in a pan of water.

"Joe, what's going on here? Why don't you just tell them the truth? That we just met last night?"

He shook his head ruefully. "You might as well know that my whole family is counting the days until I take a wife. With all these sisters I'm the only one who can pass on the family name. It's important to them that I get married, and they've deliberately misunderstood because they're so eager for it to happen. Sorry, Rachel. But it is kind of fun." His eyes sparkled.

Rachel tried to keep her cool. "Not for me. It's embarrassing."

"Rachel, what can it hurt to let them think you really are my girlfriend? I mean, it sure would take the heat off me. You can't imagine how hard these family occasions are. They're always asking me, 'Joey, when are you going to get married? Joey, when are you going to start a family?'" He mimicked Gracie's high voice and Mary Cecilia's disapproving tone almost perfectly, and Rachel started to laugh.

"No, I'm serious," he went on. "After Christmas I'll tell them the truth. But if I could just enjoy one holiday meal without all the flack, I'd be grateful."

"All right, then, I'm telling them. This is ridiculous." She swiveled to go, but he caught her arm.

"And cause a minor eruption? Mary Cecilia will get all huffy, and Lois will laugh her head off. Gracie won't speak to me for another month, and the kids won't comprehend. Think again, Rachel."

His eyes were so serious that his words gave her pause. She shook away his hand. She didn't want to add to the confusion, to spoil anyone's holiday. But he had started this—not her. They'd be annoyed with him, not her.

But would that make her feel any better?

Ever since she'd met Joe Marzinski, Rachel had had a sense of all kinds of boundaries being broken down. It wasn't only Joe that bothered her, but this whole scene— the utter familiarity of being in the midst of a family again. She'd thought those days were gone forever. They *were* gone forever. Except now, with Joe smiling into her eyes and her body responding in a way that was ridiculous, it was easy to give in to him. Or to whatever it was that was fogging her thought processes.

"Joe? Oh, excuse me."

It was Gina, and she was gazing at the baby in his arms with rapt attention.

"Gina, meet Chrissy, our Christmas baby," Joe said, his tone turning jovial.

"I know. Your mom told me how you found her in the manger scene."

"I didn't find her, Rachel did. I'm only helping out until the HSS comes to the rescue. They'll find a foster home for her." He laid Chrissy back down in the crib and was removing her wet diaper as he spoke. Rachel, letting go of her thoughts for the time being, dug a clean one out of the bag she'd brought.

"You…you aren't going to keep her?" Gina leaned against the wall. She looked exhausted, Rachel thought.

"Me? No, how could I? I'm in and out of my apartment at all hours of the day and night. No problem too big, no problem too small for Condo Crisis Control, but I have to admit that this baby has thrown a clinker in the works. Rachel, could you bring that wastebasket over here? The one next to the door?"

Before Rachel could figure out which wastebasket he

meant—there were many, all overflowing with Christmas wrappings—Gina went to get it. She planted it beside Joe and watched carefully as he finished taping the ends of the clean diaper together.

"Are you sure that's tight enough? That it won't fall off?"

Joe glanced up with obvious surprise. "Gina, who's the one who taught you to diaper a baby? As I recall, when you were baby-sitting Carson, you had a need to know."

"You taught me, Joe." Gina's smile was tentative.

"Sure I did. I know my stuff. Don't I, Rachel?"

Rachel brought the warmed bottle to him. "I'll vouch for you anytime," she told him.

Joe lifted Chrissy up and held her close to his chest. "Let's go out on the back porch, and one of us can sit in Mom's old rocker and feed her, away from the hubbub of the rest of the clan."

They stepped outside, and Rachel sat down on the rocking chair. Joe handed Chrissy over to Rachel, who cuddled the baby close while introducing the bottle to her. Joe sat down on the top porch step, and Gina eased herself down beside him.

"How's school going, Gina?" he asked.

"Great. I made straight A's."

"This is Gina's first semester at Florida State. She won a scholarship," Joe explained to Rachel.

"I wouldn't have been able to go at all if you and your family hadn't given me money for living expenses," Gina said, brushing her short hair back from her face. The expression in her eyes when she looked at Joe was frankly adoring, but Rachel noticed that Gina mostly looked at the baby. She supposed that wasn't so surprising; Chrissy was a captivating child.

"Hey, no big deal. And anyway, your sisters send you money, too."

"Not much. Anna's getting married to Mitch in June, and Dottie got downsized in the fall. She's got another job with an accounting firm, but she's catching up on past bills. She'll have them paid off in a couple of months, she says."

"Mmm. Well, Dottie's a hard worker. She did a good job for me when she worked in my office one summer."

"I was thinking that maybe I could work for you, too, Joe. Maybe this summer."

"Sure, we can always use good help. Tell me about Anna and Mitch. Are you going to be in the wedding?"

"Both Dottie and I are. It's in June."

"Anna will be a gorgeous bride, just like you will be, when you find the right guy."

Rachel caught the blush on Gina's face. "Aw, Joe, quit it. I'm going to get my education first, then get a job, and then, and only then, will I consider finding a guy."

"A good plan. I always said you have a lot of common sense." Joe got up and dusted off the seat of his pants. "What do you say we toss a Frisbee? Looks like one of the kids got a new one for Christmas."

Gina shook her head. "Not today, Joe. Please. I told you, I'm not over the flu."

Joe snagged seven-year-old Jamie as he was dashing through the backyard, and soon they had recruited more players and had a lively game going. Two kids took turns swinging on a new Mickey Mouse swing hanging from a low branch of the banyan tree, and one quiet boy nestled in a higher branch with a book.

Gina leaned back against a porch column and watched Rachel feeding the baby. The two of them were an oasis of quiet amid the clamor of the Frisbee players on the grass and the laughter and shouts emanating from the house behind them. Rachel was grateful for the peace of the moment and glad that no one was asking her questions or studying her with barely veiled curiosity.

"She seems like a very good baby," Gina said after a while.

"Oh, she is," Rachel told her. She nuzzled the baby's head.

"And you're really going to send her to foster care?"

Rachel smiled at her. "Yes, it's what we have to do. We've already reported to the HSS that I found her, we're just waiting for someone to come and get her."

"Would you mind if I gave her the rest of this feeding? I mean, you might want to play the Frisbee game with Joe and everybody."

Rachel didn't want to play Frisbee, and she was grateful to have something to do. But she found herself saying, "Why, of course, Gina, come sit in the rocker, and I'll let you give her the rest of this bottle."

Gina settled herself in the rocker with the baby in the crook of one arm. Chrissy wrinkled her nose and took the offered bottle. Gina began to rock, and Rachel sat on the top step and relaxed.

It was a sunny day with a light breeze wafting in from the ocean. A hedge of Turk's cap with its bright-red furled flowers screened the Marzinski house from the one next door where someone was playing with battery-operated racing cars on the patio. Above, a light plane flew soundlessly trailing a banner. Merry Christmas, it said.

Gina was watching the Frisbee game with interest. It now involved Joe, a couple of his brothers-in-law and four small- to medium-size boys. "It sure is good to be home," she said.

Rachel nodded in agreement. "I remember my first Christmas after I went away to college. I appreciated home a lot more than I had before."

"Yeah, so do I." This was uttered more fervently than necessary, and Rachel intuited that Gina wanted to talk.

"Tell me about your major," she said. "Or haven't you decided on one yet?"

"Ever since I got my first job in retail, I thought maybe I could be a store manager for the chain where I worked, so I just declared marketing as my major. I want to get my MBA if I can."

"With those straight A's you earned this semester, it sounds as if you're on your way."

"I hope so. Trouble is, I was a math major before. I had to make a lot of schedule changes for next semester. I'm not sure I'll get the courses I need, and I'm going to have to take some that I never planned on, so it's kind of scary."

Rachel noticed that all of Gina's fingernails were bitten to the quick. She decided to offer reassurance. "I'm sure things will work out," she said.

"It's hard keeping my grades up, working and all. But I'm going to make it. I have to! And then I want to come back to Coquina Beach and show everyone that a DeMarcos can amount to something." Gina's eyes flashed, and she held the baby up to burp her, smoothing the little red dress down carefully afterward.

Gina must have noticed the question in Rachel's eyes, and after a moment she went on talking. "You see, my mother was an alcoholic. Everyone used to laugh at her when they saw her stumbling along the sidewalk, and I got teased a lot when I was in school. I want to make up for that, you know?"

Rachel's heart went out to the girl, because once upon

a time in another life she'd heard a similar story from Nick. He said he'd always felt as if he didn't quite measure up because his father was the town drunk. And so he'd become a college professor and married the girl of his dreams and started a family, all to show people that he could.

Suddenly Rachel didn't want to talk about this anymore. It hurt to think about Nick, especially today.

"I think I'd better see what's going on in the kitchen," she said, getting up and fleeing into the house. Once inside, she went into the alcove to straighten out the sheet in the crib, which didn't need straightening but provided a way to collect herself.

"Rachel?"

It was Megan, the one with the fake tattoo.

"Yes?"

"I thought that since you're Uncle Joe's girlfriend and all, you might want to see his trophies."

"I'm not—"

"He has all kinds. Boy, was he famous when he was in high school. Come on," Megan took her hand and pulled her past the alcove into a hall lined with doors. "This is Uncle Joe's room. He doesn't live here anymore, though."

Rachel had to admit, if only to herself, that she *was* curious. After all, this guy had wormed his way into her life—no, not into her life, into her *day*—and she hardly knew anything about him.

They stopped at a room that was unremarkable in decor—plaid bedspread, curtains to match and a random assortment of battered furniture—but it immediately gave Rachel an insight into the kind of boy Joe Marzinski had been. There were pictures of Joe in a football uniform, wearing the Coquina Beach High School colors. There were trophies, both for football and for swimming, lining shelves along one wall.

Megan shrugged. "Grandma saves all this stuff. Uncle Joe keeps telling her to throw it out, but my mom and her sisters don't want her to. They're real proud of him."

Rachel wandered over to look at the trophies.

"See the cuckoo clock?" Megan asked. "It doesn't work. Uncle Joe says it doesn't matter, because a stopped clock is right twice a day anyhow. He's always saying stuff like that." She plopped down on the bed and threw her arms around a threadbare teddy bear. "This was his, too. I used to like to sleep with it when I was a kid."

Rachel had to smile at this. She could hardly imagine Joe as a child.

Megan sat up. "So, are you and Uncle Joe going to get married?"

"Well, I hadn't planned on it," Rachel said uncomfortably, unsure how to impart the information that she had no more intention of marrying Joe Marzinski than going to the moon.

"Yes, we've put the wedding plans on hold. For the time being." Joe strode in and tweaked Megan's ear. "Get going, small fry. Your mother wants you to start putting the food on the table."

"Oh, good, it's time to eat." Megan bounded up from the bed and out of the room. Rachel and Joe stared at each other across the narrow expanse of the bedspread.

"You, um, were quite an athlete," she said.

"That was a long time ago," Joe said.

"You keep in shape."

He made a dismissive motion. "I lead an active life. You know, Rachel, they like you."

"I can't imagine that they've passed judgment on me

already. There's too much going on. So why don't I see what I can do to help serve dinner?''

She started to walk past him, but at that point one of the twins—Liza? Katie?—poked her head around the door and said, ''Oh, you two lovebirds! Mommy says to come and sit down at the table so we can eat.''

Rachel jumped away from Joe, feeling guilty for— well, for what? Nothing had happened.

''Come along,'' Joe said, taking her hand, but before they reached the dining room, Liza or Katie, whichever, stopped in the middle of the hall.

''Aren't you going to kiss Rachel, Uncle Joe?'' she said impishly.

Rachel followed the little girl's gaze upward and realized belatedly that they were situated directly beneath the sprig of mistletoe. Before she could move, Joe grabbed her—that was the only word for it—and planted a kiss on her lips. ''Oh, way cool!'' squealed the twin before running to tell everyone.

'''Way cool,''' murmured Joe close by Rachel's ear, but she brushed past him into the dining room, feeling anything but. In fact, her cheeks were flaming.

There ensued a good deal of chair scraping as people found their places around the table, and Rachel continued to glare at Joe in outrage. Their interaction was obscured by the spilling of a glass of milk by one of the children and its subsequent cleanup.

''So, Rachel,'' Jim Marzinski said heartily once they were all seated, ''tell us all about finding the baby.''

''Yes, yes, tell us!'' was the answering chorus.

Rachel, still out of sorts over the mistletoe incident, was making a project out of heaping her plate with mashed potatoes. Joe, maddeningly irrepressible, grinned at her from across the table.

"Sure, go ahead," he told her.

Rachel, at first uncomfortable at being the center of attention, became more at ease as she related how she'd been coming home and heard the baby's cry, and then how the neighbors had pitched in to help, and finally how the HSS social worker had never shown up, so that she and Joe had had to take on the responsibility of Chrissy.

"You forgot the part about the Santa Claus stopping by," Joe supplied.

"Well, yes, there was this Santa—" And Rachel was suddenly struck with the thought that there had been another Santa, as well, the one at the store where she'd bought the printer paper earlier that night.

"But whose baby is it?" asked one of the older kids, the one that Rachel thought was named Paul.

"Well, it's not the baby *Jesus*," said nine-year-old Mary Grace, kicking Paul under the table.

"I *know* it's not the baby Jesus," Paul said, kicking her back.

"You two stop that," ordered Lois. "Anyway, you may never know whose baby it is."

It was at that moment that Rachel chanced to look at Gina, who was pushing food around on her plate but didn't seem to be eating any. Before she could process the girl's expression, Mary Marzinski touched her gently on the arm.

"I'm sure you can borrow any necessary baby items from one of my girls. And I have some things here— extra bottles, diapers and so on. Please make sure that you take anything you need before you leave today."

"Thank you, I will. But the baby will soon go to a good foster home. I hope to hear from the HSS people today, and then I'll get back to a normal life."

"That would be nice, wouldn't it?" Joe said affably.

One of his brothers-in-law passed him the green beans and winked. "A baby sure can put a damper on things, can't it?"

"Jackson," said Lois, who was very pregnant and, if Rachel remembered correctly, was Jackson's wife. She dimpled at her husband. "You love babies."

Her husband reached over and caressed her cheek, an open display of tenderness and somehow very touching. "And I love you. But life isn't the same after a baby arrives, that's all there is to it."

"It's better," Jenn said, curving an arm around her own son.

"Yeah, well, there's never been any shortage of babies around this house, that's for sure," boomed Jim, and everyone laughed.

Tonia, another of Joe's sisters, turned to Rachel. "Maybe someday you and Joe will have babies of your own," she said brightly.

This was too much. "We just met," Rachel managed through a mouthful of mashed potatoes, but too late she felt the toe of Joe's shoe nudging her ankle under the table.

"That's right," Joe said pleasantly. "We just might."

While everyone was exchanging meaningful but pleased glances, Joe said, "I think I'll get some ice." And he got up and went into the kitchen.

"I'm so glad that our Joey has found someone at last," Mary, his mother, whispered as she stood up to fetch the fruit compote from the sideboard.

From where she sat, Rachel could see Joe in the kitchen, and he placed a forefinger across his lips, signifying that she should remain quiet.

And so, though she didn't quite understand why, she did. Maybe it was because she was feeling comfortable in the midst of all these Marzinskis, and maybe it was also because no ghost of Christmas past was able to penetrate that tight, glowing family group of which, it now seemed, she was a part.

Chapter Six

"You never should have started it."

Joe chuckled and rounded the corner onto the bridge to the island. "What, you mean you don't like being almost engaged to me?" He glanced over at Rachel, who was leaning forward so that her breasts strained against the fabric of her bodice. He wished she wouldn't sit like that; it made it almost impossible for him to concentrate on his driving.

Rachel closed her eyes and looked as if she were praying for patience. "Of course I don't like it. You didn't mention, when you insisted that I come to dinner with your family, that you expected me to put something over on them." She leaned her head against the window.

"During the carol singing around the piano, Elliott asked me why I hadn't given you a ring for Christmas."

Rachel's head jerked up, and her eyes flew open at that. "I hope you set him straight. Who's Elliott?"

Joe supposed he couldn't blame her for being confused. Sometimes even he had a hard time recalling who matched up with whom. "Elliott is Jenn's husband. I mumbled something."

"What do you mean you mumbled something?"

"Something like, 'I'm saving it for New Year's.'"

Rachel blew out an exasperated breath. It ruffled her bangs into a little frill on her forehead. Her profile was outlined against the blinking lights at the marina below the bridge.

"You should have told him the truth, Joe."

"It was so pleasant to be able to actually enjoy myself at a family gathering without everyone hassling me that I let him go on thinking what everyone was thinking. They all say you're smashing, by the way."

"I'm not any such thing."

"You're exactly the kind of woman I'd choose if I were choosing," he threw in, just to see what the effect would be. Rachel rolled her eyes.

"So why don't you go and choose one? Just not me. What happened to that schoolteacher?"

"She wanted to get married so she could quit teaching school and never see spaghetti in the shape of *O*s or tie a kid's shoelace again." Noting Rachel's disbelieving look, he said, "Yes, she actually told me that. She clearly didn't like children, so I only went out with her a couple of times. Rachel, what don't you like about me?" He meant to tease her, but she looked at him seriously.

"You're very nice," she said slowly.

"I'm glad you think so, but do I look funny? Smell bad? Why is it that you're always trying to get rid of me?"

"Because I never wanted you in the first place. You just sort of...sort of...arrived."

"And it's a good thing, too," he reminded her with relish. As he turned into the Elysian Towers parking lot, Rachel began to gather up the baby's things. Chrissy was asleep in her borrowed car safety seat. She'd eaten her fill only half an hour ago and promptly fallen asleep.

"I'll carry Chrissy," he said as they got out of the car.

Rachel seemed to be thinking. "You know, Joe, I won't hold you to your promise to help me tonight," she said.

"Don't be silly. You can work, I can deal with everything else. Hey, do you think there are any new developments about the baby?"

"I don't know." Rachel stalked ahead of him past the manger scene with its plaster baby now firmly in place and into the building where she was greeted with familiarity by the doorman, who watched with interest as Rachel punched the elevator button.

"Ms. Hirsch, you gonna keep that baby?"

"No, Sherman. I'm waiting for the Department of Health and Social Services to be in touch. They haven't sent anyone around today, have they?"

"No, ma'am, they sure haven't. Mrs. Rink wanted to know where you and the baby went. Said she'd been ringing your doorbell and phoning and you weren't to be found."

"Great," Rachel muttered under her breath.

"Want me to call and tell her you're back?" Sherman picked up the phone on his desk.

"No, Sherman, I'd appreciate some quiet around the apartment for the rest of the evening."

Sherman shot Joe a wide-eyed and knowing look. "Heh, heh, guess I understand."

Rachel was in the elevator before Joe could make any remark at all. She was thin-lipped and silent as they exited the elevator on the eleventh floor.

"Listen, Rachel, that guy doesn't know anything about what's happening upstairs, if that's bothering you." He shifted the carrier containing the baby to the other hand and reached for the diaper bag so she could get out her keys.

She brushed his hand away. "Everybody and his brother seems to think that we're having a fling." She found the keys herself, went inside and waited until Joe was inside before closing the door with a little more force than was necessary. She almost slammed it, in fact. Joe stood there and thought about what he should do. Finally he decided to let her go on talking, which, he also decided, she might have done anyway.

"Don't the members of your family think it's a little odd that they've never heard mention of a girlfriend before and then suddenly I show up at Christmas dinner?"

"They heard of you at Thanksgiving."

"But it wasn't even me you told them about."

"Yeah, you're right. Don't be surprised if they ask you what you think of the new school lunch program."

Rachel realized that her mouth was hanging open and quickly shut it. "Joe, don't you think it's presumptuous to force me into playing a part for which I wasn't at all prepared? A schoolteacher? That's pretty far-fetched. You may be great at handling condo crises, Joe Marzinski, but that doesn't give you any right to create a crisis for me. To play havoc with my life."

Joe went into the bedroom and set the baby down in the middle of the bed. "It doesn't seem like much of a life to begin with," he said good-naturedly.

When he looked up, he was stunned to see that Rachel's face had been drained of all color. Her eyes were big, the pupils dark. Yet there was a luminosity about her, and a steeliness overlying what he thought was a rare resolve, and he sensed something terrible, too. He didn't know what that was all about. But he wanted to. He desperately wanted to.

"My life is okay," she said, almost whispering. "My life is better than I thought it would be."

"Rachel, look, I think I said something that maybe I shouldn't have." He made a move toward her, hoping to assuage, but she jerked away before he could touch her.

"You're always saying something you shouldn't have," she said, disapproval inherent in her tone.

In that moment it occurred to him in a flash that Rachel was hiding something. He didn't know why he felt that way, just the overwhelming certainty that she had created a fortress out of her reserve and her aloofness, a fortress that was meant to wall her off from all hurt.

His mind flooded with the possibilities. Had some guy dumped her recently? That would go a long way toward explaining why she didn't let him get too close and why she'd left New Jersey and settled in here. It would also account for the fact that there wasn't a man around, even though Rachel Hirsch was the kind of woman who would normally attract men in droves.

He needed time to consider this. "I'm going down to get the portable crib," he said. He strode from the room, displaying a false sense of purpose. Sure, he had to get the crib. And sure, he wanted to get away from Rachel for a minute so he could think things over undisturbed by her tantalizing sexuality and her hurt-little-girl eyes.

But most of all, he needed time to absorb the knowledge that he was utterly dazed by what he was feeling for her. And to decide if his feelings were a good enough reason to stick around long enough to try to crack the mystery.

RACHEL SANK DOWN ON THE BED beside Chrissy, who was sleeping peacefully.

"I don't know what this is, but I don't need it," she said out loud.

Not that the baby heard her. Or if she did, she didn't

respond. Babies were sweet, but they weren't much good as sounding boards.

For one wild moment Rachel had the idea of phoning Mimi in Singapore. She wanted to talk things over with someone, and Mimi had been telling Rachel for a long time that she should get on with her life. Mimi herself, at seventy-five, always had a man on hand. She believed them to be useful for many purposes, such as handyman chores, errands and, on occasion, sex and intimacy.

It was this last one on which Rachel differed from her grandmother. "I don't want to go to bed with someone unless I'm halfway serious about him," she'd told Mimi not long ago. It wasn't as if there were any suitors at the time, but Mimi had been hopeful on her behalf and had, in fact, tried to set Rachel up with a boat captain who lived on the mainland. His name had been Buford, and after the dinner that Mimi had arranged in order to introduce them, he had noisily sucked the food out of his teeth, blissfully unaware that Rachel was repulsed. Rachel had nixed Buford forthwith.

"You can't have perfection," Mimi had cautioned sternly, but Rachel had wondered, *Well, why not?* She'd certainly had perfection before with Nick, and she wasn't interested in lowering her standards.

Joe Marzinski certainly wasn't perfect; far from it. On the other hand, his torso was perfect. So was his smile. His eyes, too, might be considered perfect by some, though Rachel considered them much too penetrating.

But he was too bossy and too intrusive by far. Perfect pecs and lats couldn't quite make up for that.

YES, SHE WAS WORTH IT.

That's what Joe decided after careful consideration of all Rachel's attributes. First of all, she was a looker. He'd enjoyed walking into the family dinner with her and having everyone's eyes open just the slightest fraction more as they took in her figure, her bountiful mane of blond hair and all the other things that were so attractive about her. Her mouth. Her eyes. Her golden skin.

Not to mention that she was pleasant to everyone and they had all liked her. They'd admired his taste. Even Gina had whispered to him, "I like Rachel, Joe. She's very kind and sweet."

Rachel certainly was that, even though at the moment she was acting as if she never wanted to set eyes on him again.

"I'm back," he called out as he opened the door to the apartment. "Where do you want me to set the crib up?"

Rachel stepped out of her office. "In the bedroom, I guess. It'll be easy to check on Chrissy at night if she's in there. And by the way, I checked my phone messages. No one from HSS called."

"If I were you," Joe remarked over his shoulder as he took the crib into the bedroom, "I'd leave another message on their machine."

Rachel was right behind him. "I did. Here, put that in this corner. That's right." She kept her voice low so as not to wake the baby, who was asleep in the middle of the bed.

Joe took his time setting up the crib. Rachel, in the meantime, busied herself with taking things out of the diaper bag and putting other things into it. He couldn't figure out if she remained in the room because she wanted to speak to him or if she really needed to do those things. Chrissy slept soundly, her pacifier in her mouth, her little fists clenched close to her chest.

"I'd better put this formula in the refrigerator," Rachel

said. She went into the kitchen and he heard her let out a mild squeak of surprise. "Oh, Gladys Rink has brought over some eggnog and left it in the fridge. She has Mimi's extra key. I keep forgetting that. Joe, do you want some eggnog?"

"After that huge dinner, no thanks."

He heard her bustling around the kitchen and then she returned. "I'm glad you got the crib," she said. "It's a big help."

"Thank Gracie. She was most generous."

"Everyone in your family is. What they've done for Gina over the years was wonderful."

"She and her sisters were good kids. Someone needed to help."

Rachel turned to the baby and carefully gathered her up in her arms. Chrissy didn't wake up, only sighed deeply. While he watched, Rachel lowered her into the crib and smoothed the little dress.

"What is the attraction of a baby?" he asked suddenly.

She looked at him blankly, as if he'd lost his mind. "She's a *baby*," she said.

"No, I mean what is the attraction for you specifically? Why do you care so much?"

Rachel lifted her shoulders, let them fall. "She needs me."

Such a simple answer, but it told him so much about her. Women wanted to be needed. He wondered if she could ever be devoted to a man who needed her.

"Well," Rachel said briskly as he followed her into the living room. "I'm going to get to work now," she said. She shot him an unfathomable look. "You can go, you know."

He had no intention of leaving. It was Christmas night, and the only options open to him were to go home to his own empty apartment, to drop in on his parents or to impose on the hospitality of one of his married sisters. And he knew that there was nowhere else he would rather be than in the presence of Rachel no matter how distracted she might be.

"I have no intention of going. I promised."

She stood and looked at him for a while, and it was a look of annoyance overlaid with what he thought of as a slight amusement. He thought he knew what she'd say if she decided to comment, and that was, *I won't hold you to that promise.* But she didn't say that.

He plugged in the Christmas tree lights. "There are presents to open," he said. "You wait any longer, it won't be Christmas anymore."

"They're not for me. They're for the baby."

"There might be one for you in there."

Reluctantly she sat down beside him. He handed her an awkwardly wrapped package; he hadn't had much time to spend on wrapping things.

Rachel tore at the paper with the air of wanting to get the task over with. The gift for Chrissy was a rattle, a clear doughnut-shaped one with sparkles in it.

"That's very nice, Joe," she said.

"Now this one." He handed her a larger package.

Rachel opened it; it was a bird mobile to hang above the crib. "You wouldn't have had to buy Chrissy these things," she said. "She'll be gone soon." She sounded troubled.

"Still. A baby's first Christmas should be special."

She looked at him curiously. "You really mean that, don't you?"

"Yes."

She shook her head. In the language of head shakes,

he wasn't sure if it meant *You're a real sap* or maybe *What a nut case* or even *I don't understand you.*

"I think," he said, "there's a present here for you." He reached a hand around the back of her head, and when he again held it in front of her face, it was balled into a fist.

"Open," he said.

"I don't know what you're doing," she said.

"Bringing a little magic into your life. I wish I'd had a way to wrap this. I ran out of paper."

Keeping her eyes on his face and looking distinctly skeptical, Rachel pried open his fingers one by one. Inside was a can opener, punch type, exactly like the one Ynez Garcia had broken.

"You're underwhelmed, right? You can be honest." He grinned at her, and she looked for a moment as if she were unsure how to act. Then she laughed.

"I'd have gotten you something better, but there wasn't time."

"This is exactly what I needed. Thanks, Joe. You shouldn't have given me anything."

"I...well, I noticed that you don't have any presents around. You're supposed to have presents when it's Christmas."

She seemed, in that moment, slightly regretful. "Mimi is going to bring me something from Asia, something special. And I don't have any other relatives—except my mother, of course, and she isn't in any condition to go out and shop for the holidays."

"That's too bad for you," he said, thinking of the rollicking camaraderie of a Marzinski Christmas. Dinner at his parents' house must have seemed noisy and extremely busy to her.

"Well, I don't know," she said, but then she was all

business. "I'd better get to work. The remote control to the television is in the drawer of the coffee table, and if you want something to eat or drink, check the fridge. Formula is already mixed, and there are plenty of diapers in the bedroom." She took the can opener into the kitchen where he heard her putting it into the dishwasher. Then she went into her office, treating him to a worthwhile view of her well-rounded backside in the process, and he could hear her playing back messages on her answering machine.

Joe sank down on the couch and regarded the Christmas tree with pleasure. The tinsel twisted this way and that, magically reflecting the tiny tree lights. Chrissy's presents were still under it, and even though they'd been unwrapped, their bright colors lent an air of festivity to the room. He was glad he'd brought the tree and set it up, even though he wasn't sure Rachel had appreciated or understood the effort.

He turned on the TV, finding a football game and settling back against the couch cushions to watch it. In the next room he heard Rachel's office chair squeak as she sat down, and he heard her turn on her printer and open a package of paper.

He'd spent better Christmas nights. And, he reflected as he zeroed in on an instant replay, he'd spent worse.

JOE MUST HAVE DOZED, the effects of eating a huge dinner and not having enough sleep the night before. He woke up to the late-night newscast, some announcer acting smarmy and all-knowing as he narrated a holiday piece about Santa's not having enough chimneys to climb down in South Florida because most houses didn't have a fireplace.

It wasn't the words that caught his attention but the

Santa who was being interviewed. Joe could have sworn that this particular Santa was the one who had paid them a visit last night, crescent-shaped birthmark and everything.

"Hey, Rachel," he called.

She answered from her office, "I'm busy, Joe."

He got to his feet. "Come see if you recognize this guy. I think he's the one who came last night."

Rachel appeared in the doorway to her office holding a sheaf of papers. She was wearing glasses and squinted through the lenses at the screen. It made her look adorable, that squint.

"Doesn't he look like the same Santa?" Joe asked.

"Not sure." She pulled off her glasses, sending a shimmer through that glorious hair, but by then the newscaster was wrapping up the program.

"Well, I think he was the same guy. Strange."

Rachel heaved a sigh and rubbed the bridge of her nose with thumb and forefinger. "What time is it?"

"After eleven. Why don't you take a break?"

"Once I finish printing out this report, I will."

That was when Chrissy woke up and started fussing. "I'll take care of her," Joe said as Rachel, who seemed to be functioning on automatic pilot, headed toward the bedroom and the baby. He grabbed her shoulders from behind and steered her instead in the direction of her office. Her shoulders felt narrow and delicate, and he wanted so much to touch them under her blouse. To brush aside the neckline and slide his fingers beneath the fabric, to cup his hands to their contours. He felt a shiver run through him at the thought.

It was almost as if she felt it, too, because she jumped and put distance between herself and him.

She was already in her office before he could think of

anything to do or say to her, and besides, the baby was crying. Wondering what this would all come to in the end, Joe went and picked Chrissy up out of her crib.

He'd had, he reflected as he plunked himself down in front of the Christmas tree to feed the baby, several conversations with various brothers-in-law about how babies managed to cry at just the wrong time, but he'd never quite believed that it could be that bad. In this case it probably wasn't, but he now understood what Greg and Reggie had been talking about, and he even managed some sympathy for Jackson who had so pointedly referred to the problem at dinner earlier.

So what did people do?

"You sure are a lot of trouble," he said affectionately to Chrissy, who was staring up at him with those eyes that put him in mind of someone, and he wished he could think of who it was. Maybe she looked like one of his nieces or nephews when they were tiny—that must be it. They all grew up so fast, and sometimes it was as if they changed overnight, burgeoning into sturdy children before Joe had even become used to the way they looked as babies.

That would happen with Chrissy, too. Only he wouldn't be around to see it.

The thought gave him a pang, disturbingly in the region of his heart. And he'd thought *Rachel* was too attached to the kid! That showed just how easy it was to develop feelings for a baby.

"Joe?"

He looked up to see Rachel standing beside him. "She's fallen asleep," he said.

"I'll put her back to bed." Rachel scooped the child from his arms, and even though he wanted to, he didn't follow her into the bedroom.

When she came back, he noticed how tired she looked. Not as tired as last night, maybe, but pale-blue half circles rimmed her lower eyelids, and he thought he detected a slight slump to her shoulders.

Before she could disappear back into her office, he took her hand and drew her closer to the Christmas tree. Suddenly he wanted to get her out of here, to take her someplace where he could impress upon her the fact that he thought she was special beyond words. But they couldn't go anywhere; they had Chrissy.

"I hear that eggnog calling to me from the refrigerator," Rachel said, surprising him. "Want some?"

"Sure," he told her. He watched as she turned and went into the kitchen, and the swirl of her skirt made him notice the neat turn of her ankles. He kept finding new things about her to admire. That had never happened to him before. Where women were concerned, it was usually just the opposite—he found things about them that turned him off.

He decided that what he needed was fresh air, a fresh outlook, so he threw open the sliding-glass doors and stepped out on the balcony. The scene was still enchanting, with lights across the water and cars moving along the street below with red taillights, making them look like moving Christmas decorations. Last night—but he didn't want a recap of last night. He didn't want to make her uncomfortable, he didn't want to go beyond what she thought proper.

"Joe?"

"Out here," he called, and she came outside carrying two cups.

She handed him one, and with his free hand he pulled a chaise longue close to a chair. "Let's sit down and relax for a moment."

He took the chair, and she allowed herself to be pulled down next to him on the chaise longue. He was taken with the notion that if he got to know Rachel, really got to know her, he'd understand better what was going on in her head.

He sipped the eggnog, which she had spiked liberally with rum from Mimi's bar. How to find out what he needed to know? How to get her to open up to him?

He pondered this for a while, during which time Rachel said nothing. He glanced over at her out of the corners of his eyes. She was sitting with her head thrown back and resting against the cushion of the chair, and he was struck all over again with how utterly beautiful she was. And how alone. He supposed it made some sense for her to be alone if she was house-sitting here and hadn't had a chance to meet any other young singles, but how could Rachel stand working alone, living alone and, assuming that she did have some recreational time, spending that alone, too? Alone time was a concept that no Marzinski would ever be able to understand.

"Rachel?"

"Hmm?"

"You're so quiet, I thought maybe you were asleep."

"No, merely resting my eyes. Staring at the computer screen creates eyestrain."

"Don't you ever take a vacation?"

She laughed ruefully. "I think this stint in Florida *is* my vacation."

"When are you supposed to go back to New Jersey?"

"Mimi wants me to stay. She says she likes my company, but I think this place would be too small for us both, over a long period of time. We'd either have to share the bedroom or I'd have to camp out in my office on the futon."

The idea of Rachel's leaving gave him a twisted feeling in his gut. "Why don't you get your own place in this building?" he asked.

"I have an apartment in Lakemont."

"You can't like the weather there."

"No, I guess I can't. After living in Florida, even North Florida, I'm spoiled."

"Why'd you move from Florida to New Jersey in the first place?" he wanted to know, suddenly curious about everything that might give him a handle on her.

Rachel glanced away, but before her face turned, he recognized the familiar bleakness there.

"I...I don't really want to talk about it, Joe," she said in a low tone, and he knew then that he had somehow overstepped his bounds.

Advance and retreat. That's the way this had gone from the beginning. But he wasn't discouraged. He'd try for a change in subject.

"Well, another Christmas is over. I guess Mom and Dad have probably dug out from all the wrapping paper and put away the good china by this time." He paused. "What did you think of my family?" he asked.

She shifted and angled toward him. "Lively. Fun. The kind of family I wish I'd had. You can't imagine how lonely it was being an only child and how difficult it is now to have sole responsibility for my mother."

Joe reflected on this. "Yeah, it must be hard."

"I like your parents, Joe."

"You know, so do I. Right about now they're probably relaxing on the porch, holding hands and chuckling over the antics of the kids."

"How nice that they still hold hands," Rachel murmured.

"They're both romantics at heart. One Christmas, I

remember—'' He stopped, thinking that perhaps this story was too private to tell Rachel, but she looked so open and expectant that he wanted to share it with her.

He started over. "I went over to their house about this time of night one Christmas a few years ago. I'd left my presents there when I went out on a call and decided to drop by and pick them up. The house was open, but I couldn't find my parents anywhere, so I looked out the back door and there they were, all cuddled together under the stars in my old sleeping bag. I tiptoed away so they never knew I saw them, but they were totally wrapped up in each other—well, I guess you know what I mean.''

He could have sworn that a slow blush was working its way up Rachel's neck to her cheeks. "I...I think that's sweet, Joe,'' she said.

"So do I. Someday I hope I'll have as close a marriage as they do. They've been through a lot, raised six kids, and they're still like two lovebirds.''

Rachel looked pensive, and in the instant when her eyes met his, he saw something there—a barely concealed longing, a willingness that he hadn't sensed until now. Despite his best intentions, despite the fact that he hadn't intended to do anything of the sort, he leaned closer and kissed her on the mouth.

She was surprised at first, he could tell, but then her lips were soft and pliant. Her mouth opened beneath his as he deepened the kiss. He thought at first that she would quickly put an end to it, after which he supposed he'd go home. But she didn't pull away. He half expected the baby to wail or fuss, or the phone to ring, or someone to appear at the door. But nothing like that happened, and he made himself stop worrying that it would.

It was awkward sitting like this, and he moved forward, the better to kiss her. He had in mind a few tentative caresses, then some more caresses not so tentative. But for now there was kissing, and the sweet receptiveness that met the thrust and parry of his tongue. He was amazed when her arms slid up and around his neck, pulling him closer, and he felt her body softening in his embrace as if she would like him to do more than merely kiss her.

Which he would like to do. But not like this, with her in the chaise and him on the chair.

If he moved over to the chaise, that would interrupt what they were doing and she might very well use that momentary lull to express doubt. However, he was very uncomfortable. *Very* uncomfortable.

Carefully he disengaged his lips from hers and moved from his chair to the chaise. He was facing her, and it was only a second or two before he was able to recapture her lips. It went so smoothly that he was able to acknowledge to himself how much he wanted her. And that would have been his real Christmas present to her on this Christmas night, to let her know that he desired her and only her, to tell her how he would take her to bed and what he would do there, and also to promise her how much she would like it.

Yet there wasn't much time for talking. He was too busy feathering tiny kisses down the long line of her neck to the hollow of her throat, curving his hand around her full breast, glorying in the way her nipple swelled to his touch.

He loved the taste of her skin, salty and sweet and fragrant with a hint of jasmine. He loved her hands on the back of his neck and the way her fingers wove through the longer hair at his nape. He loved the way her body pressed against his, all pleasure and perfection. He loved—uh-oh, was it possible that he loved her? Loved Rachel?

He hardly knew her. He'd met her only a little more than twenty-four hours ago. He'd never been in love before, if this was what love was like, this crazy, heart-pounding, willful feeling, a sense of being out of control.

And Joe Marzinski was never out of control. He knew how to control everything from frozen swimming pool pumps to stuck elevators, from personnel glitches to irate condo owners. But he had the distinct feeling that he wasn't able to control the most important thing of all—himself. Because for two cents—maybe even less—he would tell Rachel how he felt about her.

And that would blow this budding relationship—if that was even what it was—sky high. Take one overardent suitor, take one reticent woman who hadn't shown a thimbleful of interest in him, and you had the makings of a romantic catastrophe.

"Joe?" A puzzled Rachel had pulled away and was staring up at him in the starlight, a host of questions in her eyes. She had realized that he was having second thoughts, no doubt, and couldn't understand why he had stopped kissing her.

"That's me," was all he could manage to say, trying to be lighthearted, trying to think, when all he wanted to do was to take this to completion right here on this flimsy chaise longue. He wanted to make her his own, and he knew that would be exactly the wrong thing to do if he hoped that they could one day care for each other the way he hoped they could.

"Is anything wrong?" Her eyes were wide and luminous, not to mention perplexed.

For once he prayed for the baby to cry or the phone to ring or for someone to be at the door. He didn't know what he could say and still be honest about things. He could hardly tell this skittishly inclined person that he thought he might be in love with her. But because he might be in love with her, he didn't want to make up some lie. He didn't think that would be a promising way to start out a relationship.

He kissed her on the forehead, very gently. He gathered her hands in his.

"Rachel," he began, but for a moment he didn't think he could go on. She was looking at him so tremulously and with such a sweet expression that he almost lost heart.

But no, his heart was exactly why he was going to speak these words. He cleared his throat and steeled himself against whatever emotion he would engender. It could be anger or perhaps dislike or even rejection.

"Rachel, I think we need to slow down. I really like you a lot, but I'm afraid we're going too fast."

He heard her catch her breath. "For an almost-engaged couple, that's a peculiar thought," she said, and at first he thought she was serious. Then he understood that she was only teasing him.

He had more to say, mostly along the lines of how much he cared for her and that he wanted to get to know her better, but she surprised him by getting up and stretching. Then she thrust her hands in the pockets of her long skirt and shrugged. "I think I'd better make sure Chrissy is still asleep," she said, rocking back on her heels and refusing to look at him. Then she went inside.

Joe sat back, not sure what to do next. If he'd hurt her feelings, she hadn't shown it. But if she cared for him, wouldn't her feelings be hurt? Even slightly?

He wasn't normally confused by women, but this one

was an exception. Earlier he had wanted to know what was going on in her head. And now he was more concerned about what was going on in her heart.

If anything.

was to recapture. Daring to feel—and to know what it was doing to her head. And then to discover in the second what was happening out in her body...

it anyone

Chapter Seven

Rachel hardly had time to think the next morning between diapering and feeding and bathing Chrissy, but when she did think, it was of Joe Marzinski.

She'd run him off. Mimi had said more than once that she would run off any man, just by acting weird. Not that Rachel had paid any attention to Mimi at the time. It had seemed like another of her grandmother's peculiar notions, like the magnetic pad under the mattress, yellow everything and her crazy friends. But now Rachel would have agreed that something had happened to make Joe lose interest, and that idea was more painful than she'd dreamed it could be.

She had to admit that she really liked this guy. Under other circumstances, she might want to pursue him or at least allow him to pursue her. But there couldn't be any future in the relationship. It was better to nip the whole thing in the bud, which was exactly what Joe himself must have decided.

Sighing, Rachel put Chrissy in the portable crib. "I guess he thought better of it," she told Chrissy. "All that stuff about Christmas and wanting me to meet his family—it must have been because he wanted to show up with a woman. And a baby in the bargain." Chrissy gave one of her vague gas-bubble smiles, and Rachel took the phone out onto the balcony to call the HSS people.

Too bad that the balcony reminded her of Joe and what had happened there the past two nights. Well, she'd better forget that. Forget him. She'd probably never see or hear from Joe Marzinski again. Chalk it up to bad vibes; chalk it up to stupidity on her part, or perhaps naiveté. But this was best. She would never have to reveal things about herself that she didn't want him to know, and that in itself was a huge relief.

Tapping her foot impatiently as she waited, Rachel listened to the HSS phone ring. Finally a woman answered. She identified herself as Madeline Ewing, social worker. Her voice was harried, and Rachel, relieved at least that someone had picked up the phone, launched into the explanation of how she'd found the baby in the manger, how she'd been caring for her over the holiday and how she'd expected someone to come to take custody of the child long before this. She even added that the police seemed to think that someone already had.

The woman listened as Rachel poured out all the details, but when she spoke, it was impatiently. "I'm not familiar with this situation. We're extremely busy and shorthanded besides, and the only reason you were able to reach me at all was that I decided to drop by the office for a few minutes and try to figure out this mess we're in. We've got sick foster parents, kids who ran away and now an abandoned baby." She heaved a giant sigh and added, "There's a shortage of licensed foster parents right now, and those we do have are full up."

Rachel made a concerted attempt at remaining neutral. Not that this was easy. To tell the truth, she didn't like to think of giving Chrissy up. As Madeline Ewing talked, Rachel listened, and as she listened, she walked inside to check on Chrissy in her crib. Chrissy was waving her little hands in the air as she tried to focus her eyes on her fists. The sight, so typical of newborns as they begin to explore their world, brought a lump to Rachel's throat. This baby deserved to be cherished and loved, not bounced around from place to place only because there was no room for her.

No room in the inn. The words from the Christmas story sprang into Rachel's mind suddenly, and they seemed to have new meaning. Everyone had turned Mary and Joseph away, and their baby had been born in a lowly stable, the cradle in a manger.

"...and so I'll send someone by to get that baby, but I don't know when. I'll have to put her in a licensed home in the south part of the county, but they're all down with the flu and I hate to do it. Where did you say you live?"

"Wait," Rachel said in a small voice.

"Excuse me?"

"Ms. Ewing, I, um, I think I can help you out."

Silence on the other end of the line. Then a cautious, "What do you mean?"

"I...I'm a licensed foster parent," Rachel said.

More silence. "In Florida? You have a license for foster care in the state of Florida?"

"Yes." The word was almost a whisper.

"Why didn't you say so in the beginning?" Ms. Ewing asked sharply.

Why? Because of Nick and Lolly and Melissa and Derek. Because of what happened. But Rachel didn't say that. "You can check if you like. It was in Cane County."

"Cane County, Cane County." Ms. Ewing was clearly annoyed, and she seemed to be riffling through cards or files. "You're aware, of course, that I'll have to do a thorough background check." She was brisk and businesslike, but at least she hadn't said that it couldn't be done.

"I know you have to be careful," Rachel said.

"And if you don't check out, we'll have to come and get the baby and put her in a proper home."

"I understand," Rachel said. This woman couldn't know that she was quaking inside. She wanted Chrissy to stay with her, wanted to be able to hold that small body morning and night, wanted so much to be able to look into those little eyes and see love and adoration and all the things she so missed from her own lost children.

Ms. Ewing sighed again. "This is a surprise, I must say. But perhaps we can work things out. I'll be back in touch soon."

"Soon," Rachel whispered, and then she clicked the phone off. As soon as she'd hung up, Rachel despaired. She must be out of her mind. The background check would show her up for what she was, a totally irresponsible person. And then Madeline Ewing, who didn't give a flying fig about what happened to this baby, would send someone to take Chrissy away, and Rachel would never see her again.

Rachel buried her face in her hands, oblivious to the boats gliding past on the waterway, tourists sauntering up and down the beach and the sun shining on the ocean. In her mind all she saw was the house that she and Nick had refurbished, and it was in flames, and smoke was everywhere. And there were sirens and shouting people running past and television cameras and an ambulance, and then she was in the ambulance, and after that she didn't remember anything until she woke up in the hospital, and then she'd remembered everything and she'd wanted to die.

IT HAD BEEN IN DECEMBER four years ago that Nick had suggested that they get the puppy. One of his friends' dogs had given birth to a litter of five, and the puppies would be ready to be taken from their mother at Christmas.

"Kids need a pet," Nick had said. "Lolly has been wanting a dog ever since she started to talk."

It was true. *Dog* had been one of Lolly's first words. She was six on that Christmas, a happy, talkative kindergartner who had never met a stranger. Melissa was four, and she was entranced with her new baby brother, Derek. He wasn't really her brother, he was a foster child, taken into their home because Nick and Rachel loved children and had plenty of room. Derek had, at the age of one, quickly become part of their family, and his birth mother had recently agreed to release him for adoption. Rachel and Nick had decided to adopt him only a few days before, and this news was going to be a Christmas surprise for the children.

Not that Rachel and Nick would stop taking in foster children. In fact, they had already applied to care for another. They planned to have lots of foster kids to fill up their big house, children that they would care for until their parents could afford to take them back, children who had health problems—all kinds of kids would enter into their care, now that they were official foster parents. They loved children, she and Nick, and Rachel thought that she'd been born to be a mother.

Nick had brought the puppy home the day before Christmas, and they'd hidden him in a storeroom off the kitchen where the kids would be unlikely to see or hear him. He'd been a cute little floppy-eared, brown-and-white mutt, and Rachel had fallen in love with him from the start. She'd bedded him down in his new doggy bed and filled his new doggy bowl with water and set up a small electric space heater for him because a cold front was passing through their little North Florida town, and she didn't want him to be cold on the first night away from his mother.

On Christmas Eve, Rachel and Nick had put the kids to bed early and had set up the tree with the presents arrayed around it. Lolly had requested a new Barbie doll, and they'd bought Melissa her first tricycle, a blue one. Derek, the baby, was getting pull toys because he had recently taken his first steps. After everything looked perfect, Nick and Rachel had cuddled close on the couch with cups of mulled wine, holding hands and anticipating how thrilled Lolly and Melissa would be about the announcement that Derek was officially to become their brother.

And they talked about how much the kids would love the new puppy. They knew that tomorrow morning, when Nick carried him out of the storeroom in the big ribbon-trimmed basket that Rachel had fixed for him, Lolly would shriek with delight, and Melissa would hang back shyly, and Derek would dimple and bounce up and down in Rachel's arms until she let him stroke Max's silky-soft ears. Max was the puppy's name, they'd already decided.

Rachel and Nick had gone to bed before midnight, and Nick had fallen asleep right away. Rachel had lain awake, snuggling close to Nick with his hand curved over her hip, and she'd thought about how happy they were. And how lucky, and how blessed. Nick had recently gained tenure in his job as a professor at the nearby university, and they had their children and each other. Things couldn't have been better.

It was much later when Rachel woke up to the smell of smoke. At first she thought it was wood smoke from a neighbor's fireplace, blown through the trees separating their properties by a rising wind that heralded the oncoming weather front. She snapped fully awake when she realized that the source of the fire was much closer than that.

"Nick!"

Beside her, he was awake too, scrambling to his feet, and he said, "I'll get the kids! Call 911!"

Rachel groped for the phone in the dark, the lights wouldn't work, and when she couldn't find it, she hurtled out of the bedroom to get another phone. The only one she could think of was in the kitchen, and she ran coughing down the stairs through a swirling curtain of smoke. She heard behind her Nick talking to the children, urging them, trying not to frighten them any more than they already were, and she heard Melissa start to cry. But she knew there was no reason to worry, not with Nick there, and when she heard Nick in the upstairs hall behind her, she thought, *Good, Nick's got them.*

The kitchen was engulfed in flames, and the worst of them were in the direction of the storeroom. She knew she should get the puppy out, but the flames beat her back. She whirled, stamping out a spark that threatened to ignite the hall rug, saw that the stairs that she had so recently descended were on fire. There was no sign of Nick and the children, but she knew he'd gotten them out. He'd been right behind her.

She ran out the door, the hem of her gown on fire, and rolled on the ground to put it out. Then she raced frantically through the woods toward the neighbors' house, knowing that she had to get the fire department there as soon as possible, knowing that Nick would look after the children, shepherd them to a safe place.

She collapsed on the neighbors' front porch, and when her friend Cindy flung the door open and said that they'd called 911 already, Rachel insisted on going back to her house. She wanted to be with Nick and the children, to feel Nick's strong arms around her and to do her part in comforting the kids.

By the time she and Cindy and Cindy's husband Stuart reached the clearing where their house stood, flames were leaping from the windows, black smoke was curling away over the trees, and sparks were flying everywhere. Other neighbors had arrived, and Rachel anxiously searched the milling group for Nick and the children. Where were they? Shouldn't they be there?

Cindy had tried to calm her with reassurances, and other friends had wrapped her in a blanket, but still there was no Nick, no Lolly, no Melissa, no Derek. Rachel tore away from Cindy and tried to run back into the burning house, tears rolling down her cheeks, but Stuart pinned her against a tree and wouldn't let her go. Finally, when she grew hysterical, he threw her over his shoulder in a classic fireman's carry and took her to the ambulance where they gave her a shot and started an IV.

She woke up the next day, Christmas Day. She hadn't had to ask; she'd seen the answer to her unvoiced question in the nurses' eyes when they found her awake. Her whole family was gone. So was Max.

Rachel learned later that the puppy had chewed through the electrical cord on the space heater that she'd put in the storeroom to keep him warm, and the resulting sparks had ignited his bedding. Flames had spread rapidly through the old house, which was constructed of heart pine harvested from the surrounding piney woods. The fire department had been slow to respond because they were operating with a skeleton crew so that their employees could be home with their families. The fire had taken her husband, her children and the puppy and left her with nothing.

Including any reason to celebrate Christmas again.

THE PHONE RANG, startling her out of her thoughts. She blinked at the bright sunlight, the blue sky and the cheery yellow of Mimi's decor. For a few minutes she'd been back in that flame-lit clearing, reliving those terrible moments. Images from that night were still so vivid, as if they were indelibly burned into her brain. So many times she'd gone back there in her mind and in her heart, and every single time she was left with one gut-wrenching certainty: she could have done more. She could have saved them if she hadn't gone to the neighbors' house before making sure everyone was safe.

She wiped the tears from her cheeks with a trembling hand and answered the phone.

"Rachel?"

Still struggling to control her tears, she recognized Joe's voice. It was amazing how happy the sound of it made her feel.

"I'm coming over. I've asked Gladys Rink to baby-sit this afternoon."

Oh, this was too much. He had no right to involve Gladys.

"Are you crazy, Joe?"

"Crazy? Maybe I am, Rachel. I'm crazy about you. Last night I was awake all night thinking about us."

Rachel closed her eyes. She felt as if she was on an

emotional see-saw—first up, then down, and sometimes landing with a thump.

"Rachel."

"Joe, what's this about?"

"You and me. Not the baby, not HSS, not the Christmas holiday, not anything. I have to see you."

"Joe," she said, wondering why all she could say was his name. Maybe it was because Joe Marzinski didn't belong in her thoughts right now. It was easier to cling to the past and all that it represented. It was easier not to move on, move out, move away.

"I'll be there in ten minutes." Joe hung up the phone unceremoniously.

One thing Rachel knew for sure, and that was that Joe meant what he'd said. He was coming over, and so was Gladys Rink. To try to stop him, Rachel knew from past experience, would be like trying to put brakes on a runaway freight train.

Rachel went into the bedroom and gazed down at the baby, who was sound asleep.

"What does he want?" she said plaintively. Not that Chrissy was going to say anything; not that Rachel wanted her to say anything.

She went into the bathroom, feeling slightly dazed. She stared at her reflection in the mirror. Unruly hair, no makeup, a T-shirt that Chrissy had spit up on, and shorts.

Should she put on something more flattering? No. She didn't care what Joe thought about her. She wanted him to go away. She wanted—

She wanted to kiss him again. There, that was the truth of it. But why? He wasn't her type. Her late husband had been a college professor. Joe was definitely blue-collar. What would they talk about? What did they have in common? Nothing except the baby. Nothing at all.

In a last-minute concession to vanity, Rachel sponged as much of the stain from her T-shirt as she could, using a solution of baking soda and water to neutralize the odor. Then she applied a pale lipstick and ran a brush through her hair. That was when the buzzer rang and she heard Sherman's lackadaisical voice. "That Marzinski fellow's on the way up."

With anyone else, Sherman would have called for permission. Oh, Joe was slick, all right. He could manipulate and maneuver anyone. Including her. Including Sherman. Including Gladys Rink, which was nothing short of astonishing.

She went to answer the knock at the door.

"Hi, Rachel. Where's that baby? Where's little Christmas Noel?" Gladys had brought an armload of baby toys, all new. Behind Gladys stood Joe, his face solemn.

"Chrissy's in the bedroom," Rachel said as she pointed the way. Gladys took off like a shot, leaving her staring at Joe. He was staring, too, his eyes hungry. He looked as if he couldn't get enough of the way she looked, and in that moment she wished she'd taken more pains with her appearance.

"Let's go," Joe said without preamble.

"I didn't say I'd go anywhere with you. I have to catch up with my work." Even to herself she sounded priggish and self-righteous. And she didn't really want him to go away. It was just that she was so torn, so confused.

"What do you have to do?" he asked tersely.

Rachel didn't want Gladys to hear this exchange, so she grabbed Joe and pulled him into the kitchen. "Don't you have a condo crisis you can control? Why do you have to try to control me?" she hissed at him.

"I don't mean to control you. Get your swimsuit on, we'll go to the beach." He looked tired, and there were circles under his eyes. He also looked undeniably handsome and male in the extreme.

"If that's not control, then what is?"

Joe rolled his eyeballs. "All right, so I'm controlling you. What's wrong with that, if it's something we both want?"

"I didn't say that's what I wanted," Rachel said, but she did want to be with him.

Gladys marched into the kitchen. "What time is Chrissy's next feeding? I'm so glad you asked me to take care of her because goodness knows I needed something to do. All my tennis partners have family in town for the holidays, so I'm odd woman out." She took one look at Rachel and Joe glaring at each other and said innocently, "Am I interrupting something?"

"No," Rachel said through gritted teeth, and she went to put her swimsuit on. A suitably modest one.

"I don't need you to create problems for me," Rachel said to Joe as they waited for the elevator. "Gladys is going to carry news of our argument far and wide."

"So let her," Joe said.

"You don't understand. News spreads like wildfire in this building. They'll have us married by the time the story makes the rounds."

"Any problems with that? We're about to be engaged." Joe grinned at her, and she looked away, chagrined at what she'd just said. Whatever had made her mention marriage? This whole thing was getting out of hand.

And it got worse as they passed through the lobby, hustling past the curious gaze of Sherman and a couple of residents whom Rachel didn't recognize. Inwardly she cringed at the thought of everyone knowing her business. She only hoped that Mimi didn't call to wish anyone happy holidays only to be informed that her granddaughter was hanging out with Joe. Mimi would be thrilled to know that Rachel had a man dancing attendance at last. She might even cut her trip short to come home and meet him.

"We'll get sandwiches at the sandwich shop, eat them on the beach," Joe said, appropriating her elbow and urging her toward the row of shops across the street from the Elysian Towers. Rachel allowed herself to be steered, not knowing how else to handle this. She kept thinking about how warm Joe's lips had been last night, but even the memory of that wasn't enough to make her forget about his rejection afterward. Well, she had rejected him once, and he had rejected her once, so it was a draw. Why he had suggested this outing she couldn't imagine.

In the deli, Rachel settled on a pastrami sandwich, and Joe ordered roast beef. Joe swung the white paper bag containing their lunch as they walked through the condo parking lot, past the Nativity scene, along the boardwalk that wound through the landscaping of sea grape trees around the swimming pool and down to the beach.

"We can sit in the chickee," he said, indicated the palm-thatched shelter built of cabbage-palm trunks in the manner of the Seminoles, and Rachel agreed. It wasn't until she was sitting across the wooden table from him, the sandwiches spread out between them, that she realized her heart was pounding as if she'd been running a mile.

She probably should have been running. Running away. But instead she picked up her sandwich and took a bite, striving to act and look normal.

"Rachel, I had to talk to you. In the clear light of day. Without people around."

She chewed and blinked at him. It wasn't as if she

could answer, her mouth being full of pastrami and rye bread. The sandwich was a little heavy on the mustard, now that she thought about it.

"I like you, Rachel. I like you better than any woman I've met in a long time. I don't know why you don't like me. I'm stumped, to tell you the truth."

Rachel watched a man parasailing over the ocean. He glided into the water, and she wished that everything was as easy as his parasailing looked.

"So could you clue me in? I mean, if I'm doing something that you hate, I'll fix it. Okay?"

Rachel swallowed and forced herself to focus on Joe's face. "You're not doing anything I hate," she said. "You do things I like, in fact."

"So what's the problem?"

"Nothing. Nothing, Joe. I'm not ready for any kind of relationship, that's all."

Looking slightly relieved, Joe finally picked up his sandwich. "If that's all it is, when will you be ready?"

Rachel shrugged. "I'm not sure. I have some things I have to work out."

Like why I want to kiss you and why I don't want to kiss you, all at the same time. She knew this would sound idiotic if she said it, so she kept quiet.

Joe took another bite. "What kind of things?" he ventured after a while.

Rachel didn't know where to begin. "Personal ones," she said at last.

"Personal," he repeated.

Rachel nodded. The man who had been parasailing was being picked up by a boat. She wished she were parasailing today. She wished she were anywhere but sitting across from Joe and being grilled on subjects she didn't want to discuss.

"That's not a good enough answer," he said.

"Excuse me?"

"I've found the woman of my dreams and she tells me that she's not interested in me because she's dealing with personal issues. Well, where I come from, we help each other with problems. We don't walk away when things get difficult."

After he called her the woman of his dreams, Rachel more or less lost track of what else he was saying. How could she be the woman of his dreams? He hardly knew her.

"You hardly know me," she blurted.

Joe carefully set his sandwich down. He stood up and walked around to her side of the table and eased down on the bench beside her.

"I know enough," he said gently. "I know you are kind and caring and thoughtful and that you make great chocolate-chunky brownies. I know that when I look at you, it's as if you were made to my exact specifications. I decided that as soon as I saw you sloshing through the water in the lobby with a baby in your arms." He picked up her napkin and wiped something from the corner of her mouth. "Mustard," he explained.

He'd known from the first moment he'd seen her that she was made to his specifications? What kind of blather was this, anyway? She wasn't sure, but she thought she'd like to hear more of it.

"You don't know everything about me," she protested, the blood pounding in her ears.

"I know I like this," he said, and slowly his face came toward hers, adjusted position, was so close that she held her breath. And then his lips closed over hers, and so help her, she responded in kind. She forgot the parasailor, the people on the beach beyond, the tall tower of the condo above. She was helpless to break the kiss nor did she want to. She only wanted to go on kissing him, and that was impossible. One kiss might be permissible, but she couldn't continue kissing him out here in plain sight of everyone, especially the Elysian Towers busybodies, any one of whom might walk past at any moment.

He was the first to pull away. "You see? We're something special, Rachel."

She struggled to regain her composure. She felt a blush of heat rising from her throat to her face and tingling behind her ears. "I must taste like pastrami," was all she could think of to say.

Joe chuckled deep in his throat. His eyes, so unusual and so all-knowing, sparkled in their depths. "Yes, you do, and it tastes good to me."

Unable to listen to any more of this, Rachel got up and tossed the remains of her sandwich in a nearby garbage can. She started walking toward the condo, then, thinking better of being confronted by Gladys while her cheeks were still flaming from Joe's remarks, she switched paths abruptly and headed down the boardwalk toward the sand. Joe was right behind her, a beach towel slung over his shoulder.

The beach was cast in bright noon light. A number of snowbirds, tourists in town soaking up their midwinter fix of sunshine, were identifiable by their pale skins. Some of them sported sunburns, sure to be painful later.

When Rachel struck out from the boardwalk, she had to swerve around a couple of children who were lobbing a large beach ball back and forth. One of them overthrew his mark, and Joe picked up the ball and tossed it back to him before catching up with her.

"This looks like a good place to settle," he said as

they reached the top of a dune. "I'll spread the towel out and we can sit down."

Not knowing what else to do, Rachel sat down beside Joe on the towel, her arms circled primly around her knees. She'd stay a few minutes, blurt some excuse to go back, hide out in the condo exercise room while her heart rate calmed down.

"I think I'll go for a swim," Joe said. He stood up and took off his shirt and then his shorts.

"Fine." Acting as nonchalant as she could, she gazed off into the distance where another parasailor was preparing to go aloft. She didn't want to look at Joe, who was now wearing only a brief swimsuit.

"You're going, too. Unless you can't swim."

"Oh, I can swim, all right," she said, and then he was pulling her to her feet, toward the ocean, into the waves.

Joe plunged beneath the surface while Rachel, knowing when she was bested, paddled a more sedate breast stroke in between wave swells. She kept glancing back over her shoulder at Joe's dark head, wet and slick as a seal's in the water. He swam with a powerful stroke; was there anything he didn't do well?

At least he was ignoring her. She had rolled over on her back and was floating toward shore when Joe suddenly broke through the surface of the water beside her. He flicked the hair out of his eyes with a quick motion of his head and grinned at her. Beneath the water, she caught a glimpse of his broad chest. She firmly averted her eyes.

"Rachel, will you go out with me tonight? Someplace special?"

She stopped floating and sought the security of the ocean floor with her feet. "I don't know, Joe."

His lips twitched with amusement. "We *are* almost

engaged, you know. Don't you think it's time for our first date?"

"I don't know. I don't know anything anymore." She felt like a parrot, absurdly repeating the same thing over and over.

"We'll go dancing, and I'll show you the lot where I want to build my house. I've never shown it to anyone before, Rachel. Will you go with me? Please?"

She didn't know why, but she looked into Joe's eyes, read the earnestness there and thought about it no more than five seconds before she said, "Yes."

The sea glittered in the sunlight, and she caught a glimpse of dark fish sliding through the clear wall of a wave.

"Good," said Joe. "I'll pick you up at seven."

Now it was her turn to swim fast and furiously, but Joe kept up with her every stroke of the way. The water felt silky against her skin, like a lover's caress.

Not like a lover's caress, she thought. *It's just water.*

But the thought lodged in her mind, and she kept thinking about how it would feel to be touched by Joe Marzinski in an intimate way.

HE PICKED HER UP after she'd written out instructions for Gladys Rink, who was delighted to be asked to baby-sit again.

"That Joe Marzinski, he's a good catch," she told Rachel after Rachel had said she was going out with him.

"Mmm," said Rachel, knowing that she'd better remain noncommittal, because if she didn't, Gladys would be more than happy to spread the news that Rachel and Joe were hitting it off.

"You know he's a natural-born manager. That's what they say around here, anyhow. And he's got a head for business. After the problems his parents had with him growing up, I'd say it's a good thing.''

Her antenna went up instantly. "What problems?" asked Rachel, but at that point Chrissy started to fuss and then erupted in a series of hearty bellows, which Gladys insisted on comforting.

"Oh, he was some sort of young hoodlum. I didn't live here then, but you know how people talk. It couldn't have been anything much, he seems like such a good person." In an abrupt change of topic, Gladys said, "You'd better get ready, dear. Leave Chrissy to me."

After a few futile attempts at trying to pry Chrissy away from Gladys, Rachel had gone to take a bath—a scented bath. She'd rubbed her skin with fragrant lotion and given herself a pedicure, all because of Joe. Her sense of anticipation built to the point where she had to stop and take a few deep breaths, reminding herself that this was just Joe she was going out with. Just Joe, and he'd seen her at her worst. But she wanted to look her best for him now.

As Joe was on his way up to the apartment, Rachel kissed Chrissy goodbye and told Gladys where she kept extra cans of formula and where she would find a fresh box of clean diapers, and Gladys said she was going to take Chrissy to her own apartment later, and didn't Rachel look nice, and then Joe arrived and spoke pleasantly to Gladys before whisking Rachel away. It all happened so fast that Rachel was out of breath before they even got in the elevator.

Rachel had piled her hair on top of her head for the evening, and she wore a saffron-yellow dress with a low-cut bustier bodice curving into a short skirt of crinkle-pleated silk that made her waist look narrower than it had ever been. Yellow was, of course, Mimi's favorite color, and her grandmother had splurged on the dress for Rachel's ill-fated meeting with Buford, the boat captain. On that night, the only time she'd ever worn the dress, Sherman had paid her a compliment, which went something like, "Wow, I mean wow!" Which was probably the doorman's ultimate form of praise.

Rachel would have been the first to admit that it was a pretty dress and that the yellow brought out the golden flecks in her eyes. "Wow, I mean wow!" Sherman said again, and Joe grinned.

"I think that means you look fantastic. And you do, by the way," Joe said.

On the way to the parking lot, she studied Joe covertly from under her lashes. She had been aware of his blatant masculinity from the start, but tonight he was an arresting figure in his blazer worn over a casual shirt open at the throat, a man overendowed with sheer vitality. She was, she realized, proud to be seen with him.

Joe's car this time wasn't the Condo Crisis van but a brand-new BMW, blue in color, and he popped open the sun roof after asking Rachel if she minded. She didn't, not at all. Maybe a healthy dose of the night breeze from the ocean would cool her cheeks, which were flushed without the benefit of blusher.

Traffic was heavy on the slender spit of the island with cars bearing license plates of other states. "Tourists," Joe said as they waited at a stoplight. "Say, I don't want to fight crowds in the restaurants. How about if we go to a little place over on the mainland? The seafood is the best anyplace, and mostly locals eat there."

Rachel agreed and remained silent as Joe drove over the bridge. She was dizzily aware of him next to her, of his aftershave lotion, of the shape of his hand as he shifted gears. Her thoughts were in a tumult. Try as she might, she couldn't stop thinking about how his hand would feel if it were to drop a bit lower and graze her knee. The thought brought her a fierce aching pleasure that she banished as soon as it surfaced. She wasn't supposed to want. She wasn't supposed to feel. But want she did, and feel, too. So help her, she wanted to feel more. Her lips tingled as she thought about the probability that this evening would end in a kiss or maybe more.

They pulled up in front of a low-slung building on the outskirts of town. It had a cedar-shake roof and tasteful low lighting accentuating the shrubbery.

"It's called Palmetto Alley, and they have the best Florida lobster on the east coast," Joe said with a grin as he handed her out of the car. She preceded him into the restaurant, where they were greeted by the proprietor, an old school buddy of Joe's. He gave them the best table, one overlooking a pond.

Joe called for a bottle of wine, and they both ordered lobster. After the waiter, who turned out to be another friend of Joe's, had left, Joe leaned back in his chair and smiled at her. He seemed relaxed and expansive, which was in sharp contrast to her own mood. She felt tightly wound and more nervous by the minute, and she was sharply aware that since learning to live alone she had lost the knack for being with someone, one on one.

Over wine they spoke in generalities—the weather, the holiday, Joe's friend and how he'd come to own the restaurant. This put Rachel slightly more at ease, and after a while she found that she was tentatively enjoying the wine, the ambiance and Joe. Especially Joe, who guided the conversation with such skill.

That is, until a lull, when he leaned over the table and smiled at her. "Tell me, Rachel, what have you heard from our favorite state agency?"

They had managed to avoid this topic so far, and she had thought that maybe, if things went well, they'd be able to avoid it all night. Now she realized that she had been deluding herself. The question was inevitable, and she couldn't very well dodge it.

"HSS? I spoke with a caseworker today." Rachel set her fork down and toyed with the edge of the tablecloth.

"Great! So what's their plan?"

"They're doing some checking," she hedged.

"Checking? Of what?" Joe looked askance, as if he couldn't quite figure out what she was talking about.

"Ms. Ewing—that's the caseworker—mentioned putting Chrissy in a local foster home where everyone is sick with the flu. But for obvious reasons she doesn't really want to do that, so she's exploring other options."

Joe looked angry, his expression dark. "I can't believe they don't have any other place for her! They can't put a newborn in a house where everyone is sick."

Rachel bit her lip. "I agree," she said finally.

"They'll have to find another place. I'd take Chrissy to my mother's, let her look after her, before I'd let her go to someplace like that. Come to think of it, why wouldn't my mother qualify? She's given birth to six kids, taken care of many grandchildren, and Chrissy would be safe with her. I suppose there's a catch, though. I bet they won't let just anyone take Chrissy."

"No, they won't," Rachel said. She stared at the lobster on her plate, her brain racing around and around. She wished she could think of some other subject to get them off this topic. Fortunately their waiter appeared and filled their water glasses.

"I suppose you have to be licensed or something to take in an abandoned kid." He glanced up at the waiter.

"Hey, Lance, do you know anything about foster parents?"

"You have to be licensed," the man said helpfully. "My sister used to be one."

"So maybe your sister could qualify to take in a baby? It's a strange story, see, but—"

"No, sorry, she can't help you. She and her family moved away a couple of years ago, opened a resort in the North Georgia mountains. Will there be anything else, Joe?"

Joe said no, there wasn't, and Rachel kept staring at the lobster and the melted butter and the lemon wedges, thinking that she really didn't have much appetite.

"So what we need is a licensed foster parent, is that right?"

Rachel set down her fork again. She saw that there was no getting around this. She'd have to tell Joe the truth. Not all of it, but part of it. Enough to set his mind at ease about Chrissy.

"We've got one, I think," she said, looking him straight in the eye.

His eyebrows shot up. "We do?"

She nodded.

"Who is it?"

"It's me, Joe. I'm a licensed foster parent. And I asked if I could be given temporary custody of Chrissy."

Chapter Eight

"You?"

"Me." Rachel looked him straight in the eye.

"You never mentioned it," he said.

"It—well, it never seemed necessary." She drained her wineglass.

"All this talk about HSS and foster parents? A baby that needs a place to go, and you never said anything?" He heard his voice rising word by word, and he fought to control his incredulity.

"I never thought Chrissy would be with me so long. I thought someone would come and get her."

Joe narrowed his eyes. "Is there anything else you think you should mention? Anything important?" There were so many more things to learn about Rachel, and this fascinated him. It was why he wanted to get to know her better, couldn't wait to understand what she was all about. He shifted in his chair, impatient to get to that point in their relationship and worried that he never would.

"All I need to say, I guess, is that Chrissy can stay with me as long as necessary. I told the social worker that, too."

"I'm glad, Rachel," he said. Still, she looked troubled.

In that moment he would have given anything to know why. It had to do with the mystery he had sensed about her, he was sure.

After that, it was as if she retreated. In another woman, he might have interpreted her mood as coyness, but Rachel was far too down-to-earth to play those kinds of games. She nibbled at her food distractedly, and the silences between them grew prolonged and pronounced. Joe figured that this might have been because Rachel was worried about the baby, who had clearly captured her heart. But he sensed that there was more to it than that.

Joe set himself to the task of drawing Rachel out, but she wouldn't cooperate and she didn't lighten up. He couldn't understand it. Most women made it clear that they wanted to talk about themselves, and some didn't want to talk about anything else. Yet here was Rachel, in whom he was mightily interested, and he got almost no response when he asked about her life in North Florida or her apartment in New Jersey or even about her friends. Didn't she have friends apart from her fellow residents at the Elysian Towers? She hadn't mentioned any.

His mind began to run away with the possibilities. Maybe Rachel was an ex-nun. Maybe Rachel had taken care of her sick mother for a long time before the mother had to go to the nursing home where she lived now. Maybe Rachel was an alien from outer space and had no knowledge of her past.

This last made the corners of his lips twitch, and Rachel cocked her head to one side in her most endearing way and regarded him with a slight frown. "I was saying that I hope whoever left Chrissy in the manger is all right. What's so funny about that?"

He hadn't even realized that she was talking about the baby again. He pulled himself back to the time and place.

''Nothing at all is funny about it, Rachel. But I wasn't paying attention.'' They had finished dessert, and their plates were already being cleared away.

Rachel bit her lip, and in that moment Joe was sorry that he'd told her he wasn't listening. What he wanted to say was that he was so bowled over by the way she looked tonight that all he could think about was holding her in his arms. But something—chalk it up to good judgment, he hoped—kept him from saying it.

''It wasn't anything you said,'' he assured her hastily, but she didn't seem convinced. When he saw a skeptical expression steal across her face, he knew he'd had enough of the restaurant and other people. What he really wanted was to be alone with Rachel. He wanted to kindle joy in her eyes, not question marks. For the first time, he noticed that her eyes were a complex dazzle of browns. At the moment he longed for those eyes to focus on him as if he were the only man in the world, which wouldn't happen as long as they sat in a restaurant where he was unable to put into play his full powers of persuasion.

''Come on, let's go,'' Joe said as he slapped a large bill down on the tray. He'd hoped that she would be as eager to leave as he was, but it was hard to figure her mood, especially when she walked stiffly ahead of him out of the restaurant and into the parking lot, not chatting, not looking back.

He breathed in the soft night air, ripe with the fresh green scent of the tropics and full of promise. ''Rachel, what's wrong?''

She seemed unapproachable and aloof, cool as polished marble. ''I think I want to go home,'' was all she said.

He felt as if she'd stuck a pin in him and deflated all his hopes. Well, Rachel might be acting standoffish, and she might be resistant to his charm at the moment, but he couldn't ignore the subtle sexuality underscored by that dress she wore. He'd always liked that particular shade of yellow, and especially in short skirts that flirted around the wearer's knees. And he'd always liked leggy blondes with tumultuous hair. The hair might not be tumultuous tonight, piled into a knot on top of her head as it was, but that was all the more reason to want to slide his fingers under its golden mass and release it from bondage.

He wasn't about to give up on Rachel Hirsch, and for that very reason, he caught her hand, swung it between them. "I don't want to take you home yet. We could go dancing, and I intend to show you the lot I'm planning to buy." He spoke as persuasively as he knew how.

"If your mind wanders when we're supposed to be chatting over dinner, I don't think we have anything to say to each other."

So that was it. She thought he'd blanked her out. "My mind wasn't wandering," he protested. Anything but. He'd been totally focused on her, almost to the point of stupefaction.

"You said you weren't paying attention. I don't know why I came with you tonight."

When Rachel was at her most off-putting, he wanted to be playful. He pulled her to him, liking the way her eyes lit with surprise at this maneuver.

"I know why you agreed to go out. So we could do this," he said, and he kissed her on the mouth.

She made a little noise, but it wasn't a protest. He kissed her thoroughly, even though he was still aware of the palm fronds rustling in the swale bordering the parking lot and the laughter of a couple who were going into the restaurant. Rachel felt pliant in his arms, not resisting, not objecting.

When he released her, she stared at him, her eyes wide but not startled. "Maybe you're right," she said in a low tone. "Maybe that's all it is."

"Would you mind being more specific?" So they wouldn't be pinned in the headlights of an approaching car, he tucked her arm through his and drew her in the direction of the pond. They could walk beside it while they sorted this out; after kissing her, his resolve not to take her home had only increased. And he was pretty sure that she really didn't want him to.

"Sex. It's about sex, isn't it?"

This flabbergasted him. They were near a small wrought-iron bench overlooking the water, and he kept walking until they were in front of it. They both sat down, and she unlooped her hand from his elbow and crossed her arms across her chest.

"It's about more than sex," he said, trying to frame his words carefully. "So much more than that, Rachel, believe me. It's about finding someone by chance and realizing that she's everything you want in a woman. It's about caring and the joy of shared experiences."

Rachel wouldn't look at him, but she pounced on the opening he'd given her. "We haven't shared that many experiences," she pointed out.

"We could if you'd let me in. You're shutting me out, Rachel. Why?"

"As I recall, last night you were doing the running," she said tartly.

He understood then that he had hurt her more than he thought by putting an end to things last night. In that instant he was overwhelmed by remorse. He hadn't meant to hurt her; in fact, his motives had been for exactly the opposite reason. Furthermore, he didn't want to hurt Rachel ever. She brought out all his most protective instincts.

Now she was looking at him, her eyes wary, her lips slightly parted and moist. When she looked like that, it was hard to think. He'd rather let instinct take over and do what came naturally.

He forced himself to focus on what he needed to say to her. "The reason I pulled back last night was that I want to do this right. I don't want to get us off to a bad start, and I was afraid that's what was happening." Even as he spoke he thought he could feel the heat from her skin across the space between them though it wasn't a particularly warm evening even for South Florida.

For a moment Rachel looked almost as confused as he felt. Impulsively he reached over and cupped his hand around her chin. "Don't say you don't know what I'm talking about. This is real, Rachel. This," and he kissed her lightly on the lips, "and this and this." He punctuated his words with kisses across her jawline and down her throat. He felt her pulse leap in the hollow there, saw her hands clench involuntarily.

She pushed him away. "Joe, the timing isn't good, I'm not ready for this, I don't know what to think when you kiss me. I don't know what to feel."

The moonlight gleamed on her hair, darkened dusky shadows in the hollows of her cheeks. If he were lucky enough to have such a woman for his own, he would never let her go. Which reminded him of something he'd been wondering, especially when she mentioned timing and not being ready and all the things that might mean that she wanted him to buzz off.

He put a few more inches between them and steeled himself to hear something he wouldn't like. A bullfrog in the reeds surrounding the pond went *Barrumph!* His words came out gruffer than he'd intended.

"Is there someone else, Rachel? A guy who is important to you? If so, tell me. Tell me now, because I won't want to hear it later."

She stared out across the pond. There it was again, that aura of sadness, that ill-concealed pain.

"No," she said finally, when he thought he couldn't hold his breath any longer. "No, Joe, there isn't anyone."

He expelled the air from his lungs. He picked up her hand again, splaying her fingers against his palm, entwining his fingers with hers.

"Well, then," he said exultantly, knowing that nothing she could have said at that moment would have made him any happier than the knowledge that she was free. "Let's go somewhere. Somewhere fun. Somewhere exciting." But he knew that it didn't matter where they went because anywhere they were together would be exciting enough for him.

"I thought you were going to show me that lot on the ocean where you want to build your house," she said.

He raised her hand to his lips and kissed her fingers. "Whatever you want. Whatever you'd like," he said, and then she smiled and he knew that he'd do anything for her, any time.

He was in love with her. He knew it in that instant just as well as he knew his own name.

RACHEL TOLD HERSELF to let herself experience the moment. To lean into it. Maybe to embrace it.

But she couldn't let herself go. It had been so long since there had been a man in her life. She hadn't had any serious boyfriends before Nick, certainly none since, and she wasn't sure how to act. Nick had been so much older than she was, a doctoral candidate at the university when she was a mere freshman; she had quit school to marry him. She'd grown up during their courtship, and now, as an adult, she felt unsure of herself when dealing with men, especially this man, who awakened needs and desires that she had thought she'd dispensed with long ago.

She knew what her grandmother would say. Mimi would tell Rachel to go ahead and enjoy herself, not to worry about repercussions, not to have regrets. One part of Rachel wanted to do exactly that, but she was afraid. She had lost so much. She couldn't bear the thought of losing again. If Joe turned out to be a hit-and-run artist, how would she feel about that? Not good.

Neither of them talked as Joe drove back across the bridge and north on the beach highway, which predated the blacktop road that had heralded condominium development on the south end of Coquina Island. They passed the old lighthouse, still lit after over a hundred years in service, and houses became sparser but grander as the road tapered to a narrow trail. On this part of the highway most of the houses were only flickers of light behind high green hedges, and some of them had heavy security gates. Wealthy people lived here; did Joe have that kind of money?

She surreptitiously studied his profile, liking the way his hair curled along his neck. He had a firm chin, no nonsense there, and from the side, she could see that there was a bump just below the bridge of his nose. She would bet he'd broken it once and that it hadn't mended well. Nick had had a bump like that, too.

She didn't want to think about Nick. But she thought of him often—every day, in fact. She'd loved her husband with all her heart. She'd never been unfaithful to him in mind or in body, not from the moment she'd set eyes on him, and she didn't want to be unfaithful now.

It was as if she could hear Mimi's scoffing voice in her head. *How can you be unfaithful to a man who has been gone for four years?* Mimi would have said. *You're only young once. Take advantage of it. Live a little, Rachel. You're alive. Act like it.*

Yes, she was alive. But she shouldn't have been. She should have died with the rest of them. With Nick and Lolly and Melissa and Derek and sweet little Max, the puppy.

Joe pulled the car over to the side of the road. The radio went on playing music as he cut the engine, an instrumental, something soft with lots of violins. Rachel stole a look at him, and he said, "I wanted to take you dancing. Come on, dance with me. Let's get out of the car."

"Dance here? How can we?"

"I'll show you," he said, and then he was around the car, opening the door for her.

The salt wind was sharp in her nostrils as he took her in his arms. All at once she felt featherlight, and they began to sway to the music. There was nothing around them but the dunes and the sea and the stars, nothing but the car and the music and blacktop stretching out in front of them and in back of them.

He was a good dancer, and so was she, but it had been a long time since Rachel had danced with anyone. She'd forgotten how music could take hold of her consciousness, impress itself on her soul and infuse her feet with such lightness of movement. Joe held her close, so close that her breasts brushed his chest, and she could feel the movement of his hips against her.

I'm alive, she thought. *Alive. Alive.* Her heart was beating to the rhythm of those words, or was it the music? The music and her heart seemed one, and she closed her eyes and allowed herself to feel this moment.

When the song was over, Joe pulled her to him for a parting embrace, and she half expected both his arms to go around her, but instead he reluctantly let her go.

"You're a good dancer," he said. "I like that."

"A little out of practice," she said, shrugging off the compliment.

"We can take care of that," he said, and after reaching in the open window of the car to switch off the radio, he drew her toward the slope to the beach.

"See that big tree?" he said. "Draw a line straight north of there for about fifty feet, and that will be my house's deck. It'll have stairs down to the sand, and the second story will have huge windows so I can see the ocean every morning when I first wake up."

"That sounds wonderful, Joe," Rachel said.

"Doesn't it? I'll have family gatherings there, and a big kitchen so we can all cook at the same time if we want to, and a playroom for the kids so they won't be underfoot, and a lot of other things that I can't even imagine at this point."

"How did you find this place? It's perfect." The moon spilled a gilt path across the water, and she thought that if she stood at the water's edge, she could step onto it and walk all the way to the stars.

He slanted a look at her out of the corners of his eyes. "When I was in high school, we used to come here to watch the submarine races. It's called Fisher's Rock."

"Submarine ra—" Rachel realized what he was saying and found herself laughing. "A make-out place, in other words."

"Yes," he said, looking amused, and he put his arm around her. "Let's walk on the beach, want to?"

She was wearing high heels. She looked down at them, and Joe caught her hesitation.

"It's either that or neck in the car."

She reached down and pulled off her shoes, tossed them through the car's open window into the back seat. "That answer your question?" He only laughed.

Hand in hand they made their way down the path, Joe going first so he could help Rachel over the rough spots. Joe took off his shoes at the high-tide mark and rolled up his pants legs as well.

"Do you come here often? I mean, now that there aren't submarine races anymore?"

He chuckled. "I've never been here at night since my high school days. Never seen the moon on the water, never walked beside a beautiful woman in the place where I plan to build my house."

Rachel tried to absorb what he was saying. He thought she beautiful. When she was with him, when he looked down at her the way he was looking at her now, she felt beautiful. She felt utterly and fantastically gorgeous even though she knew that she wasn't. Her lips were too full, for one thing, and her hair was too curly, and she'd rather have blue eyes than brown.

"Anyway, now that I'm making money hand over fist, I've hired people to help me with the business. I can afford to take time off, so I'll start building my house soon, I hope."

"Mmm," was all she could think of to say.

"And there's something else I'd like to do with all this time I'm going to have. I'm hoping you'll let me spend some of it with you." His voice was earnest and carried the weight of conviction—something that Rachel hadn't been prepared to hear.

She moved slightly ahead of him as they walked. "I'll be leaving," she reminded him. The light from the lighthouse flicked over her briefly, then left her again in darkness.

"You could stay on. You said that your grandmother would like that."

It was the second time he'd said something about her staying, and she whipped her head around. She was surprised to see such a beseeching look on his face.

"Well, think of it this way, Joe. If I leave, our 'almost engagement' will be broken. You can blame it on me, and your family will never know that you pulled the wool over their eyes at Christmas dinner." She spoke lightly, but she knew he wouldn't respond in the same vein. What she didn't know was quite what he would say.

"I don't want to blame it on you, Rachel. And I'm not at all sure I want to break our 'almost engagement.'"

"I suppose you like being 'almost engaged'?" There was no choice but to keep on with this. If she quit bantering, they'd have to confront what was really going on here, and she didn't think she could handle any more intensity.

"Yes, I like it. I could like it a lot more," he said.

She didn't look at him. She merely kept plodding along in the sand just out of reach of the little wavelets lapping the shore.

"All right. So you don't like talking about that. We don't have to. We can talk about anything you want. Pick a topic, any topic."

A glance over at Joe told her that those remarkable silver eyes were dark with unvoiced thoughts. Suddenly the breeze from the ocean took on a chill, and the night sky seemed too immense and unfathomable.

"A topic," she repeated, but she couldn't think of anything. She racked her brain, trying to think of news events, something holiday related, anything. She wanted Joe to take her hand, then she hoped he wouldn't. She wanted to bump against him as they walked, then she moved farther away so it couldn't happen.

"Let's talk about stars," she said in desperation, because the stars were everywhere, poking twinkly rays of light through the vast dark curtain of the sky, rippling on the water, too many of them by far.

"Stars," Joe repeated. "All right, we'll talk about stars. Stars are bits of fairy dust, did you know that?"

She shook her head.

"And those bits of fairy dust land all over the place. You can't sweep them up, you can't mop them up, all you can do is chase them around. Sometimes they get into the darnedest places," he said, curving an arm around her waist and pulling her closer. He stopped walking, and so did she. For a moment her breath caught in her throat. *Fairy dust,* she thought. *I can't breathe because of it.*

His hand stole up to toy with a fluttering wisp of her hair that had escaped from its knot. He touched her cheek, ran a finger along the slope of her jawline. And then he was pressing her so close that the warmth of his body penetrated her clothes. He made no attempt to kiss her, however, and she found herself burying her face in his shirtfront. He felt so solid and so real, and suddenly she wanted to hold on to that strength, to draw her own strength from it. It was what she needed—something to cling to so she wouldn't be swept away by her own doubts and uncertainties. No, not something, *someone.*

Someone who cared about her, about what happened to her, and who wouldn't let anything bad happen to her ever again.

As if that person really existed, she told herself. As if anyone could do that for another person.

"I care about you, Rachel. So very much," Joe said, his warm breath fluttering loose strands of hair in the vicinity of her ear.

She closed her eyes, inhaling the rich, male scent of him. Her arms went around him before she had time to stop them, and she felt herself tremble within his embrace. If she lifted her face just so, he would kiss her. And yet this wasn't passion, it was something else. It was tenderness and caring and incredible yearning. It was also comfortable. She could get used to being held like this, Rachel thought. Oh, she could—if only she deserved it.

She was swept with dismay. For a moment she had hoped that she'd overcome those awful feelings that had held her in their grip ever since the fire. Feelings of anguish, remorse, regret and the knowledge that she didn't deserve anything better out of life. She had believed all these years that her punishment for not getting her family out of the house was to be alone for the rest of her life.

Did she dare to hope that she could have something more?

"Rachel?"

In that moment, with the beam of light from the lighthouse illuminating his face, Joe was looking at her so lovingly that she couldn't speak. She only stared at him.

"Some of that fairy dust has settled in your eyes. Here, let me kiss it away." And he did, his lips brushing one eyelid, then the other. She thought that in all her life she had never felt a sweeter kiss.

"I want to show you where I live. My apartment. And I'll show you the house plans I've had drawn."

He kept his arm around her waist as they walked back up the beach, and after a time, because it was awkward walking so close that her arm hit him every time she took a step, she put her arm around him, too.

As they drove back to the mainland where Joe lived, her mind was reeling with thoughts too complicated to enumerate, but some conclusions began to stand out with a clarity that she couldn't have imagined a few days ago. One was that she might not deserve a lifetime of happiness, but surely she could steal a night of it. Another was that she could enjoy this gift and then she could walk away. It could be a holiday flirtation and nothing more. When the affair was over—and she was sure that it would be over sooner rather than later—she would return to Lakemont and her little apartment where there would be nothing to remind her that she had ever known a man named Joe Marzinski.

But that apartment, her home, seemed far away as she preceded Joe into the ground-floor garden unit where he lived. Inside, a small foyer opened into a large living room graced by a high, vaulted ceiling and a weathered Spanish-tile floor. The furniture was a mix of styles unified by the repeated use of a boldly striped blue-and-white fabric and the lesser use of a coordinating plaid. And there were pictures of his nieces and nephews everywhere, which created a homey feeling in what would have otherwise been a pleasant but perhaps sterile bachelor pad.

The kitchen was spacious and equipped for what Joe termed serious cooking, although he said he never did any. "Never have had much time," he said. "But now I think I might learn to cook some things. A good Polish

meal like my mom makes. Maybe something very nou-
velle Florida, like shrimp with honey-mango sauce.''

Joe flicked a switch, and mellifluous music began to
spill from hidden speakers. Rachel peeked into the bedrooms and used the bathroom while Joe played back his
answering-machine messages. This gave her time to
think, to reconsider. She knew that if she asked him to
take her home, seriously asked him, he would do it. But
after so long holding herself away from other people, of
living in virtual isolation, she ached to be with someone,
to smile and have someone notice, to be in tune with
another human being.

For a moment she forced herself to concentrate on the
fact that this wasn't merely another human being—it was
a totally masculine, dangerously exciting man. Being
alone with him in his apartment seemed like a singularly
daring exploit, but she didn't care. She would let whatever happened happen; for once she wasn't going to be
cautious. After so long without anyone, after years of
sexual starvation, Joe Marzinski was like a banquet, set
out in front of her, and she was feeling more and more
like a starving woman by the minute.

Her nerves were humming in heady anticipation when
she returned to the living room, but Joe was frowning.
She forced herself to sound matter-of-fact, as if she went
to men's apartments all the time. ''What's happened? A
condo crisis?''

''No, thank goodness. All is quiet on that front for a
change. It's Gina. Listen.'' He tapped a button to start a
message playing on his machine, and Rachel sat down
on the couch while she listened to Gina's frantic voice.

''Joe? Joe! Are you there? It's me, Gina. I just felt like
talking to you. Nothing important. Well, kind of impor-

tant. I think I've made a mistake, a terrible mistake, Joe, and I need to tell you about it."

Rachel looked at Joe in alarm as Gina began to cry. The message continued through the tears. "Well, since you're not home now, I'll talk to you tomorrow. I'm staying with Anna, and she and her fiancé and I are getting together at a friend's. Talk to you soon, okay?" Gina hung up and the machine beeped.

"She sounds really upset," Rachel said thoughtfully.

"That's just the way Gina is. She's not the most stable girl in the world, but she's doing great when you consider her background. She and her sisters actually lived on the streets until we found out about it through the church, and then my mom and dad took her in. I suspect that all this tonight is that she's worried about changing her class schedule for next semester. She probably wants to switch back to her original major."

"Why don't you call her now?"

"I think I will," Joe said. He punched out a number on the phone, and while she waited, Rachel got up and wandered over to the sliding doors leading to the patio. It was a large open-air space decorated with a number of substantial potted plants as well as a table and chairs.

"Go ahead, open the door," Joe said to her, holding his hand over the phone's mouthpiece.

Rachel slid the door open and stepped outside. A high wall surrounding the patio was overhung with bougainvillea vine, its flowers a riot of magenta, pink and purple. She took a deep breath, hoping to inhale some good common sense. Not that it worked very well; she felt a little fluttery. Slightly demented. Adventurous. She shouldn't have drunk so much wine with dinner.

After a minute or so Joe appeared in the doorway. "Gina's not home. I left a message that I called, and I'm sure she's fine. Anna is a nurturing person, and she'll look after her sister. Now. How about a glass of wine?''

"Okay," Rachel said, who even as he spoke was attempting to count how many glasses of wine she'd drunk during the evening. Well, it was too late to undrink any of it. At the moment she wanted to lose all her inhibitions; she wanted to enjoy this to the fullest.

While Joe went inside to pour the wine, Rachel lit a candle on the patio table, and soon Joe came out of the house carrying two stemmed glasses and a rolled-up set of house plans. He spread the plans out on the table in front of her, weighting the furled upper edge with the candleholder.

"This," he said, pointing to the drawing after she'd sat down beside him, "is the foyer. It's two stories high with a library loft overlooking the living room. The living room windows cover one wall for a view of the ocean, and there are two wings opening off it, one for the family room and kitchen and my home office and one for the bedrooms. Lots of bedrooms for lots of kids."

Even though she knew that Joe's house was important to him, Rachel would have gladly forgone learning about it. She could hardly think with him sitting beside her, vibrating at what she was sure was her frequency. But when she made herself look at the plans, she found that they fascinated her.

She and Nick had refurbished their old frame house themselves, and she had thoroughly enjoyed the project, which had taught her a lot about home construction. The plans that Joe showed her were for a different kind of house, but she was immediately captivated by the illustration of the house's front elevation. As for the rest of the plans, the house was grand—even elegant—but it had a family aspect to it, too, with lots of gathering places for the people who lived there. She could imagine Joe in that house.

She drank her wine quickly, all too aware of everything about Joe. His manner, his solicitousness, his eagerness to please. She found the latter especially charming, and it contributed to her comfort level so that she felt utterly and completely relaxed with him, as if she'd known him for much longer than a few days. When he got up to pour more wine, she followed him into the house.

His hand brushed hers as she accepted the refilled glass, and she would have ignored the little frisson of energy that passed from him to her. But one of them—she wasn't sure if it was Joe or if it was her—tipped the glass ever so slightly, and the wine sloshed over the side of the glass and spilled down the front of her bodice.

She stepped back and looked blankly down at the stain and the drops of wine falling from her dress to the floor. One thing she had never been was clumsy. She must really have had too much to drink, she thought; she must be getting tipsy.

"Here," Joe said, wetting a napkin with water from the kitchen faucet. He made as if to wipe the stain, but she held out her hand for the napkin and he gave it to her.

"Yeah," he said wryly as she silently sponged at the bodice of her dress. "I guess you'd better do that."

She risked a look at him. He was standing in front of her, a slightly bemused smile on his lips, his arms folded over his chest. She knew well the muscled strength of those arms and exactly how they felt when wrapped around her, and she knew how she reacted—with longing and a desire that she couldn't, no matter how much she'd tried, deny. In her confusion she dropped the napkin and without thinking bent down to pick it up.

As she straightened, Joe cupped her shoulder. "Damn," he said softly. "I can't take a view like that. Forget the dress, Rachel. I'll buy you another. I'll buy you a hundred dresses."

Too late she realized that by bending over, she'd given him a clear view down the front of her bustier.

"Joe, I'm sorry. I didn't think." It was her voice, but she barely recognized it.

She saw the muscles in his jaw working, and he caressed her shoulder before circling his arms around her. When his lips aligned with hers and then slowly came to touch them, all rational thought left her. The first kiss was gentle and tender, the second relentless. In the next few moments she realized that her feelings for him had been inescapable from the moment she'd seen him in the lobby, water pouring from the ceiling, silver in his eyes. She'd mistaken him for an angel in those moments, but he'd been real. And now, despite every reason she'd mustered to the contrary, she was willing to meet him halfway.

When he ended the kiss, she didn't dare look him in the eyes. Instead she focused on his mouth, which was directly in her line of vision. She had never noticed that sensual droop to his lower lip, nor had she cared that he had an especially deep groove in the space above his upper lip. Now those characteristics took on an irrational importance. All her senses were attuned to him, to everything about him, so that she wanted to know how it would feel to be totally in his possession. She was stunned by this feeling, this emotion, so much so that she felt lost and dizzy, suspended somewhere in time and space.

In that heartstopping moment, his hands went to her hair and curved for a moment around the contours of her head before sliding beneath the pins that held her hair fast. A few pins fell away, and then her hair was tumbling out of its knot, a cascade of golden curls. She had used lemon-grass shampoo, and the scent of it mingled with the taste of the wine on her lips as his mouth descended on hers.

She felt heavy, weighted, and at the same time an exquisite excitement seemed to curl upward from someplace deep inside. She wanted to savor the sensation and encourage it, and she knew that in order for Joe to be able to take her where she wanted to go, she would have to abandon herself to him totally.

This was about trust, and she hadn't thought she was ready to trust anyone. She certainly wasn't ready to trust herself. But here was Joe, his mouth ever more urgent upon hers, his hands sliding up and up until they molded to her breasts. She couldn't help responding to him; she hadn't known she could feel so wanton. She arched her back, and his hands slid down to her buttocks and crushed her to him.

"Oh, Rachel," he breathed into her ear, and she went limp at the sound of her name. She could feel the strong male hardness of him through her clothes, and so help her, she wanted him. She wanted—what? Something just for her. Something special and meaningful and right. And she wanted to feel again, to experience the passion and joy and excitement of holding a man in her arms and being loved by him. And not just any man—this man.

Joe loosened the circle of his arms and gazed down at her. "Let's go into the bedroom," he said. "I want to make love to you more than I've ever wanted anything in my life."

She closed her eyes for a moment, only a moment, conjuring up the four faces that had been so dear to her. But Nick and Lolly and Melissa and Derek weren't there. As hard as she tried, she couldn't see them. And when she opened her eyes, there was Joe, his face full of wonder and admiration and something else, too.

Then he was sweeping her up in his arms and carrying her across the room and through the door into a bedroom with a huge king-size bed.

When she was lying beside him on her side and he was on the bed facing her, she had one brief thought: what if he didn't like her? What if she displeased him, what if she couldn't respond to him? What if it had been so long that this didn't work?

He caressed her cheek, and he lifted her fingertips to his lips and kissed them one by one, and her mind was a jumble of thoughts. She thought about how he had danced with her on the road at the beach and how he had so eagerly shared his house plans with her. How he had capably cared for Chrissy, how he had taken charge in the beginning when she'd almost fallen apart, how he had let his family think that she was his girlfriend. They had experienced a lot in the past three days, enough to learn many things about each other, and one of the things that she'd learned was that yes, she did trust him. And maybe it was more than that, though she didn't dare hope.

Her fingers encountered a gap between the buttons of his shirt, slid inside and touched warm skin. She imagined her lips upon it, her tongue tasting him. Her mouth opening to him, exploring him. She went weak at the thought.

"Okay?" he said as his hand moved lower, feathering across the top of her breast.

"Okay," she whispered back, and she reached around

to unhook the fasteners of her dress, but he was there first. And then her breasts were bare, and then the rest of her, and after reverently expressing his approval of what he saw, his eyes, smoky now with passion, were searching her face. It was such an emotional moment that unbidden tears sprang into her own eyes. But Rachel wasn't sad, she was happy, and she knew that he was happy, too. It was gratifying to know that she could give someone else pleasure in this way because before this, before Joe, she'd thought this part of her life was over forever.

"Oh, Rachel, you are such a treasure," he breathed, and he kissed the hollow between her breasts, then found one rosy nipple and traced its outline with his tongue before teasing it between his lips.

Her hands reached lower, helped him tug off his shirt, and he rose to his knees and swiftly rid himself of the rest of his clothes. She couldn't tear her eyes away from the sight of his torso, all ropy muscles and hard belly, thick dark hair and tanned skin. She wanted to look at the rest of him, all of him, and she wanted him to look at her.

Joe lowered himself over her so that they were lying together, skin to skin, heart to heart. Her fears about what he might think of her evaporated when he said softly and with heartfelt expression, "You are so lovely, Rachel. You have a beautiful body." He slid his hand across the flat of her stomach, caressed her abdomen and wove his fingers in the curls below.

When she would have spoken, he silenced her with a kiss. "Don't say anything," he said, the words hot against her lips. His beard bit into her cheek as his mouth claimed hers with a fierceness that she hadn't expected, and she closed her eyes as doubt and longing gave way to ecstasy.

He took his time, exploring the voluptuousness of her breasts, dropping a light kiss on her navel and lower. When she didn't think she could stand it any longer, when she was virtually mindless with desire, she moved her hands down, down, across the taut muscles of his abdomen until she found what she sought. He was all man, and he was all hers.

"Are you ready for me, Rachel?" he asked, his voice ragged and uneven, and in that moment she thought she had been ready for Joe Marzinski all her life. She wanted nothing more than to be filled by him, to be part of him, to assuage the longing that was more than lust and more than sex. She wanted to know him, to know all of him, would die if she couldn't have this man and if he couldn't have her.

He slid between her legs, and she rose to meet him on a crest of wild rhythm, crying out in her intensity, and he murmured in her ear, words that fell upon her parched spirit like rain in the desert after a long, long drought, and she pulled his head down and kissed him with all the pent-up passion of her soul.

He felt the intensity of her kiss, and the love in it. In that moment he knew what was happening to her, and he was so moved by her openness to him that all control left him. Wanting to experience more, to know all of her, body and mind and heart and soul, he drove himself into her again and again, so hard that she could only cling to him and gasp. He was a man demented, ferocious with passion, and she became liquid, flowing to meet him, flowing into him until the heat of their passion swirled and converged and pulsed outward from her very soul.

When it was over, when she lay damp in his arms,

Rachel tried to remember what he had cried out at the height of their joining. She thought he had said her name and something else.

She thought he had said, "Marry me."

Chapter Nine

When Joe opened his eyes the next morning, Rachel's head was snugged into the hollow of his shoulder, and her hand was curled trustingly on his chest. Her head rose and fell with his breath, one errant strand of golden-blond hair tickling him below his left ear. He remembered, all in a flash, their lovemaking last night. She had been everything he'd ever hoped for, and he had made love to her until the wee hours of the morning.

After the first time, when they'd been new to each other and unable to get enough, there had been a second, more tender time. They had made love until the night folded over them and they slept, and they had not broken contact since.

Rachel stirred, sighed and slid her leg between his. Joe decided in that moment that this was the way he wanted to wake up every morning. With Rachel. He didn't want to be parted from her, ever.

Did Rachel feel the same way? That's what he didn't know. He was on the verge of waking her up and asking when the telephone rang.

"Joe?" Rachel murmured as he pulled away.

"My darling," was all he said, dropping a kiss on her forehead as she opened her eyes. Then he was up and out of bed, much as he regretted it. A glance at the bedside clock revealed that it was seven o'clock in the morning, and experience had taught him that such early phone calls generally announced crises of great magnitude; there was no point in letting his answering machine pick up.

"Hello, Joe, it's me, Gina."

"Gina! Is everything all right? What's wrong?" He wasn't exactly surprised to hear from her after the emotional message she'd left on his machine last night, but he didn't like the timing, not with Rachel waking up and looking all sleepy-eyed and kissable on the other side of the room.

"Nothing's wrong, Joe," said Gina. A big sigh, then a long pause. "Well, that's not exactly truthful. I want to come over this morning. I need to talk with you."

Joe glanced over at the bed where Rachel was sitting up and stretching. She wasn't wearing any clothes, and in fact her dress and underwear were tumbled into an untidy pile on the floor at the end of the bed; he smiled at her, sharing the knowledge of last night.

He made himself pay attention to Gina. "I don't know if it's such a good idea to come over right now, Gina," he said. "Can't it wait?"

"I'm just so...so...oh, I don't know, Joe. Maybe I don't need to see you. Maybe I'll get some sleep."

"Didn't you just wake up?"

"No, after I came back from the party with Anna and Mitch, I stayed up listening to music. I've been up all night. I think I want to crash. Or maybe eat some breakfast."

Typical college kid behavior, he thought to himself. Gina was probably accustomed to pulling all-nighters or maybe partying until dawn with her friends. Still, he was relieved that there was no emergency.

"That sounds like a winner," he told her. "Say, you want to call me when you wake up? You've got my pager number, right?"

"Right. That's a good idea." Gina yawned. "Sorry for calling you so early. It was really stupid of me. Say, um, Joe?"

"Yes?"

"How is the baby?"

"She's fine and healthy and being well taken care of," he said, slightly surprised at the question. But then everyone was interested in babies.

"Oh, that's good. I'm glad she's okay and all. Well, um, sorry to bother you." With that, Gina hung up.

Joe shook his head ruefully as he replaced the phone in its cradle. "That Gina. I don't know what's the story with her lately. I'll take her out for a hamburger one of these days, see if she opens up." He looked at Rachel, *really* looked at her. She was deathly pale, and she was holding her head in her hands.

"Rachel?"

"Headache. Bad one. I think I drank too much wine last night," she said.

"God, Rachel, it wasn't that much."

"More than I usually drink. I should have known better."

He went into the bathroom. "Here's a couple of aspirin," he said as he shook them out of the bottle. He brought her a glass of water, and she tossed back the pills.

"What time is it?

"Seven o'clock."

"I shouldn't have slept so late," she said, wrapping

the sheet around her and sliding over to the edge of the bed. She stood uncertainly, clutching at the bedpost. "I think I have the entire Macy's Thanksgiving Day parade marching around in my head. Which is going to pop wide open any minute like an overinflated balloon." She winced as he set the water glass down on the nightstand. "Too loud," she groaned.

He moved closer, looked into her eyes. Yeah, they looked kind of bloodshot, all right. Other than that, she was beautiful, hair all mussed and wild, lips still swollen from his kisses. But she wouldn't want to hear that at the moment. "Dr. Marzinski here. I prescribe a hot shower and breakfast," he told her.

"Breakfast? Oh, no, you don't."

"Coffee?"

"Coffee's good."

He went into the bathroom and got the shower going, and then he steered her toward it. "Towels. Washcloth. Soap. Shampoo," he said, showing her where they were.

Rachel only moaned.

While she was attempting to wash away her hangover, Joe started the coffeemaker, went and brought the newspaper in from the front step. He'd had no idea that Rachel had drunk so much last night. He hadn't. He'd been too intent on breaking through the barriers. But maybe the wine was why she'd been so uninhibited. She'd been sexy and sensual and not at all reticent.

As he was setting out mugs, Rachel, wearing a towel, stuck her head out of the bedroom and told him that she was ready for clothes.

"How's the head?"

"Still not good. The coffee smells great, though."

"It's a Kona blend from Hawaii. Special medicine for hangovers," he told her as he went to dig a Condo Crisis

Control T-shirt out of his drawer for her. She tugged it over her head before he could even express his appreciation for the way she looked with her skin still damp from the shower.

She studied the jeans he handed her with a bemused expression. "I think these are slightly too large. Do you have something else? Shorts, maybe?"

He found a pair of running shorts and she put them on, filling them out admirably. "Sherman will think I've taken up early-morning jogging," she said with a wry expression, and he thought that if she could joke, she must be on the way to recovery.

When they were on the patio drinking their coffee, Rachel leaned forward, elbows on the table, coffee mug cupped between her hands. He offered her a section of the newspaper, but she waved it away.

"I wonder if Chrissy slept through the night," she said broodingly.

Joe folded up the business section. He supposed it was only natural that Rachel would be preoccupied with the baby. "Don't worry, Chrissy is fine. Gladys was thrilled to be asked to take care of her."

Rachel sighed. "I can't help thinking about Chrissy. I can't help hoping everything will be okay for her."

"Don't worry, Rachel. Not about that, anyway. Let's not talk about the baby—I'd rather concentrate on us."

Rachel gazed at him over the rim of her mug. He got the distinct impression that she didn't think there *was* an "us." As if to confirm his suspicions, she drained the last of her coffee. "I'd better get going," she said. With that, she jumped up and hurried inside.

Somewhere a mockingbird trilled, and the sprinkler system next door switched on, whirling rhythmic splats of water against the patio wall. Joe ran a hand over the back of his neck, totally perplexed. It was just his luck that when he finally had Rachel all to himself, she wanted to leave. Besides, to his way of thinking, they had unfinished business.

He got up and followed her inside where he found her in the bathroom hanging up the wet towel she'd used. "Why go home right now? Gladys is taking good care of Chrissy, you can bet on it," he said.

Rachel refused to look at him. "Sherman comes on duty at nine. I don't want him to see me stumbling in this morning with a hangover." She walked back into the bedroom and snatched her dress up from the floor in obvious dismay.

"I liked sleeping in the same bed with you, Rachel," he said, wondering why this wasn't going well. At the same time a little niggling of annoyance twitched at him. Hadn't Rachel felt what he'd felt last night? That this was special? Hadn't she heard him say what he'd said at the last? Well, not at the last. At the end of the first time they'd made love.

If she had, she wasn't letting on.

"I'm awful to sleep with. I grab the covers. I take up more than my share of the bed."

"You didn't," he began, but she silenced him with a look. Joe was bewildered. He'd thought that last night had held meaning for both of them, and what he'd really wanted to do ever since the moment when he'd awakened with her in his arms was to make love to her again, this time letting her take the lead and showing him what she liked.

"Will you take me home?" The set of her chin told him that she was leaving whether he liked it or not.

His hopes plummeted. This meant that there would be no lazy Sunday lovemaking this morning, and he might as well accept the fact. He went to the closet, yanked out a shirt and pulled it over his head.

"Okay, Rachel, I'll drive you back to the Elysian Towers, and then maybe I'll stop by to visit Mom and Dad. Mom mentioned that she's got a drain that's kind of sluggish, so I'd better take a look." He was brisk, even brusque. He didn't want her to know that his feelings were hurt.

It worked, because then Rachel was asking him for a bag to put her dress in for the ride home, and after that the phone rang, and the caller turned out to be his mother getting frantic about the drain, which apparently wasn't working at all by this time.

Joe calmed his mother, got the real story from his dad, found a bag for Rachel's dress and held the front door for her on the way out. He transferred his tool kit from his work van to the BMW and then he drove Rachel to the Elysian Towers. It was a silent ride, neither of them talking. He turned the radio on to lessen the awkwardness between them.

He pulled over to the side of the road near a patch of sandspurs where she said she wanted to get out, at a point well before the entrance to the condo parking lot. Rachel was reaching for the door handle when he knew he couldn't let her go without telling her how he felt about her.

"Rachel," he said desperately. "Wait."

Her look was like that of a doe caught in the headlights of a car. She didn't say anything, merely looked at him.

Damn! How to get through to her? How to make her see that she wasn't a one-night stand, that she was more, much more to him than that? He drew a deep breath.

"Rachel," he said again, but she reached over and touched a hand, featherlight, to his lips.

"Don't say it," she said. "Don't."

And then she was out of the car and running along the edge of the road. Running away from him and, it seemed, the possibilities of their relationship.

She knew what he'd been going to say. She had to. And she didn't want to hear it.

But why? Why would the thought of his being in love with her scare her so much?

RACHEL DECIDED TO CHASE the remnants of her hangover by taking a long walk on the beach before reclaiming Chrissy from Gladys.

The beach was quiet, the ocean calmer at this hour than it probably would be all day. The fast-rising sun poured a wash of shimmery golden light across the gently billowing sea, a sight that Mimi had once said inspired her to decorate her whole apartment in yellow.

Right now the sun's rays seemed hell-bent on piercing little needles straight into her brain, but the aspirin and caffeine were kicking in, so maybe she would postpone burying her tortured head in the sand, attractive as the idea seemed. Farther down the shore a lone figure had propped a fishing pole in at the edge of a dune, and periodically he reeled in the line.

She focused on the figure as she thought about Joe riding across the bridge to his mom and dad's house right now. Perhaps she'd been unfair in not letting him speak his piece, but she was terrified to think that he might really care about her. Maybe she should have expected him to declare his feelings. He'd given her hints all along, saying things to let her know how much he liked her almost from the very beginning. She liked him, too. But was this thing with Joe a fling, or was it something more?

Maybe it was nothing more than overload. Rachel

hadn't been with a man in so long that all her senses were bound to be more susceptible than normal. No wonder she grew weak at the thought of Joe, ached for his touch. She was already anticipating the next time she'd see him, and she still felt guilty about the hurt and disappointment that had clouded his features in the moments before she'd jumped out of the car. What he didn't know was that it had taken every last shred of her self-control to leave him.

This was weird. It was complicated. It was confusing. But what if she was in love with Joe Marzinski?

No, she couldn't be.

Yes, she could.

Her thoughts were so contradictory, so confusing, that she actually laughed out loud at herself, sending a flock of scavenging gulls winging skyward, the wind from their wings rushing cool upon her cheeks. Her own laughter hurt her ears. And then tears filled her eyes so that she couldn't see where she was walking.

She was happy. She was sad.

No, she wasn't.

If this was love, she didn't like it. Abruptly she forced herself to think about something else, something that she thought would be more neutral territory. She thought about Chrissy, her rosebud mouth and the way she puckered it just before she let out one of those incomparable wails. She thought about round baby cheeks and tiny wisps of eyebrows. Maybe she could bring Chrissy to the beach early some morning before the sun got too hot, introduce her to the sound of the ocean, show her how the sand crabs skittered and danced around the patches of dead, dry seaweed.

If she could keep Chrissy. She shouldn't allow herself

to make plans. Chrissy might have to go—maybe even today.

But in that moment Rachel couldn't imagine *not* keeping the baby. She had almost, but not quite, forgotten that half the fun of motherhood revolved around introducing a child to the world and seeing things through her own adult eyes as if she had never seen before.

She'd be a good foster mother to Chrissy. But what if that social worker, that Ewing woman, decided that it wasn't in the baby's best interest to stay with Rachel? A lump rose in Rachel's throat at the thought of giving Chrissy up. Of *ever* giving her up.

She wanted a baby of her own. That was the truth of it. Not that she could have admitted this even to herself before she'd found Chrissy in the manger. It would have seemed as if she were betraying her own children and Derek, who would have soon been her adopted son, and even Nick and the puppy. She'd somehow thought that keeping all of them safe in her heart meant that she would have to put everyone else out of her life lest they distract from her task of memorializing her lost family.

But here was a chance to be a mom again, and she wanted to grab it and never let it go. To never let the baby go, to keep her for her very own.

Nonsense, Rachel, she told herself sternly. *You can't keep a baby that isn't yours.* But she wanted to. Chrissy had filled up that lonely space inside her, and Rachel didn't want to go back to being alone. The chief problem was that she didn't deserve to be anyone's parent, not even an abandoned child's.

"Rachel?"

She recognized the crusty voice before she even turned around. It belonged to Ivan O'Toole, who was ambling toward her wearing a jaunty canvas hat and ancient gray sweatpants. A T-shirt covered his bony chest, and he walked with the aid of a gnarled piece of driftwood. He was rapidly gaining on her.

"Good morning, Ivan," she said, greeting him graciously and hoping that she didn't still look like death warmed over. Truth be told, of the Theatrical Threesome she had always liked this man the best. So did a lot of other people. Rachel knew that Ivan was in great demand among the single women at the Elysian Towers. Rachel suspected that he was something of a heartbreaker. In his younger days, he might have been a Mel Gibson look-alike.

"Didn't think you'd be out so early, Rachel. I mean with the baby and all." He fell into step beside her.

"I have a good baby-sitter," she told him. They walked on together, Rachel clutching the bag that held her dress from the night before and hoping that her companion wouldn't guess what was in it.

"Oh, you mean Gladys? Yep, she seems to know what she's doing with kids, all right. Trouble is, we were supposed to go out last night. Instead we stayed in her apartment playing with the baby. Hey, I thought you were going to pick Chrissy up and take her back to your place early this morning."

"I decided to indulge myself with a walk on the beach first," Rachel said, feeling guilty. However, her guilt feelings were overridden by the amazing news that Gladys Rink and Ivan O'Toole had ever been anything but adversaries.

"You look kind of surprised, Rachel," Ivan prodded with a sly grin. "At the idea of Gladys and me, I mean."

"Well, you and Gladys—let's just say that you have never seemed compatible."

This elicited a hearty guffaw. "Can't say that I thought

so, either. We were going to pass some time together last night, you know, maybe go to a movie. Both our families live far away, and at this time of the year it's only natural that we would miss them, so we agreed to keep each other company this holiday season. Then I saw Gladys last night with that baby, and she seemed so much gentler than I'd ever noticed. And it's like I've never seen Gladys before. She's new to me, if you see what I'm saying."

Rachel turned to look at her companion in amazement and was further surprised at the utterly besotted look on his face. "I think maybe I do," she said slowly. "That's nice for both of you, Ivan."

Ivan nodded in agreement. "About last night. I didn't want to go home after the baby was put to bed, but Gladys made me leave, and I couldn't sleep all night, to tell you the truth. I'm going to ask her if she wants to go out to lunch. Only the two of us. That is, once you've taken Chrissy back to your place."

This reminded Rachel that it was time to head back. A glance at her watch told her that Sherman would be on duty in a few minutes, and she didn't want to run into him.

"Thanks for the reminder, Ivan," she said. "I'd better go get the baby right away. Enjoy the rest of your walk. And the lunch."

"Oh, I intend to," Ivan called after her.

An hour ago, the sand crunching underfoot would have made Rachel's head throb. Whether her hangover had gone for good was debatable, but as she hurried homeward, she couldn't help smiling to herself at the thought of the two septuagenarians getting romantic. Riding up in the elevator, she wondered what Gladys would say about the whole situation with Ivan O'Toole, and she didn't have to wait long to find out.

"He likes children," Gladys said excitedly as Rachel stuffed things into Chrissy's diaper bag. "I never knew that about Ivan. That's pretty important, you know, when you have lots of grandchildren like I do. Well, they live clear across the country, that's true, but I always spend summers with them."

Rachel was holding Chrissy, rocking her back and forth, taking in the baby's face as if she'd never seen it before. Never mind that she'd had a good time last night, never mind that she'd rediscovered how healthy and exciting making love could be, she had missed Chrissy. It suddenly struck her that she might not be sure that she was in love with Joe, but she certainly was in love with this baby.

"Rachel?"

She looked up, realizing that she'd lost track of what Gladys was saying. "Hmm?"

Gladys was standing with her hands on her hips. "I was telling you that Ivan O'Toole is one really hot guy, and what do I get? No reaction."

Rachel couldn't help it; she started to giggle at the idea of Ivan's being "hot." Lukewarm would have been her assessment, but then, what did she know?

"Well, he is, and that is the truth. Rachel, for heaven's sake, you're not supporting Chrissy's head very well. Your eyes look all veiny and red. What's gotten into you, anyway?"

A really hot guy, Rachel wanted to say. *The sexiest man in all creation.* But she didn't say such thing. What she did was smile sweetly and thank Gladys Rink for baby-sitting. And then she backed out the door, wondering when it was that Gladys Rink had started wearing Opium perfume. What was next—slinky black underwear under her tennis sweats? Judging from Rachel's earlier conversation with him, Ivan might just rise to the bait.

Back in Mimi's apartment, Rachel doctored her eyes with Mimi's eyedrops and pinched her cheeks to bring back their color. She bathed Chrissy, fed her and settled her in the crib. Then she drank another cup of coffee as she sat watching until the baby was sound asleep. *I hope I won't have to give you up,* she thought to herself.

But of course, she thought as she rinsed out her cup, she *would* have to give the baby up. Maybe she could serve as Chrissy's foster parent for a while, but the birth parents were out there somewhere in the world and might want their child back. If that didn't happen, there were more likely and more deserving parents than Rachel, parents who would adopt her.

But none who would love this baby more.

Stop it! she told herself. Nothing good could come of wanting this baby. With great effort Rachel forced herself to stop thinking about what was going to happen to Chrissy and went into her office where she surveyed the mess on her desk. She still wasn't feeling up to par, but she had so much work to do that she decided to tackle it then and there, surprising herself by finishing a typing job and sorting through a pile of bills by the time it started to get dark outside.

Then Chrissy woke up and reminded Rachel that it was time for another feeding, and afterward, as she was changing the baby's diaper, she thought wistfully that she had never really appreciated doing this for her own babies. This notion, coming at her out of the blue as it did, made her sad. But then she thought Chrissy smiled at her, and even though she knew that this baby was too young to produce a real smile, that Chrissy couldn't really be counted on to smile spontaneously until she was around six weeks old, it seemed like a real smile, and for today that was enough.

The buzz of the intercom from the downstairs reception desk startled her out of her thoughts. Rachel, with Chrissy in her arms, went to press the button that would let Sherman speak.

"Joe Marzinski is on his way up," Sherman said, sounding even more nasal than ever.

"What?"

"Joe Marzinski—"

"I heard that part. Sherman, this is the second time he's come in without an invitation. Since when do you let unauthorized people in this building?"

"Since he's got a pass from the condo committee. Mrs. Rink gave it to him so he can check periodically on repairs to that apartment that was flooding the other night. Joe mentioned coming to see you, so I thought I'd let you know. Out of the goodness of my heart," Sherman added, sounding wounded.

"Sherman," she began, but the doorman interrupted her and said wasn't the young lady with him a friend of hers, and Rachel said she didn't think so because she couldn't think of what young lady he was talking about.

It occurred to Rachel during this quick conversation to ask Sherman if he'd also given a pass to a Santa Claus with a crescent-shaped birthmark, but she never got to voice the question because she heard a peremptory knock at the door.

"I'll take this up with you later," she said to Sherman.

"Ms. Hirsch? You know anyone who wants a kitten? My cat had kittens a few weeks ago. In the washing machine."

"No, Sherman. I do not know anyone who wants a

kitten. Goodbye, Sherman.'' Rachel managed to contain her annoyance, but it wasn't easy.

Besides, it definitely wasn't Sherman who was the main problem here.

"HOW'D YOU GET GINA to agree to baby-sit?'' Rachel wanted to know. She bulldozed ahead of Joe on the beach, ignoring the pieces of driftwood and mounds of dried seaweed, walking as if she were trying to outrun him. Dusk had turned into a clear night, and the beach was deserted except for them.

Joe was already congratulating himself on his stroke of genius in getting Rachel to himself. He wouldn't apologize for his maneuvering; in his mind it was necessary.

"Gina dropped by my parents' this afternoon while I was there,'' he said.

Rachel skewered him with another over-the-shoulder glance. "Did you manage that heart-to-heart that you wanted to have with her? To find out what's bugging her?''

"No, there were too many people around. Mom was baby-sitting Gracie's kids, and they were chasing each other all over the house.''

"It was awfully high-handed of you to bring a baby-sitter over here without asking first if I was free.''

"But you were free and you did want to come with me. Didn't you?'' He caught up, aimed a grin in her direction, but she looked solemn and perturbed. "Well, I know I had to almost pry the baby out of your arms,'' he amended, hoping to appease her.

When Rachel didn't reply, he said, "Think of this as good therapy for Gina. Time seems to be hanging heavy on her hands until she has to head back to school, and she can use the money for books.''

Rachel raised her brows. Or maybe it was one brow, but the effect was the same—unbridled skepticism. "Good try, Marzinski. But don't try to pretend that this is all about Gina."

He decided to lay it on the line. "Rachel, the real reason I showed up is that I had to see you. You know that, don't you?"

"I wish I didn't."

"Why? Last night was one of the best—"

She wheeled to face him, walking backward. "Please, Joe. I'm still stuck in the same old mode." She stumbled over a piece of driftwood, and he caught at her arm to keep her from falling. The wind tossed her blond curls across her face; he reached over to brush them away. Her chin tilted up a jot, the way it did when she was determined. What she didn't realize, he'd bet, was that it also placed her lips in line for kissing.

He framed her face with his hands, unsure whether she would pull away. She didn't. He kissed her then, the kind of kiss that packed a wallop calculated to make her feel it all over. *He* certainly did. She did, too, judging from the way she took it upon herself to deepen the kiss. He didn't know how long he could last if she kept on like that.

Tonight wasn't for passion. Tonight was for straight talk, for ironing out the angles. He deliberately put space between them.

"How about if I spread this blanket and we sit down?" he asked gently. She looked so voluptuous, so beguiling, and he wondered if she had any idea of her power to move him.

He shook the blanket out and settled it in the shelter of two dunes well above the high-tide line. They both sat down, and he took her hand. She folded it inside his, and they were quiet for a time, absorbing the gentle susurrus of the waves, the scent of the ocean, the peace of the night. He dared, in those few moments, to believe that everything was going to be okay, that she was going to give in and admit that they might have a future.

"So," he said carefully, "what's the problem? Christmas is supposed to be the happiest time of the year, a time for celebration, and what are we doing? We're sitting on one of the most beautiful beaches in the world acting glum."

"I didn't ask you to come here tonight. There are some times when a person would rather be alone."

He stared at her in the darkness, thinking that the stars must have been created for Rachel, to illuminate her in silvery light. "How can you say you'd rather be alone after last night?" he asked her.

She made a little motion with her shoulders, not quite a shrug. "I don't know what to tell you about that," she said.

"Rachel, look at me," he commanded. Her head swung around, and he was utterly stunned by the fathomless pain in her eyes. This was a woman who had suffered and suffered deeply. He had sensed it, he had known it on some deep level, but he still hadn't expected this terrible degree of pain. He didn't know what it was about, but he was determined to get to the bottom of it, and before this night was over, he would. So help him, he would.

"I love you, Rachel," he said quietly. "You must know it."

She shook her head in denial of the emotion that he knew was written all over his face. Desperate emotion, he told himself. He had been looking for this woman all of his life, and he didn't want to lose her.

"I do love you," he assured her. "I have since the moment I first saw you. You're the woman I want to lie beside every night, and I want to wake up with you every morning, and I want to live with you in the house I'm going to build, and I want to raise our children together."

She closed her eyes, and when she opened them, they were filled with tears. The tears welled up and spilled over, leaving silvery tracks on her cheek. He was alarmed. He hadn't said anything that could upset her so much. In this season of hope and celebration, his love for her was one thing more to celebrate, wasn't it? It wasn't something that should make her unhappy.

Unless she cried when she was happy, but that didn't seem to be the case. Much to his discomfort, Rachel buried her head in her hands and began to sob, great gulping sobs that made him feel totally inadequate.

"What have I said? What have I done?" he demanded.

Rachel didn't answer. She only went on crying. Unsure of himself, he reached out and curved an arm around her. When she didn't push it away, he slid the other one around her, too. The sobs shook her body, and he pulled her closer so that her face rested against his shoulder.

"Rachel, are you all right?"

The crying slowed, her body trembled a little less, and she clung to him. "I'll never be all right," she said, lifting her head. "Never."

"Is something wrong? My God, you're not sick, are you?" He was overcome with dread at the thought that she might be seriously ill.

"No, no, nothing like that. At least not physically. My sickness isn't of the body. It's of the heart."

She had pulled away from him and was rummaging in the pocket of her shorts. He reached into his own pocket and handed her a handkerchief. "Here," he said.

She blew her nose. Her eyes were swollen from crying. "I need to tell you, but I can't bring myself to do it," she said, almost to herself.

"Tell me what?"

"Something terrible. Something awful. I never talk about it, Joe, not to anyone."

"What's so bad that you can't talk about it?" he demanded.

"You think I'm a better person than I am. If I tell you, you'll know the worst about me."

He already knew what kind of person she was, and nothing she could say would lessen her in his eyes. He shook his head and smiled at her. "Don't worry, you can't shock me. And you'd better talk about it because we're going to be sitting right here on this beach until you do."

She drew a deep shuddering breath and gripped his hands tightly between her own. He waited, wondering what on earth she could possibly be going to say to him. When he thought he might have to prompt her, she looked him straight in the eye.

"I had a family once. A wonderful family. A husband and three children."

This shocked and surprised him. He could only stare at her with the feeling that the bottom was about to drop out of his world. He'd thought of her as a footloose single woman, not so different from himself. To imagine her with a husband and three kids was impossible.

She watched him in the darkness, her eyes never leaving his face.

"They died, Joe. All of them. They died because of me."

He couldn't believe this of Rachel, so kind and caring. He couldn't.

"No," he said unsteadily. "That can't be true."

Tears began to stream down her cheeks again, and her pain cut through his heart like a knife. What he felt for her was more than love, it was anguish and sorrow and compassion. If he could have borne this terrible pain for her, he would have, and gladly.

He kissed away the tears from her cheeks, and he held her close.

"Tell me," he said, and so she did.

Chapter Ten

To say that he pitied her would be to do his powerful emotions a deep injustice. Joe struggled to retain his composure as Rachel poured out the awful story, as she trembled with the telling of it. He had to keep the shock from his face, had to be strong because she was so strong.

"If giving my life would have brought them back, I would have done it," Rachel said brokenly. "I wanted to die, too. Only I didn't. I had to pick up and go on. So I moved closer to my mother's nursing home in New Jersey, hoping I could make some sense out of the tragedies that had affected both of us. Somehow I managed to make a life for myself. And then I came here and met you."

He was consumed with compassion for her. "And then what, Rachel?" he said, wanting to remove the source of her pain but knowing that nothing he could say or do would ever accomplish that.

"And then," she said, lifting her eyelids, all shiny with tears, to look deeply into his eyes. "And then you say you love me. I don't deserve it, Joe."

He folded her in his embrace, wrapped his arms around her as if he would never let her go. "My darling," was all he knew to say. "My darling."

Her mouth was near his ear. "Not anyone's darling," she said. "Not anymore."

"I love you, Rachel." He relaxed his arms so that they were looking straight at each other. "What can I do to convince you?"

"I don't want you to love me. Leave me alone, Joe."

"I hear you saying those words, but I don't think you mean them. Your heart is saying something else."

"Maybe it is. But I don't have to listen."

Her words twisted something deep inside him. "I know you wanted to save your family, but you can't go on blaming yourself forever."

"You don't have to live with nightmares where you hear your children screaming and your husband calling your name. You don't smell the stench of the fire in your nostrils and know that you'll have to live with it for the rest of your life!" The words were wrung from her, each one rending his soul.

He swallowed, knowing that he would never be able to imagine what this woman had been through. He smoothed her hair, his mind groping for the right words.

"I think we all have things happen to us, things that we don't handle well," he said carefully after a time.

"Do we?" She was staring at him.

He refused to look at her as he collected his thoughts. Flashes of phosphorescence glimmered in the rise of the waves; unexpected points of light. Well, she might as well know the worst about him. Nobody's life was perfect, least of all his.

"I was in trouble when I was a kid. It was the summer between high school and what was supposed to be my first year of college," he said.

"What happened, Joe?"

Now he looked at her, and she was gazing at him, her brown eyes serious.

"I got involved with some guys who robbed a movie theater. It was the same Rio Theater where we all went every weekend when I was a kid, and a really great old guy ran it. Just a little theater where they ran second- and third-run action flicks. The guy, Ziggy, was nice to us, even let us in free when we didn't have money for a ticket, which was pretty often in my case."

"And you *robbed* him?"

"Oh, I didn't actually take the money. I wasn't even sure what was going on. These older guys I knew were driving around that night in July, saw me walking from the Dairy King to my house eating an ice-cream cone, invited me to come with them. Said they were going to catch the late show at the Rio Theater. It sounded okay to me, I'd seen them around town, thought it would be something to do. I was always ready for adventure in those days—maybe a little too much." For years he'd tried not to think about that night, and he didn't often.

"What happened?"

"We got there after the show had started, and Ziggy was counting money in the box office. We watched him doing it. The two other guys jumped out of the car and said they were going to ask him if it was too late to get in to see the feature, told me to drive around the block because the car was obstructing traffic on the street double-parked like we were." He shrugged. "So I drove around the block."

"Then what?"

"I came back around the corner and suddenly the other two guys jumped in the back seat and started yelling at me to get going. I thought maybe they'd been mugged, I didn't know what the hell was happening, so I followed my first instinct and floored the gas pedal. They were arguing between themselves, and suddenly a whole lot of money spilled across the seat.''

"The money they'd taken from the theater owner."

"Yeah, that's what it was. I started screaming at them, wanting to know what had happened, and I nearly wrecked the car. A policeman happened to be parked at a stop sign when I ran it, saw the commotion in the car, followed us.''

"And caught you?"

"He flicked on his flashing blue lights, and I was too scared to keep driving, so I started to pull over to the curb. One of the guys I was with was pounding me on the head as I slowed down, and when the policeman approached, they both leaped from the car and ran. The police officer was a neighbor, had known me since I was a baby. That really hurt, for him to be the one to haul me into the police station.''

"And the other guys?"

"Oh, they were caught. But I was implicated, they said that the robbery was my idea and that I was driving the getaway car. The getaway car! They'd hit poor old Ziggy over the head with a beer bottle. He was never the same after that, sold the theater to some adult movie house and kids didn't have a place to go on Saturday afternoons anymore. The whole thing nearly killed my parents.''

"Oh, Joe," said Rachel.

"My family stuck by me, though. I hadn't been a perfect kid—I didn't like school and acted up, sometimes went truant—but I'd never been in trouble with the law before. The judge sentenced me to community service, believe it or not. The sentence was commuted when I joined the Navy.''

"You didn't mean any harm. It's like you got caught

up in a situation that you couldn't have anticipated," Rachel said, her arm going around his waist.

He looked at her. "True. And that's what happened to you, too, Rachel. You did the best you could under the circumstances. Something bad happened. You had to make a judgment during that fire, whether to go for help or not. Chances are no matter what you'd done, nothing could have saved your family. Just as nothing I could have done when those guys jumped in the car after robbing Ziggy could have changed the fact that they'd already hurt him and taken his money."

Rachel wiped her eyes on her sleeve, and Joe took her hand in his and lay down beside her. "Rachel, I didn't tell you my story so you'd feel sorry for me. I told you so that you'd know that we've both been through a lot. All we can do now is go on. That's all there is to do."

Rachel stared down at him. "You're a wonderful man, Joe. You've overcome obstacles to get where you are today, emotionally and financially. But, Joe, none of this changes the fact that I don't deserve a family."

He lifted a hand and touched her face. "Don't say that. You deserve everything and more. It wasn't your fault that the fire started. It wasn't your fault that you couldn't get them out. Some things just happen, and we don't know why."

"Like falling in love?"

"Now you're talking my language," he answered, and he gently pulled her face down to his and kissed her.

"Sometimes there isn't a why," he murmured. "Sometimes there's only a why not." He kissed her again, enfolding her in his arms and pulling her on top of him. In their solitude out here on the beach, captured under the giant dome of stars, it was as if they existed separate and apart from the rest of the world. Apart from the world and yet still in it, apart from each other but not so far, never far again. Somehow he would convince her that they should be together forever, and making love to her on this deserted beach with the stars and the breeze and the two of them wanting each other seemed like a very good start.

He wasn't sure how it happened, but soon the two of them were lying on the blanket without any clothes and she was gasping his name over and over and he was caressing her breasts, kissing her everywhere, warming her cool skin with his breath. And then he was inside her, pure ecstasy, and he was desperate to ream those memories out of her, to vanquish them forever, but when she should have reached her peak, she only cried silent tears.

He held her in his arms, listening to her heart beating in cadence with his, and he knew that he would never rest until Rachel belonged to him. Not only her body, but her mind and her spirit and her soul. And, most of all, her heart.

LATER IT WAS RACHEL who made the first move to leave. They gathered up the blanket and shook it free of sand, and they walked slowly arm in arm back to the condo. Sherman had already gone off duty, and they let themselves in with the key to the lobby door.

Nothing was settled. Nothing had changed. And yet Rachel had begun to feel the stirrings of hope. Joe was a kind and understanding man, and he cared about her. He said he loved her, even after he knew about the fire. He'd shared his innermost pain with her. But did she love him? She didn't know.

When they arrived back at apartment 11E, it was to find Gina curled up asleep on the couch with Chrissy cradled in the curve of her body. They made a sweet picture, the two of them, and Rachel and Joe paused to look at them.

Rachel wanted to pick Chrissy up, but Joe held her back. "Don't wake them," he whispered, but with that, Gina opened her eyes.

"Oh!" she said, scrambling up, the baby in her arms. "I didn't mean to fall asleep."

"It's late," Joe said. "We didn't expect you to be awake."

"Here, let me take Chrissy," Rachel said, and she went to Gina and gathered the baby into her embrace. She kissed the baby, Joe watching her, and then she turned away. She knew that he wanted her to love him as she did this child, and she was embarrassed that she didn't. No...that she couldn't. At least not yet.

"Come on," Joe said to the Gina. "I'll take you home."

Gina went and stood close beside Rachel. "I could stay tonight and get up with the baby. I could feed her while Rachel gets some sleep. You're tired, Rachel. You must be."

"No, I'm fine. Chrissy will probably only need one feeding before morning. You're the one who needs rest, Gina." If anything, Gina's pallor was even more pronounced than it had been on Christmas Day.

"That's right," Joe said, injecting a jovial tone into the conversation. "We need to get you up to par so you can go back and tackle those new courses you're going to be taking next semester." When Gina went into the bedroom to get her sweater, Joe slid an arm around Rachel. "I'll be back after I take her home," he said.

Rachel didn't object. She wanted him to hold her all night, to feel the warm strength of his arms enfolding her. To give herself a chance to feel the emotion that she longed to feel.

She picked up the baby, and Joe held out his finger. Chrissy grabbed it and held on tight. "She likes you, Joe," Rachel said, entranced by the idea.

"Babies usually do," he said as Gina appeared in the doorway.

"Joe, let's go," she said abruptly.

Her curt tone, directly in contrast with her earlier wheedling, surprised both of them, but Joe pried his finger out of the baby's grasp and dropped a parting kiss on Rachel's cheek.

"See you later," Joe said.

After Joe and Gina left, Rachel busied herself with settling Chrissy in her crib. Chrissy fussed and grew restless, but then Joe came back, picked up the baby and comforted her while Rachel took a long soothing bath.

Joe looked up when Rachel emerged from the bathroom in her black nightgown, and he smiled. Chrissy was asleep.

"Shh," he cautioned. "The last thing I want to do right now is wake this baby."

He went into the bedroom and laid the sleeping Chrissy down as Rachel tiptoed across the room to join him at the side of the crib.

"Chrissy's so pretty," Rachel said dotingly. "A perfect baby."

"Hey," Joe said. "What about me?"

"What about you?" Rachel leaned into him, and his hand came around to cup her breast. *What about you?* she thought to herself. *What?*

"Don't you think it's time to put me to bed, too?" He was teasing her, trying to make her laugh.

And so she did take him to bed, and before she slipped

into a deep sleep, Rachel thought to herself what a comfort it was to have him there, so strong and kind and capable to the core. Furthermore, he was willing to overlook her faults.

That in itself was enough to make her love him. Wasn't it?

JOE REALIZED DURING THE NIGHT that he was sleeping on the side of the bed with Mimi's magnetic pad.

He woke himself sufficiently to get more comfortable, curving an arm across Rachel's stomach, kissing her when she murmured in her sleep. But there were no vivid dreams, only something silly about a Santa with a birthmark who kept talking about Christmas wishes.

Joe's only wish at the moment was that the dream would stop and that he and Rachel would live happily ever after. Which was worth a hearty ho-ho-ho from the Santa.

Just a silly dream, and anyway, he had promised to get up with Chrissy if she woke. Which she did. And so Joe got up with her, and in the midst of all the feeding and burping and diapering, he forgot about the dream, which was probably just as well.

THE NEXT MORNING after Joe had left, Rachel realized that she had forgotten to ask him if he'd had a chance to talk with Gina yet. Well, she would mention it later. There was plenty of time; Gina wasn't scheduled to return for the second semester at Florida State for at least another week.

Rachel played with Chrissy for a while before she managed to tear herself away from the baby long enough to accomplish some work. Work had its benefits. Rachel knew that by keeping busy she was avoiding the two most important issues in her life at present: whether or not she would be able to keep the baby and whether or not she was in love with Joe. She knew she'd have to deal with both questions sooner or later. She only hoped it would be later on both counts.

She was so absorbed in her work that the phone startled her when it rang.

"Ms. Hirsch?"

"Yes," Rachel said cautiously as she recognized the voice of Madeline Ewing, the HSS social worker.

"Ms. Hirsch, I wanted to let you know that your background checked out. It looks as if you are indeed qualified to be a foster parent in Cane County."

Rachel felt a rush of relief such as she'd never felt before in her life. It was short-lived, however.

"But there's an irregularity. Your record was amended some years back, and there is no explanation. When you were approved as a foster parent, you were married. And your record was changed to show that you are not married at present. Is this true?"

Rachel looked out at the ocean, where a curtain of rain was sweeping across the horizon. "No, I'm not married," she said.

"Since you are not presently married, you can't possibly fulfill requirements to be a foster mother. We require both a foster mother and a foster father in the home. I'm afraid that we'll have to send someone to pick up that baby, Ms. Hirsch. You should expect our people from this agency to arrive shortly."

"But...but—where is the baby to go?"

"That's none of your concern, Ms. Hirsch. Prepare the baby to be transferred to her new foster home."

"Couldn't I keep her just a little while longer? Until the end of the week perhaps?" Rachel darted an anguished look in the direction of Chrissy's crib. The baby was sleeping peacefully, completely unaware of her fate.

"I'm afraid I don't have time to discuss this further. That's all, Ms. Hirsh."

Rachel stood holding the dead phone. She thought she might be sick.

She wanted to tell Joe. He wouldn't want the baby to be taken away to an uncertain situation. He would demand that Madeline Ewing tell them exactly where Chrissy was going. Joe could fix anything, couldn't he?

She dialed his home number, his office number and his pager. He didn't answer any of them, but the receptionist in his office said that she'd pass the message along when she heard from him.

That wouldn't do. Rachel didn't know how long it would be before they came to get Chrissy, and she knew that Joe would want to see her before she left. In desperation she dialed his parents' house, and Mary Marzinski answered the phone.

"No, I don't know where Joe is working today. But they're coming to take the baby?"

Rachel was nearly in tears. "Y-yes. They won't let her stay." She didn't get into the whole story of how she had once been a foster parent and how she had been married once. She didn't have time for that.

Mary was all concern. "You shouldn't be alone, Rachel. I'll come over, maybe some other members of the family will come with me. Sit tight, dear. We'll be there soon."

Rachel couldn't sit; she had to be in motion. She fought a slow-rising panic as she mechanically moved around the apartment filling extra bottles with formula and rounding up clean diapers. Chrissy was still asleep, thank goodness. Rachel didn't think she could bear to look into those trusting eyes and tell the baby that she was going to have to let her go.

Rachel almost let the answering machine pick up the phone the next time it rang, but she hoped it might be Joe calling and so she snatched it up at the last minute.

"Rachel?" The caller wasn't Joe. It was Ynez Garcia.

Rachel wearily pushed her hair back from her face. "Yes?" As she spoke she tried to recall all the things she needed to send with Chrissy. She didn't want to forget the rattle that Joe had given her for Christmas, and she'd better disassemble the mobile over the crib.

"Have you see Ivan and Gladys? They've gone somewhere, I think together, and I want to ask Gladys if the community theater is having play practice this week or if it has been canceled due to the holidays."

"No, I haven't seen either of them. Ynez, I have to run. They're coming to pick up the baby."

"Who? Who is coming?"

"I don't know," Rachel said. "The HSS are sending people. I'm to have her ready when they get here."

"Take our little Christmas miracle? Our Christmas Noel? How dare they?" Ynez, quiet, mousy Ynez, sputtered with outrage.

"They are the agency in charge of abandoned children," Rachel said hopelessly. "They have to take her, I'm afraid."

"Rachel, I am so sorry. I will be right there."

"No, I'm coping, Ynez. There is no need." But she wasn't coping. She felt raw and battered and, yes, defeated.

"Nonsense. I will be there very soon."

It was only minutes after she got off the phone with Ynez that the phone rang again. This time it was Gladys Rink.

"I heard," she said. "Ynez told me. I think it's terrible."

"I do, too, Gladys." Rachel was sure that she sounded as grim as she felt.

"Does Joe know?"

"Not yet."

"I want to be with you when Chrissy leaves. You shouldn't have to face those people all by yourself. And I'll bring Ivan."

It was with a heavy heart that Rachel woke the baby, who was grumpy because she wasn't ready to get up, and while she tried to get Chrissy to take her bottle, Rachel fielded several more phone calls from Joe's sisters and Sherman, who had been clued in by the condo grapevine.

"It's just a shame," Sherman kept saying. "Just a damn shame."

"There's apparently nothing to be done about it. Will you call me as soon as you see the HSS car drive up?" Rachel said distractedly. Outside, rain had begun to spatter against the sliding-glass door in big drops. The day had turned gray and gloomy, which seemed highly appropriate to her mood.

"Sure. I'll let you know when they get here," Sherman said.

Rachel dressed Chrissy in her red velveteen dress, the one Joe had bought her for Christmas. The baby cried so hard that Rachel couldn't think. Chrissy refused her pacifier; Rachel gave up on trying to get her to take it.

"I know, I know," Rachel said, rocking Chrissy in Mimi's plush yellow swivel rocker. "We all hate it that you have to go." This only made Chrissy cry harder, and if Rachel hadn't known better, she would have believed that Chrissy understood every word she was saying.

A knock at the door heralded the arrival of Gladys and Ivan; Ynez was not far behind.

"There, there," Ynez said, taking the baby from Rachel's arms. "Dear little Christmas Noel. We love you, *querida,* you know that?"

"It's been like a breath of fresh air, having a baby at the Elysian Towers," said Gladys.

Ivan put his arm around her. "We'll all miss her," he said comfortingly.

Rachel favored them with a bleak smile. "I'm going to miss her most of all," she said. She got up and stuffed the mobile into the diaper bag. A cursory look around the apartment showed no signs that a baby had even been there. "Well, Chrissy is ready. Even if we're not."

As if on cue, Sherman buzzed. "That car is here," he said. "The one from HSS."

"Oh, they're here. So soon," Gladys lamented.

"If only they'd come the first night, Christmas Eve. We wouldn't have gotten to know the baby so well," Ivan said.

"I'm glad I got to know her," Rachel said. And she was. She was grateful for having given every feeding, changed every diaper. She'd been reminded by this experience that babies were special, and she'd learned that she still knew how to be a good mother. Her confidence in herself—and her self-esteem—had been restored as a result, and that was no small blessing.

But the time had come to give the baby up.

"I'll carry Chrissy," Rachel said, holding out her arms.

"You should, Rachel. You found her."

"Yes, yes," said Ynez. The gravity of the occasion had apparently inspired Ynez to liberate her hair from its pink foam rubber prison, and she had fluffed it into a becoming halo around her face. She was even wearing makeup.

"Rachel? Are you ready?"

Rachel drew a deep breath. She didn't dare look down at Chrissy. She didn't think she could stand it. She had well and truly bonded with this baby, and she would have given anything not to be turning her over to people who didn't know her, who didn't care about her and perhaps never would.

Ivan, always the courtly gentleman, opened the door, and all of them proceeded to the elevator. They wore solemn faces. "This is too much like being a pallbearer," Ivan said suddenly.

"Hush, Ivan," Gladys told him, but Rachel noticed that they were holding hands.

The elevator landed with a muffled thump on the ground floor, and the doors soundlessly slid open to reveal a lobby full of people. Rachel was stunned at the turnout; there were Mary and Jim Marzinski as well as all of their daughters, each of whom had brought her children. And Gina was there, too, but there was no sign of Joe.

"We couldn't locate Joe," Mary said. "We left messages all over the place. Oh, Rachel, I know he'd want to be here."

Rachel was so overcome with gratitude for everyone's support that she couldn't speak. She could only gaze at them mutely, trying not to let her tears overflow.

"I don't want the baby to go anywhere," said one of the kids, who, if Rachel remembered correctly, was named Todd.

"Me, neither," piped Emily, who was four. Her mother, the enormously pregnant Lois, pulled her daughter close by her side.

Rachel managed an awkward smile of thanks. The Marzinskis were the kind of people who would always be there for you, and they had proved it today. She was glad for the Theatrical Threesome, too. She had been alone for a long time, but she wouldn't want to have to do this alone as well.

Outside the full-length glass door, under the portico with rain streaming off it in sheets, waited a white car bearing a government logo. Two people climbed out, a man and a woman. Looking grim, surprised to see all the people standing around, they walked into the lobby.

The man advanced first. He pulled an identification card out of his pocket. "I'm Hugh Saleevy, State Department of Health and Social Services. Are you Rachel Hirsch?"

Rachel swallowed. Chrissy stirred in her arms, making a little mewling sound.

"I am," said Rachel. Her heart was beating much too hard, and her throat was dry.

"We've come to take the abandoned infant," he said.

Rachel tried to swallow past the lump in her throat. "I know."

The man stepped forward and the group around Rachel moved even closer, flanking her. Mary Marzinski slid an arm around Rachel's shoulders.

As the man held out his arms, Rachel said a little prayer for the baby. She hoped that Chrissy would be placed in a good home and would eventually be adopted by parents who would love her as a child deserved to be loved—unreservedly.

At the precise moment when Chrissy was actually transferred to the HSS man's arms, Rachel glimpsed a streak of blue denim flashing through the rain and past the car outside. She recognized the tall, muscular figure, the deep suntan. The man burst into the lobby.

"Joe!" Rachel said. "I knew you would come!"

He went straight to Rachel and put his arms around her. He was damp and smelled of the rain, and his hair was plastered across his forehead, but Rachel was so glad to see him that she didn't care. His mother moved away, but her hand remained on Joe's shoulder in a show of solidarity.

"You can't take this baby away!" Joe growled as he glowered at the people from HSS.

This caused an eruption of agreement among the onlookers, a development which caused Hugh Saleevy to look momentarily disconcerted. "Those are my orders." The woman with him had the good grace to look doubtful, but she reached for the baby's bag and took it from Ynez, anyway.

"This baby is coming with us. If you have any questions, you'll have to call the local office," Saleevy said officiously. With the baby in his arms, her small fists flailing the air, he turned and began to walk swiftly to the car. It was no small satisfaction that Chrissy chose that moment to spit up profusely on his burgundy blazer.

Rachel clung to Joe, not wanting to watch but unable to look anywhere but at the baby, who was now being buckled into a child safety seat. After she'd finished fastening Chrissy, the woman slid into the car beside her and sat gazing straight ahead, ignoring the indignant group who had gathered to watch Chrissy's departure. The baby continued to cry, great gulping sobs that were heartrending in the extreme.

Rachel had gone numb. She was aware of Joe's arms around her, but just barely. To think that she would never see the baby again...to think that she would never know the joy of watching her grow up... It was an unbearable pain. She knew that Chrissy's face would be indelibly carved on her heart, right alongside the faces of her own lost children.

The car started and began to move. Rachel bit her lip, trying not to cry. But it wasn't Rachel who had the greatest reaction. It was Gina.

She fainted.

MIMI'S LITTLE APARTMENT was aswarm with people. Gladys had produced smelling salts, Ynez was crying quietly as she cowered in a corner, and Ivan paced the floor. A gaggle of Marzinskis muddled around, chasing children, getting glasses of water, exploring the refrigerator.

Rachel sat beside Gina, chafing her wrists. Gina was propped up on the couch, her feet on the coffee table. Joe sat on the other side of her, his expression dark with concern.

"Maybe you should see a doctor," he said to Gina.

"No! I'm fine."

"It *was* awfully hot and humid in the lobby," said Gladys. "I was fanning myself with a newspaper. Wasn't I, Ivan?"

"Yes, the crush of people was claustrophobic. Too much excitement."

"I couldn't get any air. I couldn't breathe," Gina said. She struggled to sit up straight. "Can someone take me to my sister's place? I feel okay now."

"I'll take you, but not until later," said Joe. "I want to make sure you don't pass out again."

"I won't," Gina said, and it was true that color had returned to her cheeks.

"Is the baby going to a nice family?" Megan wanted

to know. She sported a different artificial tattoo today, this one on her hand.

"I'm sure she will," Rachel managed to say.

"Will she get to come visit us?" Todd's big blue eyes focused on her with worry.

"I don't think so," Joe told him.

"You mean we'll never see her again?"

Mary Marzinski slid an arm around one of the twins—Liza? Katie? "Perhaps not," she said.

"We're going to have our own new baby soon," said Lois's Jamie with an air of self-importance.

"Nobody will come get our baby, will they, Mommy?" asked his younger sister.

"No, darling, of course not."

"But the HSS takes babies away." This was Jamie again.

"Wait a minute, fella," said Jim Marzinski. "They only take babies that have nowhere else to go. They find homes for them."

"Our own baby will always have a home, won't it?"

"Yes, Emily." Lois caressed her daughter's cheek.

Rachel felt heartsick at this conversation. She hadn't thought about the effect the baby's leaving would have on these kids. She doubted if their parents had, either. A glance at Gina told her that the teenager was also upset by this talk; she supposed that wasn't so surprising considering that Gina had been a throwaway kid herself. No one had wanted her and her sisters. This whole episode probably brought back memories that Gina would rather forget.

Rachel decided that it was time for everyone to cheer up. Not that losing Chrissy to HSS was easy, not to trivialize their loss, but it was important to make an attempt at normalcy for the kids' sake. "Tell you what," she said, rallying with effort. "There's a big container of Rocky Road ice cream in the freezer. Who wants to dish it up?"

Megan volunteered, and soon everyone, even Ynez, was eating ice cream.

"One thing I don't understand," Joe said conversationally after a while. "Why didn't you qualify to keep the baby, Rachel?"

"Because she isn't married," volunteered Gladys Rink. "Isn't that right, Rachel?"

Rachel's mouth was full of ice cream; she couldn't answer.

"Yes, they've got this silly rule. There have to be two parents in a foster home. Never mind that we'd all help," Ivan said huffily.

"Never mind that I had not yet had a chance to babysit little Christmas Noel," said Ynez, sniffing and dabbing at her eyes with a hanky.

Joe stood up abruptly. "Is that true, Rachel? Is that the only reason?"

Rachel swallowed the ice cream. It was painfully cold and sat in her chest in an icy lump.

"I'm not sure that's the way it was before, or maybe it's the difference in counties, or…I don't know. But that's why they took Chrissy away," she said.

"Well, I have the solution." All eyes focused on Joe, who looked expansive and confident.

"It's about time someone did," said Ivan.

Joe stood looking down at her, hands on his hips. "We'll get married. They can't take her away then."

Rachel's mouth dropped open, and then she shut it. All around the room Marzinskis stood watching and waiting for her answer.

"Why not get married? I'm nuts about you, Rachel."

"I'm thinking. I can't think. Oh, I don't know," she said.

"Of course you do. We'll be a family—you, me and Chrissy. I care about her almost as much as you do, and we can't let her go to people who don't love her. She was abandoned once. I'm not going to abandon her again."

"Oh, yes, you could keep the baby," breathed Gina. "If you got married, I mean."

"Will you, Rachel?"

Rachel opened her mouth. She closed it again. No words came out.

"Of course she will," said Gladys Rink. "She's madly in love with you. Anyone can see that."

"Rachel?"

"Could I have a word with you, Joe? In the kitchen?" She didn't want to discuss marrying him in front of all these people.

She got up and marched into the kitchen, where she shut the door and leaned against it. Joe regarded her across the kitchen table, and she thought he had never looked so handsome. But how could she possibly marry him?

A long intake of breath shuddered through her. "Are you serious? Are you out of your mind? We've known each other all of five days, and I can't imagine what you're thinking."

He took two steps across the room and pinned her against the closed door with his full weight. She heard the hammering of his heart beneath his shirt; she heard her own pulse beat in her ears.

"I'm thinking we should get married," he said his breath warm on her cheek. "There's Chrissy, and I could get more specific as to other reasons. I could kiss you, like this,'' and he demonstrated, "and like this."

This wasn't the kind of summit meeting she'd had in mind, and she wished he wouldn't do that. She pushed at him furiously. "There are people on the other side of this door," she hissed. "Your family is there, for Pete's sake. How can you—"

"I believe in living dangerously."

"You must if you're serious about marrying me!"

"I've never been so serious in my life." He nibbled on her earlobe.

"I want to have a serious discussion," she said indignantly.

He shoved back, walked across the kitchen and leaned against the countertop, his arms folded across his chest. "Okay, so discuss."

Rachel swallowed. Her lips burned from his kisses. "Married forever?" she asked. "Or until we can adopt Chrissy and we could be divorced?" She was afraid to hear his answer.

His eyes were direct and unyielding. "I don't believe in divorce, Rachel. But I do believe in us. Marry me. Give us a chance. If you're not happy, you can leave."

"And take Chrissy with me?" She couldn't imagine marriage to Joe. She couldn't imagine living with him day by day. What was more, she couldn't imagine divorcing Joe even if it didn't work out.

"I wouldn't fight you for custody, if that's what you're worried about. You and the baby—you look natural together. You must have been an incredible mother."

No time to object that if she'd been a better mother, she'd still have her children. No time to even think about it. This was about Chrissy and how to save her; this was about the two of them, about her and Joe, who could so easily become the three of them. A family. A unit.

"If we *did* get married, no one could take Chrissy away again," Rachel said. "If we adopted her, I mean." She well recalled the situation with little Derek. When Derek had first entered foster care, his birth mother had thought she would reclaim him eventually, but she'd finally acknowledged that she wouldn't be able to provide a stable home for him and had gladly released him to Rachel and Nick, who could. Once the adoption was final, Derek would have been irrevocably theirs. It would be the same with Chrissy.

Someone knocked impatiently on the kitchen door. "Are you two through in there?" called Ivan.

"Are we?" Joe asked Rachel pointedly.

Looking across at this charming man who had expressed a heartfelt desire to marry her, she almost melted. But she'd been happily married once before, and she knew that marriage was a lot of hard work. It wasn't to be entered into lightly for even the most altruistic purpose.

The kitchen door opened. Ivan was standing there. "Well?" he said. "Are you through keeping us in suspense?"

From the living room everyone was still staring at them, and Rachel was embarrassed. They didn't know her. They didn't know anything about her. Joe's family still thought she was a schoolteacher. She and Joe needed to talk about that, he needed to inform his family that she wasn't who they thought she was, that she was Rachel Hirsch, a widow. She had lost three children. If they knew the circumstances, would all these Marzinskis think she was good enough for their Joey?

Joe's little Christmas ruse had complicated things beyond belief, and she was about to pull him back into the kitchen for further discussion and negotiation when it occurred to her that this was a very private matter. It was bad enough having to have this discussion with Joe, but for all these people to be party to it was difficult, to say the least.

"What are you going to do, Rachel?" asked Gladys.

"Yes, yes, what are you going to do?"

Rachel stood uncertainly, wishing she could walk out of the kitchen, go in the bedroom and shut the door. She wished she'd never found the baby in the manger, and she wished she had never met Joe Marzinski.

No, that wasn't exactly true. She wished she could have met him under more normal circumstances.

"Maybe this setting is not romantic enough for Rachel," suggested Ynez.

Joe stepped out from behind her. He had a funny little half grin on his face, one of his most endearing expressions.

"Oh. Well, maybe what we need is a little romance. You know, I haven't had much practice in proposing to people." To Rachel's utter amazement, Joe dropped to one knee and took Rachel's hand in his. "In the presence of all these witnesses, my love, I do humbly request your hand in marriage. I adore you. I have since the moment I first saw you. Marry me, Rachel. Marry me soon."

If this wasn't such a solemn moment, Rachel might have dissolved in hysterics. She still might. She looked from Joe to Gina and around at all the people, all of whom seemed to be holding their breath. What was she supposed to say? What was she supposed to do?

"Well, Rachel?"

She drew a deep breath. "I don't know, Joe," she said. "I'll have to think about it."

Chapter Eleven

After such an anticlimax, everyone left. Joe did, too, saying that if Rachel needed time to think things over, he'd understand. Rachel took to her bed, downed by a nasty headache that no doubt owed its origins to the distressing and unsettling events of the afternoon. She had no intention of going to sleep, but she must have dozed for a while because suddenly she was dreaming that the phone was ringing. And then she realized that it wasn't a dream—the phone really *was* ringing.

"Hello?" she said fuzzily into the receiver.

"Rachel?"

She swung her feet over the side of the bed. "Mimi! Oh, Mimi, I'm so glad it's you. You wouldn't believe what's been going on."

"If it has something to do with that guy who showed up fixing things on Christmas Eve, I might. What's happening, dear?"

"Where are you?"

"In India. Today I rode an elephant."

"Well, something almost as exciting happened to me. Joe Marzinski asked me to marry him."

Her grandmother indulged in a stunned silence for almost thirty seconds at expensive international telephone rates. "What did you tell him?" she asked cautiously.

"I said I'd have to think about it."

"Rachel, I don't know how to give grandmotherly advice when I haven't even met the man, but I have one question to ask you. Do you love him?"

"I've only known him for a few days."

"I didn't ask how long you've known him. I *know* how long you've known him. What I asked is if you love him."

"I think so. I'm pretty sure. He's a good man, Mimi, and he's crazy about me."

"Oh. Well, it sounds like something hormonal. I'd better call Gladys or Ynez and get the real scoop."

Rachel jumped up and began to pace the floor. "Don't you dare call them! They like him. And guess what—Gladys and Ivan are falling in love."

Her grandmother gasped. "Rachel, that is simply not possible. Not Gladys and Ivan. They were always nattering at each other. She's always called him a pompous old fool, and he thinks she's an obnoxious busybody."

"They might both be right, but listen, Mimi. Gladys wears perfume now. Ivan gets this ridiculous idiotic expression on his face whenever he looks at her, which is all the time."

"I'd better cancel the rest of this trip and come home. It sounds as if you've all lost your alleged minds. Tell me, is Ynez part of this madness?"

Rachel thought for a second. "She's unwound her hair from those pink foam rubber curlers and looks better than she's ever looked. She seems to have taken more of an interest in life in general."

"That's a good thing. Ynez folded up and gave in when her cat died, and it was like she simply didn't choose to participate in life anymore. Why, she even quit the community theater. But back to this marriage proposal from this Joe Syzinski. Wasn't it a bit sudden?''

"Marzinski. Joe Marzinski."

"Sorry, dear. But answer my question. Hasn't this all happened much too fast?"

Rachel thought back over all that had happened during the past days. "Sort of. But there was a natural progression. And, oh, Mimi, the HSS came and took the baby. We all love her, and we didn't want to see her go. And I'm a foster parent but couldn't keep the baby because the state requires two parents in a foster home, and Joe asked me to marry him. If we were married, we could make a home for the baby. Don't you see, it's the perfect solution."

"Rachel, I'll be home as soon as I can get a flight. I can't believe this—I leave town for a month and everyone goes bonkers."

"I have to call Joe in the morning. I have to tell him what I want to do. And I have a terrible headache, I can't even think."

"Lie down on my magnetic pad. The one on my bed. I know you never believed in it, but it will cure your headache and help you dream good dreams. But don't—and I repeat don't—*do* anything."

"Mimi—" She was going to tell her grandmother that she didn't believe in the magnetic pad's ability to cure anything, but Mimi wouldn't listen.

"I'm hanging up right now. I can't believe this. I'll see you soon, Rachel."

"Mimi!"

But her grandmother had already hung up.

FOR THE FIRST TIME IN HIS LIFE, Joe Marzinski had asked a woman to marry him. And with most of his family watching and listening and waiting to hear her answer.

And what had she said? "I'll think about it."

She'd *think* about it! Sheesh. He thought he'd done his part by accepting the challenge of converting her from one of the walking wounded into a woman who was ready to move forward with her life. All she had to do was say the word, and a whole new vista would open up for both of them.

It was all right with him if Rachel needed time and space to think things over, as long as she came to the right conclusion in the end. To maximize her chances of doing that, Joe had ushered everyone out of apartment 11E, kissed Rachel goodbye and driven Gina back to her sister's house. Then he'd gone straight home.

Now he was doing some much-needed repairs around his own apartment. What was that they always said about the shoemaker's children never having any shoes? It was like that with him and his apartment. He might always be fixing someone's drain or dealing with air conditioner problems in the condominiums he serviced, but he needed screens replaced in his own apartment, and so that was what he'd decided to do tonight.

He had a roll of screening stretched over the door and was tugging it into place, trying to get it to fit inside the grooves of the aluminum frame. If only dealing with Rachel could be this easy! He pushed and pulled at the screen, making it fit, using the tool that would fasten it tightly. He was sliding the refurbished screen experimentally along its track when the doorbell rang.

He almost didn't answer it. It was late for unannounced visitors, ten o'clock at night, and he had work to do. But perhaps it was Rachel. In case it was, he left his task and went to the door. A look through the peephole revealed Gina standing there.

He was worried about her, fainting like that today, and now here she was at his place. He opened the door, and Gina gave him a tentative smile. She was all dolled up, and she looked as if she might have been out on a date. He hoped so. A boyfriend might be exactly what she needed to get her mind off more serious matters.

"Well, come on in," he said heartily, glad to see her. He hadn't expected her to be out tonight, and he certainly would have advised her to stay home if she'd mentioned going anywhere, but now that she was here, maybe they could have that heart-to-heart that he'd been planning.

"You're not busy, are you?" Gina seemed nervous and uncomfortable.

"I'm doing some work around the house. I find that it helps to keep busy when I'm concerned about something." He ushered her into the kitchen. "Want a snack or something? I've got tortilla chips and maybe some salsa in the refrigerator."

"I'm not hungry."

"Where have you been? You look nice." She was wearing a navy blue dress, high heels and gold earrings. He realized that she had grown into a beautiful woman in the past year or so.

"Anna and Mitch took me out to dinner. They asked me to go to a club with them, but I thought they might like privacy and, anyway, I didn't want to overdo."

"How'd you get here?"

"Drove Anna's car."

"Come on out on the patio while I put the screens back on the track. Then you can keep me company while I install a new faucet on the kitchen sink."

Gina followed him outside and perched on one of the patio chairs while he finished with the screens.

"Have you heard from Rachel? About whether she wants to get married?"

He glanced over at her. "Nope. My offer is still on the table."

"Aren't you worried, Joe? I mean, what if she says no?"

Joe tossed a screwdriver back in his tool kit. "I hope she'll say yes. I haven't allowed myself to think that she might not."

"I hope you and Rachel get married. I hope you live happily ever after."

Gina's impassioned words made him look at her closely. It seemed to him that her emotions were teetering on a fine edge. Maybe she just needed to talk. Maybe he could find out what had been bugging her lately by encouraging her to open up to him. He'd always been her first choice for confidences and advice. In the early days after she'd moved in with his parents, Joe had been the only one she trusted. He didn't know why there had always been a special bond between them, but that's the way it was.

"Let's work on that faucet," he said easily. They went into the kitchen, where he showed her the new faucet and explained how he was going to install it, and she seemed interested in the way it worked.

"Maybe you don't want to get an MBA in marketing after all," he teased, hoping to make her smile. "Maybe you'd rather learn condo crisis control." This, he thought, was the perfect opening for her to talk about her change in courses, which was what he thought had been worrying her ever since she'd been on break, but she didn't pick up on it. Instead she moved closer and watched as he removed the old faucet.

He completed the attachment of the new one quickly, perhaps too quickly. Something went wrong—perhaps he hadn't tightened it enough—and when he turned on the water again, water sprayed all over the place, inundating him and the kitchen and Gina, as well.

It was only a few moments before he had matters completely under control, but by that time he was soaked. So was Gina.

He ruefully wiped the water from his face and handed Gina a clean towel so she could do the same. "I'm sorry," he said, but Gina didn't seem unduly upset.

"It's an old dress," she told him. "It's completely washable. Being wet doesn't feel so great, though." She picked wryly at the wet fabric.

"I'll change clothes and find you something else to wear," he said.

Gina had already taken her shoes off and was padding around barefoot by the time he came out of the bedroom with one of his Condo Crisis Control T-shirts and a pair of shorts for her to wear. This reminded him of how he'd found Rachel something else to put on when she'd spent the night, and the memory tugged at him. He wanted to call her. But it was eleven o'clock. He thought she might be asleep.

Gina changed clothes in the bedroom and hung her dress to dry on a hanger on the patio while Joe sliced each of them a piece of the chocolate cake that his mother had sent home with him as a reward for fixing her stopped-up drain.

"This reminds me of old times," Gina said as she sat down across from him at the breakfast bar in the kitchen. "Remember how you used to come to see me when I lived at your parents' house? And we used to raid the pantry?''

"Mom always has something good to eat around," he said.

"Yeah, like fresh-baked bread. And she always made extra fried chicken because she knew I liked to nibble on cold drumsticks."

Joe exchanged a smile with Gina across the table.

"You were lucky, Joe. To grow up in a home with parents like you had, I mean."

"I know."

There was a silence, and Joe dug into the cake. It was good, his favorite. He wondered if Rachel knew how to make chocolate cake. He wondered if it mattered.

"Joe," Gina said suddenly. "I need to tell you something."

Here it is, Joe thought. *This is what Gina's been worried about.* He thought he was prepared for whatever she might have to say. But he still didn't believe his ears when she spoke.

Gina shifted uncomfortably in her chair and looked as if she'd rather be anywhere else. "Joe, I've done something awful. Chrissy—well, Chrissy is my baby."

AGAINST HER OWN better judgment, Rachel slept on the side of the bed with Mimi's magnetic pad. It took her a while to get comfortable on it, but she eventually fell into a deep sleep. The sleep was accompanied by vivid dreams, one after another, and she knew she was dreaming but was powerless to stop it. Then the dreams slowed, and she fell into a deeper sleep. It was then that she had the strangest dream of all.

She was floating through the Marzinskis' living room, and all the children were watching. She was looking for

Joe and couldn't find him. She felt scared and lonely, or as lonely as anyone could feel when in the company of all those kids. And she thought she might never find Joe again. There was also someone else she couldn't find, someone who might be waiting for her in another room of the house.

But she couldn't move very fast. It was as if she were swimming through the air, similar to when she and Joe had swum in the ocean. She rounded a corner and saw the entrance to the sunporch. On the doors was the mural of the Santa scene, complete with elves. She vaguely recalled that one of the children had painted it on the door, and although she hadn't paid a whole lot of attention to the mural on Christmas Day, when she'd been there for dinner, now she was aware of every detail.

What surprised her was that she walked up to it and then took one more step, only to find that she was actually inside the picture. And Santa, who was standing at a table helping an elf cobble together a toy house, glanced up and smiled at her.

"Come in, Rachel," he said. "I've been expecting you."

Rachel looked wildly around. She saw the glass door through which she had gained access to the picture, and on the other side were all of Joe's nieces and nephews, their faces pressed to the glass and listening to every word.

"Rachel?"

"Why am I here?" she said. It had not escaped her that this Santa had a crescent-shaped birthmark exactly like both the store Santa on Christmas Eve and the Santa who had called at Mimi's apartment later.

"To learn," said Santa.

This was ridiculous. She wanted to be back in bed in Mimi's apartment, but she didn't know how to get there.

"Learn what?"

"To know."

Rachel hated riddles. She hated guessing games. "I'm leaving," she said abruptly.

"Not yet."

"I have some serious thinking to do," she said, feeling slightly frantic.

Santa laid a finger alongside his nose. "Ho-ho-ho," he said. "As if you haven't been thinking seriously already."

"How do you know?"

Santa looked wise. "Your Christmas wish."

She had to think hard for a moment to remember what she'd wished. Oh, yes. "I wanted a reason to celebrate Christmas again," she said.

"I gave you one. You're not going to throw it away, are you?"

"Uh—"

"Think carefully, Rachel. And do the right thing."

She was on the verge of asking him exactly what the right thing might be, but he spoke again.

"A baby is a symbol of new beginnings," he said, and suddenly she woke up with a jolt. She was lying in Mimi's bed, and her shoulder hurt because she was sleeping on something hard and uncomfortable, and she'd been dreaming a stupid dream.

The magnetic pad. She never should have slept on it. Mimi was out of her mind if she thought it could help cure anything.

But her headache *had* gone away. And outside, a fragile, pearlescent light was creeping up from the horizon. It was morning, and she had to talk to Joe.

She got up, showered and dressed, caught an elevator and ran out the lobby door past two startled condo residents who had ventured out early to buy their daily newspapers.

"Hello, Mrs. Cohen," she said. "Hi, Mrs. Winstrom."

"Rachel, I just wanted to tell you how sorry I am about little Baby Christmas's leaving," said Mrs. Winstrom.

"We're going to get her back," Rachel said, determination in every syllable.

"But I thought—" Mrs. Cohen began, wrinkling her forehead.

"Not to worry," Rachel said cheerfully, leaving the two women staring after her with confused expressions on their faces.

She jogged past the manger scene, sniffed the brine in the air appreciatively and unlocked her car. The sun was shining, the sky was a bright azure-blue unsullied by clouds, and today was going to be a wonderful day, perhaps the most important day in her life. She sang "Hark, the Herald Angels Sing" off-key as she zipped her car across the bridge to Joe's apartment house, where she squealed to a stop at the curb and started to get out.

The song died on her lips as the front door of Joe's apartment opened. Joe stood there in the doorway, smiling down engagingly at a woman whose face was screened by the fronds of a small palm tree. Rachel slid back into her car, her heart beating wildly. Who could be leaving Joe's apartment at this hour in the morning?

Not only that, but his visitor was wearing a Condo Crisis Control T-shirt and shorts exactly as Rachel had when she'd spent the night. The woman was also clutching a plastic bag, and, recalling that she'd carried her own dress in such a bag on the morning after spending the night with Joe, Rachel had a pretty good idea what was in it.

Shock, disbelief and rage curdled her blood. Here she was, prepared to tell Joe that she would marry him, and he was bidding goodbye to a woman who had obviously spent the night with him in his apartment. A wave of nausea rose up from her throat and threatened to choke her.

Trust, Rachel believed, was one of the most important aspects of a relationship. It was the cornerstone on which a marriage should be built. She, Rachel, was not stupid enough to marry a guy she couldn't trust, and she most definitely did not trust Joe Marzinski now.

She couldn't marry him. And she wouldn't.

Blindly she rammed the key into the ignition, and her car's engine sprang to life. Joe looked up. He froze in place, his face blanching visibly, and the woman with him turned around so that Rachel got a good look at her for the first time. The uniquely shaped eyes and the close-cropped dark hair left no doubt about who the woman was.

It was Gina.

RACHEL, HIGH ON THE ADRENALINE of her anger, made two trips downstairs carrying clothes and file boxes before Sherman arrived on duty that morning.

"Ms. Hirsch, what's going on?" He blocked her way to the elevator.

"I'm driving back to Lakemont, New Jersey. Today," Rachel said curtly.

"Oh. Guess that means there's not going to be any wedding bells. So to speak."

"Guess so. I might need some help with my computer when I've got it packed up and ready to go."

"Sure. Just call me. Oh, and you might like to know that I've given away all the kittens. You know, the ones that were born in the washing machine."

"Good, Sherman." Rachel started to brush past him, but he didn't step aside.

"And guess who took one of them? A little gray tabby, real cute?"

"I can't imagine." She didn't feel like having this conversation. She didn't feel like having any conversation. All she wanted was to get out of there before a delegation of Marzinskis descended on her with the idea of changing her mind or before Mimi arrived home from wherever.

"Ynez Garcia took the gray tabby. She said that having the baby around made her realize how important it was to enjoy life while we can. She said she'd missed her cat Rubio so much that she didn't think she had anything to live for. A baby gives you hope for the future, you know? So she wanted a baby. A baby cat. Neat, huh?"

Rachel blew out an impatient breath. "Right. I'm glad for her."

"Look," said Sherman. He delved a hand into his uniform pocket and extracted a tiny, fuzzy, gray tabby kitten. "See? This is Tabitha."

The kitten was adorable, and normally Rachel was not immune to such enchantment. On any other day she would have exclaimed over the kitten and cuddled it, but today was different. "She's lovely, Sherman. And I wish I had time to get to know her. But I'm eager to get on the road."

Sherman stroked the kitten's gray-striped fur, and it opened its mouth and uttered the squeakiest mew she'd ever heard. "No problem. Mrs. Garcia will be down to get her in a few minutes. You let me know when you need help with the computer, 'cause there's no need for you to lug it down by yourself.''

"Thank you, Sherman.''

Rachel fidgeted all the way up to the eleventh floor. Now that she'd decided, now that she'd made up her mind, she never wanted to see Joe Marzinski again. She did want to see Chrissy, however. But that wasn't possible. She'd never see Chrissy again or hold her or sit with her in the middle of the night soothing her colic. She'd never get to celebrate another Christmas with Chrissy or her first birthday. She felt inconsolably deprived.

She blinked tears from her eyes as she emerged from the elevator into the hall, and she was so blinded by them that she almost bumped smack into Gladys and Ivan. Gladys was wearing a pink linen dress, a sharp departure from her usual tennis whites or sweats, and Ivan was nattily dressed in green golf pants and a matching striped shirt.

Gladys pounced. "Rachel, dear, how good it is that we ran into you! I know you're going to marry that nice Joe Marzinski. I mean, why wouldn't you? But that's not the reason I'm so happy. Ivan and I are getting married, too! Aren't we, Ivan?''

"We certainly are. As soon as we can buy the ring and find a preacher.'' He rocked back on his heels, smiling a smug little smile.

Rachel blinked. The two of them were holding hands.

"Isn't this a bit sudden?'' she said.

"When you're our age, you don't have a lot of time to waste. We want to spend all our time together. For the rest of our lives. Right, Ivan?''

"That's right, my little Googie.'' Ivan beamed at her.

Googie? Gladys Rink was Googie? Rachel was speechless.

"And you know, Rachel, it's all because of Chrissy. We never would have spent quiet time together—"

"—and we never would have gotten to know each other," said Ivan.

"If it hadn't been for Chrissy. So maybe Ynez was right. The baby *was* a Christmas miracle," added Gladys.

It wasn't lost on her that Gladys and Ivan were finishing each other's sentences, but Rachel almost couldn't swallow around the lump in her throat. "Yes," she said wistfully. "Perhaps Chrissy was a Christmas miracle."

"We're going out to choose a ring, and then I want to hear all about you and Joe," Gladys said, patting Rachel's hand.

But Rachel didn't think they would want to know that she had seen Gina leaving Joe's apartment very early this morning. They wouldn't want to know that she wouldn't marry Joe now if he were the last man on earth. And she wasn't going to tell them. She would be long gone from Coquina Beach before the Theatrical Threesome even knew she had left.

The phone rang as she reached her office, and she'd already unplugged her answering machine. Against her better judgment, she answered it.

"Rachel," Joe said. His voice was gruff, the way it was when he was upset. She had grown to know that about him in the past several days—not that it was important.

"I don't have anything to say to you." The fist around her heart tightened, twisted. She closed her eyes, tried not to picture his face.

"I can explain. I can explain everything."

Pain and disappointment spewed out of her unabated

and unedited. "Maybe you want to tell me that Condo Crisis Control T-shirts are standard issue for every woman who spends the night at your apartment? Or that asking me to marry you was some kind of weird joke you perpetrated on your family to make them think that you were finally going to settle down?"

"No, Rachel, I'm in love with you. I *want* to marry you." The words pierced straight to her heart.

"So last night, I suppose, was one last fling." There was no point in keeping the bitterness out of her voice, and she didn't even try.

"It wasn't anything like that," Joe said on a note of desperation.

"I only have two words for you, Joe Marzinski—drop dead." She slammed the phone down and tried not to think about his silvery eyes gone cold, about his strong arms never again enclosing her, protecting her, holding her close as he made love to her.

You could lose in life. You could lose the things you loved over and over again. But you could also survive those losses, and that was what she intended to do, mainly by putting a lot of distance between herself and the man who was the cause of her pain.

But would distance ease this ache in her heart, the knife in her gut? She loved Joe Marzinski, she'd wanted a lifetime with him. She treasured the time they'd spent together and the way he'd made her feel worthwhile. The way he'd loved her and, yes, cherished her in spite of her faults.

She'd foreseen a future with him, bright and new and untarnished by pain or guilt. She'd reached for it—and it had been yanked away.

Life was cruel, and you couldn't count on anything,

so she might as well get on with the life that was left to her now.

Mimi's apartment was in chaos. Rachel had haphazardly tossed clothes into her two suitcases, and they lay open on the floor. Papers in the office needed to be packaged and mailed to her New Jersey apartment, where she could sort them later. She needed to call Gilberto Perez and tell him she was leaving; she needed to clean the apartment so that Mimi wouldn't have to do it when she came home.

But first she would box up her computer and printer.

Once that task was accomplished, she called Sherman to carry them down to her car, and he answered his phone right away. Rachel was in no mood to listen to any more protracted stories from him, no matter how interesting they might be.

"Sherman? My computer is ready. Could you please load it into my car? Thanks." He was still talking when she hung up, but she didn't want to hear what he had to say; she didn't need to. She'd be out of here in less than an hour with any luck.

When the knock sounded on the door, she opened it right away. But it wasn't Sherman who stood on the threshold. It was Gina, and she had been crying.

"Rachel, please, you have to listen," Gina began.

"No, I don't," Rachel said firmly, and started to close the door.

But Gina had slid her foot into the opening. "It wasn't what you thought," she said. "There's nothing between Joe and me."

Gina spoke with such resolve and determination that it gave Rachel pause.

"And there's something else you need to know," Gina went on. "Please let me in."

"I'm going back to New Jersey," Rachel shot back. "I don't have time to talk to you."

Gina's eyes widened perceptibly. "Oh, gosh, then you have to listen. You have to. Because I don't want what I did to break you and Joe up."

"What you did was spend the night with him. Right?"

"Yes, but—"

Bitterness rose like bile in her throat. "Go away, Gina. Leave me in peace." *To pick up the pieces,* Rachel added to herself. But then you always want what you can't have, and Joe was just one more thing that was lost to her. The thought of a lifetime of losses threatened to make her break down right here, but she would save that for later. She wouldn't give Gina the satisfaction of letting her know that her heart was broken.

"Not until you listen. I have something really important to tell you, Rachel. It's…it's about Chrissy."

"Chrissy!"

As soon as Rachel said the baby's name, Gina's face crumpled and tears began to course down her cheeks.

"Gina," Rachel said reasoningly, not understanding what this was about.

Gina began to sob quietly, not covering her face, not doing anything to hide her raw anguish. Rachel knew it would be only a matter of time before Ynez popped out of the door to her apartment on her way to pick up her new kitten and asked what was wrong. To forestall that development, Rachel reached out and pulled Gina inside.

"You might as well sit down," she said ungraciously. She brushed a pile of papers and books off the couch and indicated that Gina should sit there.

Gina scrubbed at her eyes with a fist. "You weren't supposed to find the baby in the manger," she said.

Gina's tone gave Rachel pause. "I wasn't?"

"No, Joe was."

"What on earth are you talking about, Gina?" She stared at the girl, whose eyes were so puffy that Rachel knew she must have been crying for hours.

"I didn't know what else to do with her. Joe was always so kind to me, so levelheaded, that I thought he'd be good to a baby. I was going to leave Chrissy on the doorstep of his apartment that night, but I waited and waited for him to come home and he didn't come back. Then I found out from Mrs. Marzinski that he was working a condo crisis here on the island, and I rode over here to see if I could talk to him. So—"

Rachel sank down on a chair; her knees refused to hold her. "You mean Chrissy is *your* baby?"

Gina, eyes downcast, nodded. "Yes," she whispered.

Rachel's thoughts were scrambling as if through a minefield where sections of the landscape had been blown sky-high. In the meantime Gina went on talking.

"So I was sitting in my car in the Elysian Towers parking lot and I was getting so tired. I'd lost a lot of blood, and I was very weak. I mean, I'd just given birth to a baby all by myself."

"You were all alone? Oh, Gina," Rachel said, but Gina silenced her with a wave of her hand.

"No sympathy, please. I don't deserve it. Anyway, the baby was born three days before Christmas at Anna's house. I knew I couldn't stay there in the parking lot on Christmas Eve. I wanted to be at Anna's, safe in bed when she and Mitch came home from a three-day visit to his parents that night. Joe's van was parked outside this building because he was inside working, but the van was locked, so I couldn't leave the baby in it as I planned. I knew that Joe would have to walk right past the Nativity scene to get to his van when he left that night. I figured he'd find the baby if I left her in the manger.''

"And that's why you left Chrissy outside the building?'' Rachel's outrage was exceeded only by her incredulity.

"Uh-huh. It seemed safe enough, behind the ixora hedge, under that little roof of the stable where Mary and Joseph were. I laid Chrissy in the manger, told her goodbye, and then I went away. And you found her.''

"What if I hadn't? What if something had happened to her?''

"I wasn't thinking rationally. I was so exhausted.''

"Your sisters never knew you were pregnant?''

Gina's head drooped. "I never told them. I went away to college before I got really big. I wore lots of baggy clothes and didn't tell a soul.''

"The baby's father?''

"A college boy who was in Daytona Beach for spring break last year. The only one I ever—well, I know he's the father. I never even knew his last name or where he went to school.''

Rachel couldn't help it; her heart went out to this naive young woman who hadn't known how to deal with such a grave mistake. "You should have told someone you were going to have a baby. You should have had help.''

Gina looked as if she were at the end of her rope. No wonder she looked exhausted, though—no woman should have to handle pregnancy and birth all alone. "I know that now,'' Gina said, looking straight at Rachel for the first time since she'd embarked upon her tale of woe. "But I've been on my own for a long time, and I thought I could deal with this by myself.

"I was in denial for months, but when I finally admitted to myself that I was pregnant, I was afraid I'd have to give up college—and it means so much to me, Rachel! Everyone who helped me get there is counting on me. I'm not nearly ready to be a mother. I can't keep that baby. But you and Joe could. You could adopt her.'' She leaned forward hopefully.

Rachel's head was spinning with all these revelations. ''I'm not going to marry Joe. I won't marry anyone who spends the night with another woman, especially on the very night that I'm considering his marriage proposal,'' she said slowly.

''Rachel, oh Rachel. I slept at his apartment, all right, but not with Joe. Last night I went over there to tell him about the baby and what I'd done, I had to get it off my chest, and I was helping him fix a faucet and the water spurted all over me, so I changed into some other clothes of his, and when I got around to telling him that Chrissy is my child, he got really upset and started yelling.

''And I began to cry and he apologized for yelling, and I cried some more, and if I had gone home looking upset, Anna and Mitch would have demanded to know what was wrong. I know I'm going to have to tell them, but I couldn't face them, not so soon after admitting everything to Joe. Joe was real nice. He let me sleep on the couch. He cooked breakfast for me, and I was getting ready to drive home when we both came out and saw you there. You took off before we could explain that it was perfectly innocent.''

''Oh,'' Rachel said. She hadn't thought that it was possible for the scene at Joe's to be anything but incriminating. But now, knowing what she knew, understanding Gina's state of mind and Joe's nurturing nature, everything began to make sense.

Neither of them spoke for a long time. Gina sighed heavily. ''Now you know what happened.''

There were still loose ends, and Rachel's mind struggled to tie them all together. "But the Santa..." Rachel said, her voice trailing away when she realized how silly it would be to say that she'd thought that the Santa whom she had first met on Christmas Eve when she was buying paper had put Chrissy in the manger.

"The Santa?" Gina repeated, looking confused. "What did Santa have to do with it?"

"I don't know," Rachel said truthfully. "I honestly have no idea."

"I mean, it was Christmas Eve and all. But I'm too old to believe in Santa Claus."

Rachel thought about the kindness of the Santa in the discount store and the way his eyes had seemed to pierce right through her soul to the pain that she'd thought would never go away. "I'm not sure I'm too old to believe, Gina," she said, meaning it.

Gina was twisting a sodden handkerchief in her hands. "The thing is, Rachel, I feel so awful. I failed to live up to the responsibility of having a baby."

Rachel moved to the couch and curved an arm around Gina's shoulders. The girl felt so fragile, so tiny. "Yes, Gina, I suppose you did. The baby might not have been found until morning."

"I'm so ashamed of what I did that night! If anything had happened to my baby, I would have wanted to die. It's just that...that I thought I didn't have anywhere to turn," Gina said, beginning to weep again.

"I know why you felt that way. Believe me, I understand."

"How could you?" Gina wailed. "I bet you've never done anything so awful."

"Oh," said Rachel, "but I have."

Gina dried her eyes and stared. "Not you, Rachel. You look so perfect, so pretty, so…so *okay*."

"Maybe," Rachel acknowledged. "But I did something I'm not proud of."

"You, Rachel?" Gina looked unconvinced.

Ever since Joe had told her about his shame over his involvement in the robbery, Rachel had felt better about the way she had acted on the night of the fire. So now it seemed to her that the most helpful thing she could do for Gina was to hold Gina's hand and tell her about Nick and Lolly and Melissa and Derek and the puppy and the fire that had claimed their lives, and how she almost couldn't live with herself because if she hadn't left the burning house, if she had made sure that everyone else got out when she had, they might have lived.

In the end, after the telling of it, they both had tears in their eyes.

"Rachel, I'm sorry. I didn't know," Gina said.

"The best advice I can give you—or anyone else—is that bad things happen to people sometimes. The only thing we can do afterward is to move on. To get on with our lives." This was what Joe had told her. It was what she now believed to be true.

"But, Rachel, what makes that possible?" Gina asked tremulously.

"Love," Rachel said with sudden certainty. "In the end love is what we live for. It helps us move beyond the tragedies."

"There's not going to be any love for me," Gina said with dark certainty.

Rachel couldn't believe her ears. "Gina! That statement makes me want to shake you until you come to your senses! How can you say that, when all the Marzinskis care about you so very much and when you have two sisters who, from what I can tell, love you a lot?''

"Oh," Gina said, understanding dawning in her eyes. "I thought you meant love as in, well, romance."

"There are lots of different kinds of love, which is a lesson I've learned only recently. Look at Gladys and Ivan, at Ynez, at Chrissy and what a difference she made to all of them!''

"And she made a difference to Joe and to you, Rachel. She brought you together. He really does love you, you know. You were all he could talk about last night after I told him about the baby. You and his hopes that you could all be together.''

Something lightened in her heart then, and a great burden seemed to lift from her shoulders when she thought about Joe. She had resisted him long enough; now it was time to reach out and take the gift of love that he had offered her almost from the very beginning.

"Joe has given me the strength to move on with my life. I guess I'd better tell him so, don't you agree?'' There was a lilt in her voice and gladness in her heart for the first time in many years.

Gina smiled shakily and squeezed her hand. "You're going to marry him?"

"If he still wants me."

Gina perked up at this. "He does, Rachel. You'll see. Oh, but he's not at home. He had a call this morning. Something about an elevator at some condo down the beach.''

Rachel went to phone Joe, her heart doing little joyful triphammer things as she dialed his pager number. In her mind she was already rehearsing the words she would say when she heard Joe's voice, but to her surprise the person who answered the page wasn't Joe.

"This is Andy, Joe's my boss. He can't answer your page. There's been an accident, and they've taken him to the hospital." The words were terse, the information chilling.

"What hospital?" Rachel felt as if a cold knife had been driven through her heart.

"Holy Angels. But I'm not sure you can see him."

"Is he going to be okay? Is he—"

"I don't know. I haven't heard. He looks as if he's in pretty bad shape."

WHEN RACHEL AND GINA arrived at the hospital, other Marzinskis were gathered in the emergency room.

Mary Marzinski gathered Rachel into an embrace, and even the prickly Mary Cecilia seemed glad to see her.

"What happened?" Rachel asked, her heart in her mouth.

"An elevator shaft accident. He's unconscious," Jim Marzinski told her. He looked worried and much older today. Maybe it was the harsh fluorescent lighting overhead, but Rachel didn't think so.

"Unconscious!"

"They aren't telling us much," Mary Cecilia said.

"Is anyone allowed to see him?"

"Not yet."

Rachel turned to Jim, who seemed the calmest. "What went wrong?"

"There was a problem with the elevator cable, and Joe leaned into the shaft to look. Somehow he lost his footing and fell. That's all we know," Jim said.

"Andy said Joe seemed distracted this morning," Gracie said into the awful silence.

Rachel exchanged an anguished look with Gina. What if Joe had been so upset by her actions that he'd become careless? And she was haunted by the last words she had ever said to him when he'd called and tried to explain. She would give anything to take them back, she'd give anything to have never uttered them. She had told him to drop dead.

"The accident couldn't have been your fault," Gina whispered when no one else was paying attention, but Rachel's stomach had tied itself in knots and she didn't know what to think. All she knew was that Joe was hurt and that she felt responsible. It was like the fire all over again, only Joe was alive and there was still a chance that he would recover. She closed her eyes and willed him to be all right.

After a time—Rachel had no idea how long—a nurse ushered them into a waiting room where Jackson handed Rachel a cup of coffee that she couldn't drink. They all sat down and tried to look more cheerful than they felt. A loud TV on the wall provided dubious distraction.

Some of them made attempts at desultory conversation.

"I guess you're looking forward to starting back to school in January," Jenn said to Rachel.

Rachel thought for a split second that Jenn had her confused with Gina, who would be returning to college soon. "Oh, I'm not—" she began, then realized that they all still thought she taught school. Now what?

"What grade do you teach?" Reggie, Tonia's husband, asked in an attempt to be polite.

This was it. She would have to tell them the truth about herself. And in that instant she realized that she could. She could talk about her past without feeling like a failure. No more was she the pathetic, bereft woman who had come to Coquina Beach to hide from life.

She inhaled a shaky breath. "I...well, I'm not actually a teacher," Rachel said.

"Excuse me?"

"I'm not the schoolteacher Joe was going out with at Thanksgiving. That was a misunderstanding."

"Misunderstanding?" Mary, his mother, wrinkled her forehead.

Rachel wasn't sure how much to say, but she knew that she couldn't let Joe's family go on thinking that she was someone she wasn't. If she were going to marry him, they would eventually need to know the truth.

"On Christmas Day everyone assumed that I was this other woman he'd dated, and Joe didn't correct anyone, but I'm just visiting Coquina Beach to house-sit my grandmother's condo. I've never taught school, I run my own secretarial service. I found the baby on Christmas Eve, and Joe helped me. You see, I don't have any family here, and that's why he invited me to Christmas dinner." She knew this sounded jumbled and confused, but at the moment she wasn't capable of organizing words into neat little sentences. This was as logical as she could make it.

"You have no family?" asked Tonia sharply. "None at all?" It was as if she couldn't imagine anyone's being so deprived.

Rachel took a deep breath. "My grandmother's in Asia doing some long-awaited traveling. After that there's only my mother, but she's in a nursing home in New Jersey. She doesn't know who I am anymore. And I did have a family—a husband and children. Once."

"What happened to them?" Gracie, Joe's quietest sister, asked.

"They died at Christmas four years ago. In a house fire."

This statement produced a long silence.

"How terrible for you," murmured Mary at last.

"How awful." Mary Cecilia reached over and touched Rachel's hand.

Rachel looked around at their concerned faces. "I thought I would never be able to celebrate Christmas again. And then I met all of you. I felt so welcome in your home." She tried to smile.

Jim cleared his throat. "You *are* one of us," he said comfortingly. "You're family."

Rachel felt their love reaching out to include and embrace her. "I feel that I am. Thank you—all of you. And I hope you know that I love Joe very much."

"We've wanted to see Joey settled for a long time," said Lois. This elicited a round of agreement.

"Chrissy isn't your baby, is she?"

Rachel stared back at Mary Cecilia, who had zinged out of left field with that question and dropped it right in her lap. "No," Rachel said quietly. "She isn't."

"Chrissy's mine," Gina said into the hollow silence.

Rachel swiveled to look at Gina. She remained composed, her hands folded quietly in her lap, even as everyone's jaw dropped.

"And I hope that she will soon be Rachel and Joe's," Gina said.

No one spoke for a long time as their minds grappled with this unexpected revelation. "I guess there's more to this story," said Mary gently. "More than you'll want to tell us right now?"

"Yes, and I want to share it with all of you soon," Gina said, her head held high. "After I've talked to my sisters. I just hope that…that you won't think less of me. I couldn't bear that." Her voice broke slightly, but she looked at Rachel and seemed to take heart.

"Whatever you've done, we love you, Gina," Mary said firmly.

"You had the baby," said Tonia. "You didn't get rid of it."

Gina's eyes opened wide. "I would never—I mean, I couldn't."

Gracie went to Gina and slid an arm around her shoulders. "Tell us about it only when you're ready, okay?"

Gina, tears in her eyes, nodded.

Lois glanced around at the group before she spoke. "Well, guys, we all wanted Joey to have his own family. Looks like Gina has given him a head start, if you ask me."

A few tentative smiles, and then Mary got up from her chair, walked to Rachel and hugged her. Rachel was framing what she wanted to say to them, something about love and loyalty and how she admired those traits in them, but she didn't have a chance to speak before a doctor arrived carrying a clipboard.

Unaware of the mix of powerful emotions humming in the air, he greeted them quickly and began to brief them on Joe's condition.

"Joe's got a few nasty bruises, and we've set his broken arm. We're also monitoring him for internal injuries. There are no signs of any yet, which is encouraging. He has a concussion, but I'm happy to report that as of fifteen minutes ago, he has regained consciousness. The only thing is, he keeps asking for Rachel. I don't recall a sister named Rachel." He raised his eyebrows questioningly.

"I'm Rachel."

"She's his fiancée," supplied Mary.

The doctor grinned at her. "Ah, I see. In that case, Rachel, won't you come with me? He won't be pretty to look at, but I think it would be good medicine for Joe to see you."

JOE OPENED HIS EYES. The pain had receded into a huge white void, and hovering above him was the most beautiful woman he'd ever seen. She was gazing at him with love and trust and a lot of other emotions that were too complicated to enumerate. Her hair was bunched around her face in a wondrous welter of curls, and she had a face like a Madonna, or was it an angel?

"Joe?"

Drifting in from wherever he'd been, he realized that this wasn't a Madonna, nor was it an angel. It was Rachel. He hadn't expected her. She was furious with him. At the moment he couldn't recall why she was so angry, only that he'd been devastated. He roused himself, tried to concentrate, couldn't. So was he alive, or had that accident with the elevator shaft sent him straight to heaven?

She touched his hand. She bent close and kissed his lips. This wasn't heaven. It was decidedly real. It hurt when he smiled at her, even though the balm of her tears fell on his eyelids.

"Oh, Joe, I've been so worried about you." She wiped the tears from his face with gentle fingertips and laid her cheek against his. This he could feel. This he liked. Suddenly he remembered. Oh, God. Gina. This morning. Rachel hanging the phone up on him. What to say?

"Well, I was so upset about what you thought that I went out and threw myself down an elevator shaft," he said.

She straightened and frowned. "Don't joke, Joe. I know nothing happened between you and Gina. She's told me everything."

Relief sent him spinning. He squeezed her hand, and she squeezed back. His lips were painfully dry. "I would have come over to explain after you hung up the phone on me this morning, but I got the call about the Crowne Point's elevators malfunctioning, and it was a safety issue, so I knew I had to go check things out myself. I didn't trust anyone else to deal with the problem." The long speech wore him out.

"Joe, I shouldn't have jumped to conclusions about you and Gina this morning. I should have known better."

"It looked bad," Joe conceded. "From your point of view, I mean."

"Don't talk, my love. Save your strength."

"For what? Looks like I'm going to be laid up here for a while."

"For wedding vows. Marry me, Joe."

"I second the emotion," said someone behind her, and she turned to see Joe's parents, all his sisters and Gina, who proceeded to crowd into the small hospital room.

Joe's lips curved into a wry and painful smile. "I guess it's unanimous," he said.

"Well? I asked you something," Rachel said, holding tightly to his hand.

"I asked you first," Joe reminded her.

"The answer is yes," Rachel said.

"When? When?" All the Marzinskis circled the bed.

"As soon as we can," Rachel said firmly. "As soon as Mimi gets home. I want her to be my attendant. And I want Chrissy to come."

As everyone else began to chatter among themselves, Joe gazed up at Rachel. "I love you, Rachel. With all my heart."

"And I love you."

He felt better now. Fantastic, in fact. "We'll make a wonderful life together, you'll see."

She leaned over the rail at the side of the bed and kissed him on the forehead. At least it didn't hurt. "One thing for sure, I'll always have plenty of reasons to celebrate Christmas from now on," she said.

"For instance?" Joe murmured.

"You and Chrissy and Gina, and your mom and dad and Mary Cecilia and Greg and Paul, Megan, Mary Grace, Todd, Amanda—"

"I get the picture. The very big picture. And I hope that before long we'll be adding some new names of our own to that list."

"We will, my love."

Oblivious to the other people in the room, Joe reached out and gripped Rachel's shoulder, because for this he had amazing strength. And he kissed her properly, with everyone watching.

"Oh, Joe, don't you think there's something to this Christmas miracle business?" Rachel said unsteadily, her lips close to his.

"Maybe so, my dearest. Maybe so." And with that, Joe kissed her again.

Epilogue

June, Eighteen Months Later

A slightly pregnant Rachel, with Chrissy straddling her hip, stepped out onto the deck of their new house on the beach, where Joe was finishing a cup of coffee while thumbing through a maintenance report before going to the office.

"Daddy," said Chrissy, holding out her plump little arms.

Joe set aside the report and reached for her. "How's my girl?" he said, smoothing Chrissy's pale bangs back from her face.

"Go bye-bye," said Chrissy as she bounced on his lap. "See Mimi."

"Mimi's baby-sitting this morning while I shop for maternity clothes," Rachel explained.

"Buy something pretty. I'm taking you out dancing Saturday night," Joe said, smiling at her.

Rachel smiled back. "Even if I am a little heavy on my feet?" she teased.

He slid an arm around her hips. "You're as light on your feet as ever, and you're twice as sexy."

Rachel knew he loved her rounded look now that she was pregnant; he swore that she'd never been more beautiful than when she was carrying their child. "That's because I love you. And because you love me."

"You're right about that," he said.

"How about meeting for lunch?"

"Gina's coming to the office at eleven for her summer job interview. After that I'm free. Want to check with me later, see what time I can get away?"

"Sure. Do you think Gina will come by to see Chrissy?"

"I doubt it," Joe said. He nuzzled the baby's rosy cheek. "I think Gina wants to put the past behind her as much as possible."

They'd heard from Gina only sporadically throughout the school year. Still a straight-A student, Gina concentrated on her course work and was still intent on pursuing her MBA. She often asked about Chrissy, but the adoption was final now, and Gina seemed relieved that the baby had a good home. Her role in their lives, as well as in Chrissy's, was as a family friend, much the way it had been for the many years that the Marzinskis had helped her to pursue her dreams.

"Tell Gina that she's welcome to come over tomorrow for dinner. We're grilling steaks out here on the deck, and I've invited Mimi and Gladys and Ivan and Ynez."

"Aren't Gladys and Ivan leaving soon to spend the summer near her grandchildren in Seattle?"

"They're going next week. That's why they want to visit with Chrissy before they go."

"Are you sure Ynez is coming?"

"Oh, it'll be hard to tear her away from the new calico kitten that she got to keep her Tabitha company, but she'll be here. She says she has first dibs at baby-sitting our new baby.''

"Do you think it's a coincidence that our new little Marzinski is due on Christmas Eve this year?" Joe asked.

Rachel bent down and plucked Chrissy out of his arms. Chrissy grabbed a fistful of Rachel's hair and gave her a big smacking kiss on the cheek.

"I suppose so. Only—" She disentangled her hair from Chrissy's fingers.

"Only what?" Joe stood up and put his arms around them.

"Only it seems so strange that I was lonely on Christmas Eve, and the discount-store Santa asked me to make a wish. And I wished that I'd have a reason to celebrate Christmas again, and almost immediately there you were—you and Chrissy. And now, next Christmas Eve, a new baby.''

"Don't forget Gladys and Ivan's falling in love. Or Ynez's renewed interest in life after she realized that she didn't have to give up because her cat, the only thing that meant anything to her, had died.''

"If all this isn't enough to make us believe in Christmas miracles, I don't know what is," Rachel said. "Not to mention Santa Claus." But she would always believe, in the depths of her soul, that the real Christmas miracle had been Joe's healing of her heart so that she could find the courage to love again.

"Oh, after the past year and a half I believe," said Joe with great conviction. "I definitely believe."

"How about you, Chrissy?" said Rachel.

But Chrissy didn't say a word. She only winked one

of her eyes, which were the same distinctive almond shape as Gina's.

And although Rachel thought she heard a distant ho-ho-ho ringing out over the sunny beach with its breaking surf and fringe of sea grapes, she kept it to herself.

If you enjoyed what you just read,
then we've got an offer you can't resist!

Take 2 bestselling love stories FREE!

Plus get a FREE surprise gift!

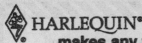

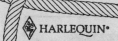

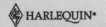